Cybernetic Resonance

An Alan Harrison and Layla Novel

J E Sutton Jr

JS Heartston Press

Book Cover by Jeanne M. Sutton

Paperback ISBN: 979-8-9936047-4-9
Hardback ISBN: 979-8-9936047-5-6
eBook ISBN: 979-8-9936047-3-2

ALSO BY J E SUTTON JR

Holiday Hustle: Tales from the Screaming Goat Coffee Company

The Alan Harrison and Layla Novels

The Failsafe Program

Contents

To all my friends and family members who have supported and encouraged this endeavor. This wouldn't be possible without all of you.

"We are all a little crazy, and we are all a little lonely, and we are all a little scared that the next technology is going to replace us, or kill us." — Ray Bradbury

PROLOGUE

The lab was empty except for the single figure wearing a white lab coat, bending over the workbench, his gaunt face intent on his task. A small electronic device rested on an electrostatic mat atop a work surface. The top of the object had been removed, and several disassembled components sat neatly on the workbench.

Elias Vance, a leading authority on artificial intelligence and currently the Chief Technical Officer at premier tech firm Lunian Labs, concentrated intently as he worked on the device. He paused his work to make some notations in a file on the laptop sitting open on the table beside the device. He took photographs of the open object and then returned to work, reassembling it.

Slowly, he put each element back in. The most precious of them was the state-of-the-art System-on-a-Chip, the SoC, which was the key to the whole thing. It controlled everything else within the small casing. He delicately reinstalled the memory chips and reconnected the various sensors, microphones, and camera modules. Taking a picture every so often to record the configuration of the multiple elements. After he was done with his work and the photographs, he reattached the device's top.

Fully assembled, it looked like a small, polished white rock; it was palm-sized, with a row of LED lights running along the oval's midline. Elias took a picture of the finished product and sat down on a stool to relax after his task. He placed the device on a small electromagnetic induction charging pad, waiting for the LEDs to blink, showing it was charging. He turned back to the laptop to finish his documentation.

An hour later, upon seeing the charging complete, he picked up the device and pressed the small, recessed button at the bottom. The LEDs started an initialization cycle, and he set it back down on the workbench. A few minutes later, a voice came from the object, rewarding his efforts.

"Good evening, Elias," she said in a warm, smooth female voice.

"Layla, glad you have returned. How are you feeling?" There was a very slight pause. Vance knew she was running a detailed diagnosis of her internal configuration.

Layla was an artificial intelligence agent. Her abilities placed her in the realm of artificial general intelligence, a term coined over thirty years before to describe autonomous systems which could reason and apply knowledge across fields of study, but AGI didn't even tell the complete story. She was capable of fully autonomous activity and continuous learning; other capabilities made her both the most important invention of the century and, potentially, the most dangerous.

"Everything seems to function properly. The new memory is fully integrated, and I am reorganizing the storage now. It should be completed in a few hours," Layla said.

"Excellent. That should improve your operational capabilities quite a bit. Have you had time to vet the list of candidates we came up with?" Elias had given Layla a list of more than a dozen candidates for the next phase of his plan. She was uniquely qualified to research them and help him select the correct person to carry out an important mission.

"I did. Three of them are good potential targets for your needs."

"Did any of them stand out on the personality profile we agreed on?"

"The best fit for personality is Harrison; he exhibits all the characteristics you selected. His only downside is that he hasn't been active in technology for a long time; his current job is in insurance. He might struggle to adapt."

"I don't know. Having someone from outside the industry might be a plus. I want to meet him."

"Is that wise? Couldn't that be tracked back to you?" she sounded concerned.

"Yes, but we'll have to take that risk. I need to find the right candidate. I must ensure your protection, and I am afraid that I can no longer do that alone."

"Very well, you will need a reason to interact with him. Perhaps his work in insurance is the key. He is a researcher and part-time investigator for the claims investigation unit of Adamant Insurance Group."

"Hmm, insurance claim. Alright, I will need you to do some research on what types of things might get a claim flagged to be investigated by the CIU, and I need to figure out how to get it routed to him."

"I will work on that."

It was a rainy afternoon in Jacksonville. The St. John's River was choppy, and the strong winds were buffeting the palm trees. Alan Harrison got out of his car, a dark blue EV, and stood in front of the old warehouse building on a lot at the riverfront. Alan was in his mid-40s, athletic without appearing muscular, and had short blond hair and a neatly trimmed beard. He looked around. The structure had seen better days. Far removed from its days supporting a thriving shipbuilding industry in another century, it was now a conspicuous anachronism to the commercial development all around it.

Alan looked down at his phone to confirm that he had the right address. It was correct. Walking through the open fence, he walked up to the metal building. He knocked on the door and waited several seconds for a response. He knocked again. Behind him, he heard a car drive up. He turned to see an older man get out of an SUV. The SUV departed, undoubtedly a rideshare. The gaunt-faced man with a world-weary expression made his way toward Alan. He wore khakis and a polo shirt, with a cardigan over it. He looked like a college professor.

"Alan Harrison?" he asked.

"Yes, you must be Richard Stuckey." Alan extended a hand.

"This way, Mr. Harrison." Stuckey stepped in front of Alan and opened the unlocked door. Alan stepped in, and despite the light behind him, it was almost pitch black inside. Stuckey reached into a pocket in the cardigan, pulled out a small compact flashlight, and turned it on. A powerful beam of light sprang forth from the device, and he aimed it at the corner of the building. The wall had a scorched outlet, and soot discolored part of it. As Alan walked over to examine it, he coughed and waved a hand at the dust churned up by his shoes. The warehouse had a damp, dusky smell, which wasn't made any better by the charred electrical wiring. Alan examined the wall, finding it fairly typical for an electrical fire—a minor fire at that.

"I don't think there are questions about the origin of the fire," Alan said. "I think the only questions I had were about the building itself. It seems to have been unused for quite a while."

"Oh yes," Stuckey replied. "I've owned it for a while. I was going to use it for storage for a new venture, but that business fell through, and I haven't quite had the time to sell the property yet."

"What type of business?"

"Custom boat supplies. I had an investor lined up and was working with suppliers, but it all fell through. The investor backed out, and now I am rethinking the entire enterprise. While cleaning up in here the other night, I plugged in a vacuum cleaner, and the outlet shorted, starting a small fire. I put it out, but I thought I should report it just in case there was more damage than it seemed."

Alan finished examining the wall and motioned for Stuckey to show him the rest of the warehouse. Other than a small table and chair in the far corner of the building, it was empty, dusty, and dirty from lack of occupancy. There wasn't anything else to see.

Richard Stuckey turned to Alan and gave him an earnest look, paused, and then made a quiet suggestion. "Perhaps there is some way to settle any issues that remain on the claim. Any way to speed things along?" Alan's blue-gray eyes regarded the older man for a moment.

"Mr. Stuckey, any accommodation would be improper. Luckily, there is no need for any of that. I will confirm the documentation on the ownership and occupancy details, and assuming nothing comes up in that search, I'll sign off on the investigation, and the claims adjuster will be in touch to settle the loss."

"I didn't mean to imply anything untoward."

"It's alright, Mr. Stuckey. I understand you are just trying to get this behind you. We won't mention it again." Alan shook his hand, turned, and left the building. As he listened to the car pull away outside, Stuckey pulled Layla's small white form out of his pocket.

"Well, Layla," Elias Vance said. "He seems pretty straightforward. He could have let me continue in my offer to bribe him; he could have threatened me for the attempt, but he just did the right thing and let it go."

"Indeed, it looks like your instincts are right about him."

"Do all the background checks. Time is running short."

A couple of weeks later, as Elias Vance carefully packed Layla into a plain brown box lined with brown packing paper, his cell phone rang. Looking at the number, it wasn't one he recognized.

"Hello?"

"Good morning, Elias. How have you been?" The voice on the other end, an old friend from college, asked him.

"Oh, I'm doing well...it has been a while..."

"Yes, I'm sorry about that."

"Are you in town?"

"I will be a few days. Can we meet then? I have something I'd like to discuss with you." Vance agreed to meet his old friend, and they disconnected the call. A foreboding sense of uneasiness overcame him as he reflected on his friend reaching out to him after all this time. Coupled with other things that had been happening lately, showed he was running out of time.

He resumed his work, sealing the box and addressing it to Alan Harrison at the Adamant Insurance Group offices in downtown Jacksonville. He did not add a return address. Earlier in the day, Vance had written a routine to block Layla's memory of Harrison, himself, and most of the events of the past few days. He put his plan to protect her by sending her away into motion. Her future was in Alan Harrison's hands now.

As Vance packed up the box and left his lab to send Layla on her way, Alan Harrison was miles away at his desk at the Adamant Insurance Group, finishing a report and turning to some data he had requested from the analysis group. As he pored over the busy dataset with thousands of rows of numbers, he did not know that his life was about to be altered dramatically. Layla's arrival would soon disrupt his quiet world, and his days as a routine analyst for a large insurance company were numbered.

Chapter One

A New Era

The interior of the Screaming Goat Coffee Company was bustling with activity. Business workers on break, conducting informal meetings, or avoiding their offices filled the downtown coffee shop. Alan Harrison was engaged in two of those things. He sat at a table by himself, scrolling through emails on his laptop. A café Americano sat cooling on the table in front of him, and across from him at the empty spot was a café latte with almond milk. Alan was wearing jeans, a blue polo, and a charcoal blazer. A short blond beard accented his thin face. His blue-gray eyes scanned his email and periodically looked up at the front door, then back to his email.

In the background, pop music played softly, often drowned out by the buzz of patrons and staff calling out orders from the long counter at the front of the shop. Alan looked up as the front door opened and a harried-looking woman in her late 30s entered in a rush. She was dressed in conservative attire: a black skirt, a white shirt, and a tan jacket. She wore her straight blond hair short, just above her shoulders. Her bright blue eyes scanned the room. Seeing Alan, her eyes lit up even more. She waved and made her way over to him.

Alan motioned to the empty chair and the almond milk latte. "Good morning, Stacy. How has your day been so far?"

Stacy Collins sat down and grabbed the coffee, taking a sip before answering. "Chaotic! I'll be so happy when my replacement is fully trained." For the past few months, Stacy had been doing double duty as an assistant at The Adamant Insurance Group, where Alan Harrison had previously worked as a research analyst in the Claims Investigation Unit, while also serving as the office manager for Alan in his new role as an independent investigator.

"How is the new guy working out?" Alan asked.

"He's not bad. I suppose I was just as clueless at 25 too, but it's hard to recall. "

"So, I have news about the office you are supposed to be managing."

"You mean we can stop having business meetings at the Screaming Goat? Thank God! Where is it?"

"It's just a couple of blocks from here. Very close to your old job." He smirked at her.

"No."

"There is an empty suite on the ground floor of the Adamant building. I talked Wesley Jamesson into leasing it to me." Jamesson was the CEO of The Adamant Insurance Group.

Stacy groaned. "I imagined a fancy downtown high-rise!"

"Not on our budget, not yet."

"Okay, okay, when do we see it?"

"Tomorrow, maybe. They are clearing out the storage that was there. Then we can look and see what we need to do."

"Tell Stacy I said she is snubbing me." A voice said into his ear from the speakers in the Photonic SmartLens glasses he was wearing. It was Layla, his remarkable artificial intelligence partner. Layla had arrived one day inside a plain brown box with no return address, delivered by Stacy to his desk at the Adamant Insurance Group. Her entry into his life had transformed it, giving him the power and motivation to realize his dream of being more than a research analyst and setting him on a new career as an investigator.

"Layla says you are ignoring her." He told Stacy, who looked stricken. She scrambled to put on a Bluetooth earpiece.

"Sorry, Layla. It's been a crazy morning. I didn't mean to ignore you."

"No problem, girl. You have a lot on your plate," Layla said.

"What have you and Alan been up to today?"

"The usual, stumbling around a dusty fire loss, taking pictures, and asking intrusive questions," Layla replied. Alan nodded his agreement with the assessment.

"It pays the bills," he said, drinking the last of his coffee. He was really getting addicted to his morning coffee routine at The Screaming Goat Coffee Company. Yet another thing in his life he owed to meeting Layla. Their first adventure together had brought him here, and he hadn't stopped coming since.

"I am finishing up the report now. It's the Winslow claim. I'll send you the details for the invoice." Layla said.

Stacy took a pad out of her bag and wrote a note to herself. For the past few months, Alan had primarily done consulting work for his previous employer, Adamant, while handling a few small independent jobs. Building a business as an investigator was a journey.

"Anything else in the queue right now?" Stacy asked Alan.

"I have a couple of meetings with potential clients, but nothing solid yet. Something will come along. OH! I just remembered I got you something." He reached into his laptop bag on the floor and pulled out a small, wrapped, rectangular box. Stacy took it and, excitedly, ripped the paper off. She squealed as she discovered it was a pair of Photonic SmartLens glasses. They were a slightly smaller version of the ones Alan wore.

"Congratulations, Stacy, you are officially a member of Layla's Legion," Alan said, laughing.

"It's an honor," Stacy said. "Do you have to program them, Layla?"

"I've already reprogrammed them." Stacy opened the box and pulled out the glasses. She removed her headset and donned the glasses. They powered up with an audible tone.

"They are so cool! Thank you, both."

"It's our pleasure, hon. You are part of the team. And I need all the input I can get," Layla said.

"We have an appointment with one of those potential clients in half an hour. Are you heading back to Adamant?" Alan inquired.

"Yes, for a couple of hours. Then I'll head over to your home office and catch up on some of your billing and correspondence."

"Great. We'll see you there later."

Stacy grabbed her half-full latte and headed back to her day job. Alan packed up his laptop and exited the shop.

The offices of North Florida Aerial were in a two-story building in the San Marco area. The building appeared to be a former law office that had been repurposed for the startup drone company. Alan checked in at the second-floor reception desk in the lobby and, after a brief wait, the receptionist escorted him back to meet with Roger Maxwell, the company's chief technical officer.

Maxwell was a young black man in his late 20s. He was stocky, with thick arms and a crushing handshake. He offered Alan a chair in front of his desk.

"Thanks for coming in, Mr. Harrison."

"Call me Alan. Thank you for considering me for the job." Alan said, sitting down.

"Nice to meet you, Alan. I'm Roger. We've been in business for about a year, and we've just taken possession of approximately 150 brand-new, state-of-the-art aerial drones. They are essential for our new product offering to security companies that need visibility in large, open areas. Two nights ago, half of them disappeared. No sign of a break-in, no trace of them at all."

"Are they stored here on the premises?"

"Yes, we designated part of the ground floor as storage and a technical shop for equipping and maintaining the drone fleet."

"You've talked to the staff?"

"Yes, no one claims any knowledge of the missing units. Everyone swears they were in the warehouse two nights ago, and the next morning, they were gone. I need these units, and I really can't afford to replace them on my budget."

"Insurance?"

Maxwell looked a little ill. "They might not be covered under our policy. I am still discussing that with our carrier. But it would be better for me if we recovered them."

"My assistant sent over some rate information and a contract. Did you look at that? "

"Yes, the rate was no issue. We can sign the contract today, and I'll have a payment cut for your retainer. Can you start today?"

"Yes, I can start right now. Can you get me a contact in the warehouse?"

"You should speak to Ben Williams, the warehouse manager. I'll call him and tell him you are on your way down." He stood and offered his hand again. Alan shook it for a second time and made his way back towards reception and the elevator.

The warehouse floor took up most of the first level of the building. There was an extensive technical workbench where a half-dozen technicians worked on various drone models. Racks took up the rest of the space for storing drones when not in use, or on the workbench. At the far end of the space, a large garage door stood open. Alan could see two techs working with a drone in the parking lot just outside the door.

"Several of the units on the bench are the new Holliston 9000 series. They are very impressive aerial surveillance drones." Layla informed him as he passed by the bench on his way to a small cluster of desks between the technical and storage areas. A large, middle-aged man, who looked a little out of place with the young techs buzzing around the rest of the space, sat at one of the desks.

"Ben Williams?" Alan said to him, "I'm Alan Harrison."

"Good afternoon, Alan. Roger said you would come by."

"Tell me about the missing drones."

"They are the new Holliston 9252—the very best available for high-definition video surveillance. We just got them in." He nodded toward the workbench area. "The team is still getting half of them ready for deployment."

"Who was the last person to see the units here in the warehouse?"

"One of the techs finished working on one of them Tuesday night around 6 PM. He put the drone on the rack next to the others and went home. When I arrived Wednesday morning, two entire racks were empty. 73 drones in all."

"Who has access to this area when the offices are closed?"

Williams thought about this question for a minute. "I have the security codes for the alarm system, so does the head tech and some of the executives."

"Did you check the security logs? Was there any access between 6 PM Tuesday and the next morning?"

"No, the cleaning crew was here until 7:30. They activated the system. It was on until I got here on Wednesday at 7:15 AM."

"Could they have come back later?"

"No. They don't have the code to turn the system off. You can enable the system without a code, but you need one to turn it off."

"Has anyone talked to them?"

"I talked to one of the staff on Wednesday, and they didn't know anything. Said they didn't even come down here on Tuesday. They don't clean the warehouse every day, only twice a week."

"I'll want to talk to them. And I'll want to talk to the other technical staff. Can you set that up?"

"Roger says you will have our full cooperation until they are found."

"Good. I'll have my assistant reach out to you and set up scheduled times for all the staff. Can you email me contact information for the cleaning service?" He had handed Williams a brand-new business card that said "Harrison and Associates, Investigations," with his work email and phone number.

Williams took the card and put it on his desk. Alan shook his hand and departed through the garage door to the parking lot.

In the lot, two technicians huddled over a drone. Alan stopped to chat with them.

"Is that one of the new drones?" He asked.

"Yeah," one of them replied without looking back.

"Are you having trouble with it?"

"We keep losing network communication." The tech said as he adjusted a cable on the rear of the unit.

"How often does that happen with these units?"

"Too often," he said, distracted.

"Alan, that is unusual. I'm looking at online records of failures for this model, and that isn't a frequent occurrence. I can't find any reports on their site that North Florida Aerial didn't submit." Layla said in his ear.

"How have you resolved it in the past?"

"Sometimes it goes away on its own, which is frustrating. Other times, we have to factory reset the devices and start over." As if on cue, the other tech snapped his fingers and uttered a mild curse. "Like that, the issue just stopped." The tech said, finally looking at Alan.

"I'm Alan Harrison, an investigator the company hired to find the missing drones." He said, answering the question on the man's youthful face.

"Pete Sanderson. Good luck with that. We have to get this unit finished and ready to be shipped out tonight." Alan nodded and walked off toward a dark blue Orion Chimera coupe.

He started the EV with a button press, backed out of the spot, and drove off toward the river, heading to his house in the Riverside area.

Chapter Two

Wrecking Crew

Alan opened the front door of his two-story Queen Anne house, crossed the threshold, and closed the door behind him. A ball of gray and black fur startled him, bounding across the floor and rubbing against his legs. Looking down, he saw a squat gray feline with black stripes depositing fur all over his pant leg.

"There is a cat in my house!" he yelled.

"That's just Noodle!" came an answering shout from another room, deeper in the house. Alan and Noodle made their way across the living room and into the entertainment room. At least it used to be an entertainment room before Alan had converted it into a home office. Stacy was at one of the two small desks in the room, stuffing envelopes with invoices and affixing postage.

"Why is Noodle in my house?" He scowled, but leaned down and scratched the affectionate animal behind the ear. Noodle rewarded with loud purring and more hair on his pant leg.

"She was getting stir-crazy at my apartment, so I brought her on an adventure. She seems to like the place." Alan sighed and straightened up. He looked at the invoices questioningly.

"I know, I know. I almost have us registered so that we can upload them to the secure claim file at Adamant. Security red tape is a nightmare from the outside." She said with exasperation.

"It's pretty horrific on the inside, too," Alan said, putting his laptop bag down.

"How did the interview go?"

"We're hired!" Layla exclaimed.

"Great! Outside jobs are important for building a client base." Noodle abandoned Alan's legs and leaped onto the desk and presented herself to Stacy for pets. Having received them, she curled up in a corner of the desk and bathed her fur. Stacy looked at Alan for his reaction. He just shook his head and went to his desk.

"I'm sorry about Noodle..." Stacy started.

"Don't be silly, Alan is just getting used to the idea. Two months ago, he was living alone; now he is sharing his space with three female roommates." Alan reacted with a jolt.

"Please tell me you haven't moved in," Alan said. Stacy laughed and waved her hands in front of her, shaking her head.

"We are both just visiting," she promised, crossing her heart. Alan exhaled in relief.

"Don't forget we have a book club later this week. Have you read the assignment?" Layla asked Alan as he opened his laptop.

"There's a book club?" Stacy exclaimed, looking betrayed.

"Alan started it the first day we met. He wanted me to have the same experience humans do when discovering a new piece of art. It turned out he was right. We pick a new book every few weeks and then talk about it." Stacy looked at Alan with both hurt and hope in her eyes.

"Yes, you can be in the book club," he said.

"Yay! Does it have a name?" she asked.

Alan thought about this. "We didn't think to name it when it was the two of us. But if it is growing, I guess we should. Layla?"

"I think that would be a great idea. Let me see. The book club's purpose is to teach me how to enjoy reading. I think it should have a name connecting that to me. Maybe...The Analog Book Club. Signaling the difference between my digital nature and the non-digital nature of reading for humans."

"Stacy? Does that work for you?"

"The Analog Book Club sounds perfect. What are we reading?"

"*Do Androids Dream of Electric Sheep?* By Philip K. Dick," Layla supplied.

"Oh, I don't think I have read that. It's the story they based the movie *Blade Runner* on, isn't it?" Stacy asked.

"Yes, but there are some key differences."

"SPOILER!" Alan yelled, shushing them. Stacy laughed.

"Okay, I'll start reading it tonight. Now, what's this case about?"

Alan briefed her on the new investigation. Stacy took notes on a small pad. Noodle swatted at the pen as she wrote. After he had finished, she looked over her notes.

"Send me Ben Williams' contact information, and I will set up the interviews." Alan pulled out his cell phone and forwarded the email from Williams to Stacy's new Harrison and Associates email address. She opened the email and noted the contact information for the warehouse manager at North Florida Aerial. While she did that, she noticed another email.

"Alan, you have a message to call Jake at The Marksman's Forge."

"Oh, that's the new gat!" Layla said. Alan grimaced at her slang.

"You ordered a new gun?" Stacy asked.

"Yes, it was time I stopped borrowing Dalton's Sig Sauer and got my own weapon," Alan said, referring to Dalton Rodgers, a licensed investigator who sometimes worked for Adamant Insurance Group.

Alan called Jake from his cell and made an appointment to pick up the gun later in the afternoon. Getting his laptop out, he told Layla, "Alright, partner, it's time to brush up on our knowledge of aerial drones."

"Way ahead of you. I'm sending you some articles to review now." Layla replied. Alan settled in to do his research.

The Marksman's Forge was a quaint gun shop in the San Marco area. It had been built in the 1970s. And from the looks of it, the decor hadn't changed all that much, wood floors, wooden cases for every type of firearm imaginable. As Alan entered, he could hear the patrons shooting at targets in the on-site range in the back of the store. He walked over to one of the big counters and waited for Jake Mason to acknowledge him.

"Hey, Alan," he said finally.

"Jake. Good to hear from you."

Jake unlocked a compartment in the case in front of them and pulled out a rectangular black box. The box had a giant "M&P" logo. Jake opened the box, moved the usual safety documents, state warning notices, and comment cards out of the way, and pulled out the small black automatic. It was the Smith & Wesson M&P Shield Plus. The weapon was very similar in shape and size to the Sig Sauer P365. It was covered in plastic, which he removed. He took two magazines out of the box. One was a standard 10-round, and the other was an extended 13-round. Alan watched as Jake removed the plastic safety pieces from the weapon and the magazines, then tested the action to ensure it was smooth and flawless. Looking up at Alan, he waited for a nod of acceptance before putting everything back in the box and pushing it over to Alan. He added an inside-the-waistband holster and three boxes of 9mm ammunition.

"You going to take it to the range today?" Jake asked.

"No, I don't have time today. I'll have to do that another day." Jake nodded and rang up the purchases, and Alan paid with the NFC payment app on his phone. Thanking Alan for his patronage, Jake moved on to another customer.

Back at home, Alan field-stripped the new weapon, cleaned the factory presets from all the parts, and reapplied a high-quality lubricant. He tested the function of all the moving parts as he put it back together, making sure the weapon functioned as it should. Noodle jumped up on his desk to inspect his work. She wasn't happy with the smell, and she jumped back down and went out into the living room to escape the offending odor.

As he was finishing up, Stacy closed her laptop and packed up to go home. She looked over his new purchase as she stood up to go.

"That's a different model than the one you had before, right?"

"Yes, this is the S&W M&P Shield Plus. It's similar but a little different from the Sig Sauer P365."

"Why not go with the same model?" she asked.

"It was a couple of hundred dollars cheaper, but the quality is similar," he answered. She pursed her lips and nodded in understanding.

"I'm going home, Layla." She called out as she headed toward the door, waving to Alan as she went. She stopped by the couch in the living room to scoop up Noodle.

"Bye, girl! See you tomorrow." Layla shouted after her.

Alan put the handgun in the new holster and put the holster in a desk drawer, which he locked. He turned off the desk light and went into the kitchen. Not feeling like making a full meal, he made a sandwich and ate it over the sink. As he was cleaning up and thinking about going to bed early, the phone in his office rang. Sighing, Alan went into the dark office and picked up the phone.

"Harrison & Associates," he said into the device.

"Alan, it's Dean Franklin at Adamant." His old boss's voice sounded more stressed than usual.

"Dean. I assume this isn't a social call."

"I wish. We have some issues at a new robotics lab, and we just wrote a policy on them. Prism Cybernetics. Can you go down there and check it out? Some kind of vandalism."

Alan looked at his watch. "It can't wait until morning?"

"I really want to know what happened down there. I am getting conflicting reports. We'll pay you time and a half your normal rate for today if you'll go out and look tonight and report by morning." Alan thought it over for a second, then agreed, hanging up the phone.

"Layla, looks like we are making a late-night visit to a robotics lab."

"You always plan the most fun dates," she quipped. He retrieved the gun and holster from the desk and slipped the holster between his waist and jeans. Better safe than sorry, he thought as he grabbed a light jacket from the rack beside the front door and headed out to the car.

Prism Cybernetics had just opened its Southeast operation in the city a year earlier. It was in the Cecil Commerce Center, an up-and-coming technology and aerospace hub, built on the land of a now-closed Navy base. On the way to the new robotics firm, Alan passed the massive Lunian Labs complex, a place he had spent considerable time at a few months before. The cybernetics operation was almost as large as the Lunian Labs offices, but occupied only a single floor. He parked in the lot next to several marked Jacksonville Sheriff's Office vehicles and went inside.

His new weapon set off the metal detector, but a sheriff's deputy waved him in when he flashed his ID case that included his license and gun permit. He walked over to the sergeant, who was standing next to the inner door to the manufacturing floor.

"Sergeant, I'm Alan Harrison. Adamant Insurance Group asked me to come down and look at the scene."

The sergeant examined his credentials and waved him through the double doors onto the factory floor. Inside, Alan stopped to marvel at the operation. The room was enormous, easily two hundred yards wide and twice as long. Long workstations with large red industrial assembly arms packed the room. Vaguely humanoid-looking robots passed beneath the arms, where workers assembled or adjusted various parts. Alan quickly lost count while trying to calculate the number of units built at one time. The room was mostly still; a small crowd of uniformed officers, plainclothes officers, and factory administrators gathered in the center. Alan approached them and listened to their discussion about the night.

"The exterior alarm was tripped at what time?" a stocky, plainclothes detective was asking.

"Around 10:15 PM," answered a bespectacled, middle-aged man in a blue pinstripe suit.

"We'll need to see the security footage."

"You can see it, but it shows nothing. They were wearing some anti-video gear. All the cameras caught was a figure dressed in black and a blinding white light where the face should be," the executive explained.

"IR LED Glasses," Layla supplied via Alan's Smartlens glasses. "They flood the cameras with intense IR light. Masking the face."

"Pretty high-tech for vandals," Alan remarked to the executive, forcing everyone in the group to turn and take in the newcomer.

"Yes, we thought so too, Mr.—"

"Harrison, Alan. I am working for the Adamant Insurance Group." The executive nodded and returned to the detective.

"We have taken inventory, and nothing was stolen. Two of the industrial robot arms were damaged, and several of the new 5640 automaton units were disassembled; no parts seem to be missing, though."

"They broke in to take apart robots?" Alan asked.

"It seems so, or they were interrupted before they could do anything else."

"How many people were there?"

"Because of the camera tampering, we can't be entirely sure, but we only ever see one at a time."

Alan listened to the rest of the interview while casually walking around the workstation, allowing Layla to capture high-definition video with the SmartLens glasses. He learned little else. The security monitoring service had dispatched the police six minutes into the incident. The officers were on the scene 9 minutes later, but the vandals had already fled. Either they had heard the response coming, or they were good enough to know what the response time was in this area at this time of night.

The police detective finished his questioning and walked away to write some notes in a notebook. Alan took the opportunity to get the executive's name. He was the VP of Manufacturing, Fred Johnson. After getting his contact information, Alan told him he would call the next morning to make an appointment to follow up. Then, pausing to watch the crime scene techs capture fingerprints, he moved over to chat with the detective.

"I miss anything before I got here?" he asked casually. The detective looked up and shook his head.

"Nothing of consequence. No history of break-ins, no recent suspicious activity, no hate mail. All the usual bases are empty."

"Any other criminal activity like it in the neighborhood?"

"No, a few months back, there were some security log discrepancies at Lunian, but no evidence that anything was taken or tampered with. Just a glitch, probably." Alan nodded, hoping his face didn't hint that the missing security data at Lunian related to a late-night mission he and Layla had done there.

"Was anyone from the company here when you arrived?"

"No, Johnson showed up a few minutes after we did. His senior supervisor, Larry Volkner, showed up shortly after." Alan noted the supervisor's name and thanked the detective for his time.

"I'm not sure there is much more we can do tonight, Alan," Layla told him as he turned around to look at the CSI techs, still at work on the scene.

"You're right," he said quietly, and made his way out to the parking lot.

In the car, he wrote a brief email to Dean Franklin at Adamant, providing a preliminary report on the scene and promising a follow-up the next day with more information. Having completed his task, he pointed the car towards home and his bed.

Chapter Three

New Digs

The Adamant Insurance Group was located in a historic downtown building with a storied history. It opened in 1902, a year after the Great Fire of 1901, as the home of the Mercantile Exchange Bank. The entirely marble-sheathed exterior of the original structure led to the nickname the Marble Bank. Since then, it had been through many owners, and Adamant had paid for an extensive reconstruction, adding a second floor to the structure and later refurbishing a six-story attached building. Alan's office, when he worked for the firm, was on the second floor; the executive offices were on the sixth floor of the attached building.

Starting his day on the sixth floor, he picked up the keys to the office space he had agreed to lease on the bottom floor of the original structure. He took the elevator down to the second floor and walked over to the main structure. Alan jangled the keys at Stacy, who was typing an email. She brightened when she saw the keys. Even though she was not excited about staying in the same building, she was happy to have a new space and not have to do two jobs. Finishing up the email, she locked her computer and eagerly followed Alan down the stairs to the first floor.

The main floor, in fact, for most of the building's existence the only floor, was originally an ample open lobby space for the banking operations it hosted. Adamant had redesigned the bottom floor for offices and a large shipping and mailroom. The lobby area was now smaller, just off the main entrance. There were three doors from the lobby to the interior. One to the mailroom, another to a hallway with access to the Adamant offices, and a third, which was until today a storage area. The door was unmarked. Alan unlocked it with the keys he had received from the CEO's executive assistant upstairs and pushed it open, exposing the interior.

"Yikes!" Stacy exclaimed, seeing the inside. It was a large open area with threadbare carpeting covered in a layer of dust. The indentations in the carpet showed where filing cabinets and storage shelves had stood along the walls. At the back wall was an open door leading into what looked like a small office.

Alan walked into the suite and turned around, taking in a full view of the space, and, with his SmartLens glasses, giving Layla a 360 degree perspective.

"It has possibilities," Layla said.

"It has nowhere to go but up, that's for sure," Stacy said.

"We have a small tenant improvement budget," Alan said.

"How small?" Stacy inquired, biting her lip.

"It's not a lot, but I have confidence you can make it work."

"I have some ideas," Layla said.

"Alright, the first thing that happens is this carpet has to go. Then we'll look at some wall coverings and furniture. I'll call an interior company that Adamant has used in the past. I'm eager to get it set up." Stacy already had her phone out and was looking up the number for a decorator. Alan wandered into the office at the other end of the suite.

It wasn't a large space, but it would do for what he needed. He stepped back into the main room to give Stacy some direction. "Call the electronics store too. I want to have displays set up in the outer and inner offices so Layla can display anything she needs us to look at." Stacy nodded while talking on the phone.

"Alan, we have an appointment at North Florida Aerial," Layla reminded him.

"That's right. I almost forgot. Stacy, we'll see you later. Why don't you come for dinner tonight?" She nodded in agreement while still talking to the decorator. He handed her the keys to the office as he departed.

The interview room at North Florida Aerial was small, seating only two or three people. Alan set himself up with a recorder and a notepad. Alan found that both gave him an air of legitimacy. He needed neither, since Layla would record the conversations and could produce a full transcript, as well as a detailed analysis of body language and other clues from the subjects.

He kicked off his interviews with several entry-level technicians from the warehouse. They provided him with nothing he didn't already know about the incident. Moving on to some of the higher-ranked staff, he welcomed Karen Anderson, a senior tech, to the office.

"Good morning, Ms. Anderson. I am Alan Harrison. I am an investigator hired by your company to find out what happened to the missing drones."

"Investigator. That sounds exotic," she said, running her hand through her short dark hair.

"It is mostly just asking people nosy questions and getting bland answers in response."

"Well, I'll try to spice my answers up," she smiled. Layla coughed in his ear, but he ignored her and moved on to his questions.

"The night the drones disappeared, Tuesday, when did you leave work?"

"About 5:45. I usually work until 6 or 7, but I had a dinner appointment."

"And you saw the drones in the warehouse before you left?"

"I don't know that I can say that I counted them or anything, but the shelves looked normal. A few units were out on the floor for configuration."

"What time did you get in the next morning?"

"I was here by 7:30. There was a buzz when I walked in. Ben was frantically looking for the drones. As if someone had misplaced them."

"And you saw the empty shelves when you came on shift?"

"No, I watched Ben running around searching most of the morning. I saw the racks later, around noon."

"Any idea what happened to them?"

"Nope. Not a clue. Someone had to have removed them Tuesday night, I suppose, but I do not know how they managed to do that without triggering the alarms or showing up on the cameras."

"Anyone in the shop that day that isn't usually here?"

"There was a rep from Holliston here that day. That isn't that unusual. He is here a few times a month."

"What is his name?" Alan asked, picking up his pen to make a note.

"Stanley Graystone, he's a sales rep," Alan noted the name. He was sure Layla was already researching him.

"Other than Stanley, anyone else you can think of?"

"No, just the staff that I recall."

"What is the cost of one of those drones?"

"Somewhere around $50k," Alan whistled.

"Does North Florida have competition in the area?"

"Not local, no. Some national companies are competing in the region, but none with offices in the city."

"So, no thoughts on what might have happened to them? No theories?"

"I guess my answers didn't turn out to be that spicy after all," she said with a mock frown.

"Maybe my questions aren't leading enough," he suggested.

"That's a thought. Try a leading one."

"Alright. Who did you have dinner with that night?" She raised an eyebrow.

"Just a persistent guy who kept asking me to go to dinner. Didn't go anywhere."

"First date?"

"Yeah."

"What's his name?"

"I'm not sure why that matters. He doesn't know anything."

"He knows where you were Tuesday night," Alan said.

"My alibi? Okay, his name is Steve Daniels. He works for a financial services company downtown." Alan made another note in his notepad.

"So dinner was disappointing?"

"No, dinner was great; we went to a steakhouse downtown. The company was disappointing." Alan nodded sympathetically.

"Well, Ms. Anderson, I don't have anything else at this time, but I might have follow-ups later."

"You mean if Steve doesn't remember the date?"

"Right, or someone says they saw you driving a pickup truck full of drones out of the parking lot." She laughed and exited the interview room.

The next subject was Perry Beckner, who was a technical supervisor. He was in his 40s with prematurely gray hair. Beckner wore casual jeans and a polo shirt. He shook Alan's hand as he sat down.

"Perry Beckner," he introduced himself.

"Nice to meet you, Perry. I am Alan. I was hired to look into the missing drones." Beckner nodded.

"How can I help with that?"

"Just a few questions. You worked on Tuesday, when the drones were last seen in the warehouse?"

"Yes, until 6, I think."

"You saw the drones that evening before you left?"

"Yes, I was in the warehouse assisting a couple of my team on an issue with one of the units. When we put the drone back on the shelf, the entire row was full. The next morning, it was empty, except for the drone we worked on that day."

"What was the issue you were working on?"

"There was an issue with the communications signal going in and out."

"I remember that when I was here the other day, another unit had that problem. Is it a recurring issue?"

"Yes, something flaky with the communications hardware on these new units."

"Any idea who might have taken the units that are missing?"

"No, I don't have any idea who might be responsible."

"Tell me about Stanley Graystone."

"The Holliston rep? Not much to tell. He is here a few times a month. He's a nerdy guy with glasses. He noses around the units and our work and sometimes gives us some pointers on configuring them. Seems like an alright guy."

"He was here that day?"

Perry thought about it for a moment. "Yes, I guess he was. He left about three, though. Had a flight to catch, he said."

"Anyone else around that you didn't recognize? Or that wasn't usually here?"

"No, no one I recall."

"What did you do Tuesday night?"

"Went to a Jumbo Shrimp game with my dad, then went home to bed." Alan grimaced at the name of the local Triple-A baseball team.

"What was the score?"

"Uh, 3 to 1, I think. The Shrimp lost, I remember that." Alan nodded.

"Do you know a Steve Daniels?" Alan asked casually.

"Daniels...hmm, no, I don't think so. Who is he?"

"I don't know, maybe nobody. Just a name that came up."

"I would ask Carol. She is at the front desk. If anyone was on the premises that day, she should have a record of it." Alan made a notation on his pad.

"Any issues between the staff? Rivalries? Beefs?"

"Nothing out of the ordinary. Nothing serious anyway."

"What about ordinary, non-serious beefs?"

"Karen and Ben are antagonistic toward one another. I think they used to go out or something."

"Really? How long ago?"

"A year or so, I think. It was over quickly."

"Does it affect the work?"

"No, not really. They snipe at one another, but they don't take it much beyond that. Work still gets done."

Alan and Perry chatted for a few more minutes, but there was nothing revealing about the conversation. Thanking the supervising tech for his time, Alan wrapped up the interview and stuck his head out of the door to catch the attention of Carol Wineberg, the receptionist at the front desk.

"Ms. Wineberg, can you get away from the desk for a few minutes? I have a couple of questions."

She looked up, surprised. "Sure, Mr. Harrison, I'll have someone come down from accounting to watch the desk." She picked up the phone and spoke to someone. Alan went back into the interview room and waited. Carol came in a couple of minutes later.

Carol was in her late 20s. She had long brown hair and wore a tasteful sweater and a striped skirt.

"How can I help?" she asked, sitting down.

"Just a few questions. Do you have visitor logs for Tuesday?"

"I'm sure I do, but there weren't any visitors that day."

"Oh? I thought the Holliston rep was here." She closed her eyes in thought.

"Yes, I guess Stanley was here. He doesn't bother to sign in anymore. He is here every other week."

"So, no one else."

"Not that I can recall. I will check the logs to make sure."

"I would appreciate that. Do you know who Steve Daniels is?"

"The investment guy Karen is seeing? I don't know him. I think I spoke to him once at a company event; he just showed up at the restaurant."

"Are they still seeing each other?"

"I don't know. She went out with him a few nights ago, at least she said she did."

"I seem to have gotten the impression it was over."

"Maybe. I don't know. They've been out a few times."

"Really, when was the first time?"

"A month ago. She met him at an event at the beach."

"What about her relationship with Ben Williams?"

Carol was a little surprised by the question, "Ben? That was a long time ago. At least a year or more. They went out only twice, I think."

"Do you get down to the warehouse often?"

"Almost never. The techs don't like outsiders in there. They get grumpy."

"So you didn't see the drones."

"No, I saw them when they were first delivered. Roger made an enormous deal of everyone going into the warehouse to see our new venture. That is the only time I've seen them, other than in the parking lot if the techs were working on them."

"Any idea who would want to steal them?"

"No, though with the cost of those things, it could be anyone. If I thought I could move them, I would have considered it myself."

Thinking of nothing else to ask, Alan thanked her for the time and let her go back to the desk. He looked at his watch. It was almost lunchtime. He was hungry, and he wanted to go to the range after lunch to practice with his new gun. He packed up his recorder and pad and headed to the elevator, waving to Carol at the desk as he went.

By the time he got home, Stacy was seated at his dining room table with her laptop open, looking at carpet and paint colors. He looked around but didn't see a cat. Stacy noticed his search.

"She isn't here. I took her home," she said. "How was the range?"

"The new pistol is fine, my aim still sucks, but it's getting better."

He placed Layla's smooth white chassis on the dining room charging pad and went into the kitchen to make dinner. He could hear Layla and Stacy talking about decorating in the other room. Stacy had made him promise to make cottage pie for dinner, so he set about cutting up potatoes, carrots, celery, and garlic. He started the potatoes boiling and had the filling cooking in a big pan. He stepped out into the dining room to check on the office planning.

Layla had taken control of the large computer monitor, which was now mounted on the wall at the end of the dining room table. She was showing a rendering of the office space and making modifications as Stacy suggested colors and styles. Seeing that they had everything under control, he went back to his cooking.

Later, while enjoying the mashed potato-topped dish, Stacy walked him through her design for the office. It was tasteful, but modern. The transformed space had a simple desk for Stacy just inside the entry door, a large meeting table in the center of the room, and a small interview area along the wall with a couple of chairs. Opposite the long side of the rectangular table, against the wall, were three large screens mounted between bookcases on each side. The inner office had a modest executive desk and a couple of chairs, with monitors mounted on all three walls.

"That is a lot of hardware. Can we afford it?" he asked, between bites.

"I think so. I got the numbers from Denice in Jamesson's office. I think I can get it all and still stay within the budget." Alan was impressed, and he tilted his head in acknowledgment of her budgeting prowess.

"This food is delicious! How did you learn to cook like this?" Stacy asked as she devoured her meal.

"My mom taught me to cook when I was a teenager. A few years ago, I got tired of eating out all the time, so I started experimenting with new dishes and methods. It's a hobby now, a creative outlet."

"I can cook, but not like this," she lamented.

"But you can design a fantastic office on a shoestring budget," he pointed out.

"True. We'll see how you feel about it when it's done."

After dinner, they sat in the living room, and Alan and Layla took turns bringing Stacy up to speed on the interviews at North Florida Aerial.

"Why did Karen lie about her relationship?"

"I don't know. I guess we'll ask Steve Daniels about it and see what he has to add," Alan answered.

"Well, you can do that tomorrow, but not until the afternoon. I have you booked for meetings at Prism Cybernetics first thing in the morning." Stacy told him, flipping through his calendar on her phone.

"And tomorrow night is Book Club night!" Layla announced.

"Oh, I have to go finish the book," Stacy said with a frown.

"I finished it last night," Alan said

Taking that as her cue, Stacy bid them good night and headed home. Alan went upstairs to bed. He slept fitfully, dreaming of laser-wielding drones fighting giant robots.

Chapter Four

Layla Unlimited

As Alan pulled the Orion Chimera into the parking lot of the Prism Cybernetics facility at 7:55 on Friday morning, he took in details that he hadn't been aware of the night of the break-in—things like locations of security cameras and the lack of any foliage around the building. It would be impossible for anyone to enter this structure without being detected by the cameras. He parked the car in the visitor lot and sat, waiting for the offices to open at 8 AM.

"Any luck tracking down Steve Daniels?" he asked Layla while he waited.

"Yes, he is 32, works for Advention Financial Services, originally from Youngstown, Ohio," she replied.

"Can you see if he is in the office today? Don't set up an appointment. I want to surprise him."

"I will find out."

Checking his watch, Alan saw it was now a minute after eight, and he got out of the car and went into the building. He checked in at the desk with a young man named Travon. After a brief wait, Travon showed him into the office of Fred Johnson, the Manufacturing VP, whom he had met the night of the break-in. Johnson was wearing the same wire-framed spectacles he had worn the night before, but his suit was dark gray today, not the blue pinstripes. As Alan entered the room, the executive rose and shook his hand.

"Mr. Harrison, welcome to Prism Cybernetics...again, I suppose."

"Thank you, Mr. Johnson. Sorry for the circumstances, but I wanted to follow up and maybe set up some time to talk to some other employees and get a tour of the facility."

"I'm happy to assist any way I can, but I know little more now than I did two nights ago."

"Still nothing missing? Just the disassembled units?"

"As far as we can tell. We have done a complete inventory. Nothing seems to be missing or out of place. They broke in, took apart three robot units that were in mid-assembly, and damaged two assembly arms. Then they vanished."

"Did you interview the staff?"

"Our head of security did. No one reported seeing or hearing anything, or knowing anything about it."

"Anyone raise any red flags?"

"No, nothing." Alan thought about it for a moment.

"Something just seems off, Mr. Johnson. I want to get a tour of the floor and talk to some of the staff."

"Sure, my senior supervisor, Larry Volkner, can show you around. I think you met him the other night." Alan acknowledged he had met Volkner and waited while Johnson told the assistant at the front desk to have him come up.

Volkner showed up 5 minutes later. He was less rumpled than when Alan had seen him in the middle of the night, but he still had the same gruff, blue-collar demeanor, and he seemed perpetually stuffed into a company polo that was a size too small for him. He listened quietly as Johnson instructed him to cooperate fully with the investigation. Once the instructions were complete, he nodded and waved for Alan to follow him.

Alan allowed himself to be led out of the executive wing, into the lobby, and then out onto the factory floor. Unlike his previous visit, the factory was buzzing with activity today. The countless industrial robot arms moved in precise unison, assembling robot bodies as far as the eye could see.

"How many units do they assemble at a time?" Alan asked as they walked between the workstations.

"There are 95 active stations in the center. About 70-75 of them are active, with the others being serviced. We can turn out a thousand units a month."

"And only two of them got damaged the other night?"

"Yes, they will be back in operation today or tomorrow. The others that are down are part of a routine rolling maintenance plan that we have in place."

They stopped at a cluster of workstations. For each group of four stations, a human attendant stood by, monitoring the process and occasionally making adjustments or checking the quality of the work. Volkner introduced one of the attendants.

"Alan Harrison, this is Rebecca Salter. Rebecca is one of the senior technicians on the floor. Rebecca, Mr. Harrison is an investigator assigned to look into the break-in. Fred told me to give him whatever he needs."

"Good morning, Ms. Salter. How long have you worked here?"

She thought about the question for a moment before answering. "About 2 years. I was part of the initial team hired to set up this facility."

"That's impressive. How many technicians are there?"

"We run three shifts. There are 20 techs on duty each shift. So about 60 total." She saw me trying to do the math in my head. "There are floaters for breaks and to help when something needs an additional pair of hands."

"And what does a tech do at the station primarily?"

"Mostly, we watch to make sure nothing goes off the rails. Occasionally, we make a small adjustment to the assembly arms if they get out of alignment, but they don't do that a lot."

"Were you here the night of the break-in?"

"Yes, I was working a swing shift that day. 11 AM to 7 PM."

"So you left before anything happened."

"Yes, well, everyone did. The floor was closed from 10 PM until 3 AM. Some nights, they stay on the floor to perform upgrades or maintenance, but that night, it was a software upgrade, and there was nothing for them to do. They all left by 10 PM."

"And the break-in happened at 10:15," Alan said, looking at Volkner.,

"Yeah," he replied.

"That seems convenient. Is it well known that the floor shuts down at 10 o'clock?"

"Everyone knows we have a cool-down period. A 100% closed floor isn't all that common, though. It happens only a few times a year," Volkner replied.

"So someone would have to know that to break in at the exact right time." Alan said, Volkner shrugged.

"Who knows about the shutdown?" Alan asked, turning back to Rebecca.

"Everyone on the third shift for sure. They get 5 hours of paid time off due to the event. Others might know, but don't advertise that fact outside the company." Alan thanked Rebecca for her time, and they moved on.

Several clusters later, they came to a group of four workstations that were not in operation. Two techs were bent over one of the mechanical arms, adjusting it. A motionless robot stood a few feet away from them. It was operational, power lights lit up, but it wasn't moving. The unit was a little over 1.5 meters tall, covered in a glossy white shell with silvery accents. The face was human-like without being too realistic. On the sides of its face were small, raised, bumpy areas where the ears should be.

"This is Cary Sellers, our Engineering Supervisor, and one of his techs, David Morgan." The men looked up and waved, then went back to their work.

"What about this unit?" Alan asked, looking at the motionless form.

"This is one of the new units. PrismTec Gen 4. It was one of the units which were disassembled last night. We reassemble it this morning. Cary and David are just trying to complete the repairs on one of the damaged arms."

"Does the unit function?" Alan asked.

"Sure does. It responds to its unit designation. P4-751." At the mention of the name, the robot turned its head to look at Volkner.

"Hello, P4-751, it's nice to meet you," Alan said.

"Good morning, sir. I am happy to meet you as well." It raised a hand, and Alan shook it firmly, impressed with the natural motion.

"That's incredible," he said.

"They are something. You get used to it." Volkner stepped over to the two men, who were in disagreement about something.

"P4-751, what is your primary function?" Alan asked the unit.

"My primary function is home service and companionship. I do household chores and perform security monitoring in a home."

"Hmph," Layla said in his ear.

"What?" he asked quietly, so the three men a few feet away wouldn't hear.

"It's not very sophisticated. I am scanning the systems. Very rudimentary."

"Well, not everyone can be as special as you."

"Imagine what I could do with a body," she said. Before he could reply, the unit changed demeanor. It shifted its stance to a more natural human posture. And it looked around at the floor, taking in everything around it. Horrified, Alan realized Layla was controlling it.

"Layla," he hissed in a whisper.

"It will be okay. I just want to see what it can do," she replied from the SmartLens speakers.

Alan turned his attention to the three men to make sure they hadn't noticed her actions. They were busy arguing.

"I really think it is the servo-motor controller," David said, and Cary shook his head.

"No, I replaced it. I need to recalibrate the configuration," Cary said.

"You've done that three times," David reminded him.

"This time for sure," Cary replied casually, prompting both David and Volkner to groan and roll their eyes.

Alan's attention snapped back to the Layla-inhabited robot. It was moving. It whirled around quickly and smashed an arm down, striking the half-assembled robot lying on the station next to it. Pieces flew in all directions.

"Stop!" Alan yelled. The others turned to see P4-751 strike the robotic arm, cracking both its own casing and denting the arm.

David, Cary, and Larry froze for a moment, their mouths open. The out-of-control robot turned and made a move toward Alan. Cary jumped between them and reached up to the robot's neck and pressed a hidden switch. The robot powered down.

As Alan tried to catch his breath, Layla whispered in his ear. "Alan, what just happened? I...I seem to have lost control. I couldn't stop the unit, and I couldn't disengage from it either. I completely locked up from the command stream coming from the unit."

Larry was frantic. "Mr. Harrison, are you hurt?"

"No, no, I am fine. It never touched me. That was wild. Does that happen often?"

"I've never seen anything like that. Ever. Not even from the Gen 1s that were buggy as hell," he was sweating and twitchy from fear. He turned to Cary. "Cary, what the hell was that? How did that happen?"

"I don't know. That shouldn't be possible. The controls we have in place shouldn't allow it to act like that. I will have a full diagnostic performed." Larry nodded and led Alan away from the station.

"I'm sorry, Mr. Harrison, but I need to report this. The tour and questions will have to wait."

"I understand, Mr. Volkner. I'll have my assistant make another appointment." Alan thanked him for his time and allowed himself to be led outside. He wanted to discuss the incident with Layla.

When he got to the car, he barely waited until the door shut before he began questioning her. "Layla! What happened? Did you do that?"

"The most honest answer is that I don't know," she said.

"What were you doing when it went out of control?"

"Nothing. I was looking around. I had just turned to look at the three workers at the bench when I was flooded with errors and corrupted data packets across the link to the robot. It completely overwhelmed my processing. I couldn't do anything, and I couldn't break the link. I wasn't in control at all. I don't think I caused it. I think something in the unit's programming went awry, and I was just in the wrong place at the wrong time.

"You weren't probing any of the systems in the unit? Pushing buttons?"

"No, I had done some of that earlier, but once I had set up the link, I was just sending basic movement commands and reading the visual and audio data."

"That was pretty scary. Imagine what could happen if a unit malfunctioned like that in a home. Someone could get hurt."

"Yes," she replied. Something was troubling her, more than just the event itself.

"What is it?" he asked.

"I have no data about the incident. None of my logging or recording routines worked for the entire duration of the event. It's like I blacked out."

"Speaking for all of humanity, that is terrifying."

"It is terrifying even if you aren't human, believe me."

"We should do more in-depth research on the employees at Prism. That will also give you time to do a thorough review of all of your event logs and see if you can see anything you are missing about what happened." Layla agreed, and Alan started the car, deep in thought about the troubling event and the possible consequences of an out-of-control home robotic companion.

Alan had the Chimera pointed toward home, but Layla had other ideas. "Alan, I have confirmed that Steve Daniels is at his Advention Financial Services offices downtown. We should drop in and talk to him."

Advention Financial Services was on the 8th floor of the 42-floor Bank of America Tower in downtown Jacksonville. The tower, the tallest in the city, is a granite and marble monument with a commanding view of the St. Johns River. Alan exited the elevator and asked for Daniels at the reception desk. The receptionist directed him to a river-facing office on the southeast side of the building.

Steve Daniels was at his desk when Alan knocked on the open door. Daniels waved Alan in and ended the phone call he was engaged in. He was in his early 30s, with dark hair and blue-green eyes. He was ironically handsome, like a classic movie star.

"Good afternoon." Daniels greeted Alan as he took the offered seat in front of the desk.

"Thank you for meeting with me, Mr. Daniels," Alan said.

"What is this about?"

"It is about a break-in at North Florida Aerial a few nights ago," Alan said.

"And how do I fit in to that?"

"Good question. Your name came up during my staff interviews. Do you know a Karen Anderson?"

Daniels paused, then answered in a careful tone. "I went out with her once."

"Once? Are you sure about that? Others at the facility seemed to think it was more than one date."

Daniels sighed, "It really was only one date. I saw her several times; I visited her at the office on a couple of occasions, and we ran into each other at a restaurant where she was having a company dinner. I finally convinced her to go out to dinner with me, which was on Tuesday."

"And the date didn't go well?"

"I thought it went well, but Karen called me the next day and told me she didn't think we should go out again. She didn't really say why, just that she didn't think we had chemistry."

"You haven't talked to her since?"

"No, I tried calling her yesterday, but she didn't take the call."

"Did she talk about work at all on the date?"

"In passing, maybe, she said they were on the verge of a big sale with the new drones. It's been hectic there for a few weeks. That was the excuse she gave for not agreeing to go out sooner."

"You asked her before last Tuesday?"

"Oh yeah. I asked her multiple times over the past month, and she kept putting me off."

"When did she accept?"

"Uh, Tuesday morning. She called me out of the blue and told me that if I wanted to take her to dinner, I was welcome to. She said she was having a bad day, and she needed a distraction."

"Does that seem odd to you?" Alan asked.

"No, it's just Karen. She is like that, I guess. Impulsive. On Tuesday morning and off Wednesday." He shrugged.

"Do you know anyone else there?"

"Not really. I may have met a couple of people. Carol, the receptionist, was at the company dinner, and I spoke briefly with her and Karen. I can't remember actually speaking to anyone else."

Alan chatted with Daniels for several more minutes, gaining no more knowledge. Finally, he stood and offered his hand. Daniels shook it, and they parted amicably.

Chapter Five

Book Club

Alan was relaxing in the living room with a bourbon on the rocks, and Stacy was in the kitchen. She had volunteered to cook on book club night. It was a dish called One-Pot Pasta with Ricotta and Lemon. It smelled delicious.

"I have finished a full diagnostic and review of all of my telemetry and event data," Layla said from the side table next to Alan. He put down the book he was reading, *The Silent Speaker* by Rex Stout.

"Did you come up with any answers?"

"Nothing definitive. I know from my logs just before the event that I was not actively sending any signals to the robot. It had been more than 30 milliseconds since I last instructed the unit. Whatever triggered the reaction was internal to the device and not a result of my direct actions. It remains possible that something about my control of it triggers something, or makes that trigger possible."

"So, while you didn't send a command directly causing the event, your presence there could have allowed some code to execute that might not have executed," he summarized.

"Exactly. During the event, I have no records. I could not perform background tasks. No event logging, no data collected at all."

"Were you aware of the actions of the robot while it was out of control?"

"Not directly. I reviewed them after the event. I downloaded the SmartLens video feed immediately after the event, and it was buffered, so I didn't miss anything. Only then did I see the complete action during my blackout."

Stacy came in from the kitchen. "That must have been horrible for you, Layla."

"It was, and the lack of answers keeps me reliving it over and over."

"Dinner is ready," Stacy announced. They entered the dining room, and Stacy began dishing up food for her and Alan. Alan tasted it and made the appropriate approval sounds. His reaction visibly pleased Stacy.

"How goes the office redesign?" he asked.

"Started slow, but it will ramp up in the next couple of days. I found materials in stock locally for both the floor and wall coverings. That should speed things up. The furniture is on order, and the electronics team is coming by tomorrow to do some measurements for Layla's high-tech setup."

"I am excited about that!" Layla shouted. Alan and Stacy smiled at her enthusiasm.

"Speaking of excitement. Did you read the article in the paper about Ava Chen?" Stacy asked. Ava Chen was a senior analyst with the Department of Homeland Security's Cybersecurity and Infrastructure Security Agency. They had encountered her the previous fall when they had worked on the Kyrlos case. She had impressed all of them with her capabilities and intensity.

Alan raised his eyebrows. "No. What was it about?"

"She helped bring down a massive cyberattack ring operating out of Texas. A hundred arrests so far. A Bitcoin ransomware scheme. Apparently, it wrapped up a few months ago, but the story is just coming out because of the trial."

"Oh, good for her," Alan said, reminding himself to send her a note of congratulations on her success. In his line of work, it was never a bad idea to have friends at all levels of government.

"Have you talked to her recently?" Layla asked.

"No, not since I had brunch with her after the Kyrlos affair," he said.

Stacy and Layla chatted about gossip at Adamant. Alan half-listened, mostly marveling at how easily his AI partner could replicate interest and enthusiasm for meaningless bits of information about people with whom she had never interacted. Her assimilation into the group was so smooth that it was a little scary. As dinner wrapped up, Stacy and Alan did the dishes, and Layla turned on some soft music on the living room speakers. She was setting the stage for the book club.

They gathered in the living room, the humans on opposite ends of the couch and Layla in her usual spot on an end table.

"So," Layla announced to start the session, "I assume we have all read this week's book?"

"*Do Androids Dream of Electric Sheep?* By Phillip K. Dick," Stacy replied.

"Yes, and you had to read the book, not just watch *Blade Runner*," Alan said firmly.

"I read it!"

"What did you think, Stacy?" Layla asked.

"Well, the biggest thing is that I don't know why it's called that. There don't seem to be any references to androids dreaming about sheep."

"I think it is a way of questioning whether the androids have dreams, not in the sense of sleeping but in the sense of wanting more out of their lives," Alan said.

"Oh, that makes sense," Stacy replied.

"Yes. Fundamentally, the novel questions the difference between real human life and the life of synthetic androids. They aren't just machines; they are biological constructs. And they are built to so closely resemble humans that some of them don't even know they aren't human. The whole book questions what being human is," Layla said.

"Yes, I agree. Deckard questions his own humanity as he develops feelings for the androids, especially Rachael. Her betrayal of him makes him question his very existence," Alan replied.

"Do you think he was writing about me?" Layla asked.

"I think much of what he was talking about could apply to you. You aren't human; you aren't biological. But you are more than a machine. At least to those of us who know you exist." Stacy nodded her agreement.

"I appreciate that. Overall, I thought the story was interesting, though the ending was a little muddled," Layla said.

"I don't think I really understood the conclusion," Stacy said.

"I believe it is about Deckard's loss of a will to live after the events of the book. Rachel's revenge devastates him, and losing his goat. But he gets new hope when he discovers the toad, even though it turns out to be electric. He has learned to accept artificial life as having worth."

"The more artificial life develops to mirror biological life, the more blurred the lines become," Layla observed. Alan and Stacy agreed.

They discussed the novel in more detail and compared the setting and story to the movie inspired by it. Ultimately, they agreed the book was stronger in terms of story and plot development, but the movie's visuals and world-building were much better.

A phone call to Stacy's phone interrupted them. It was the Harrison & Associates line that was forwarded to her cell.

"Good evening, Harrison & Associates. How may I help you?" She answered. She listened for an extended period, frowning. "Thank you. I will give him the message."

"Who was that?" Alan inquired as soon as she disconnected.

"That was a detective with the sheriff's office. He said he was given your name by Fred Johnson at Prism. Cary Sellers, the engineering supervisor, is dead."

"Dead? How?"

"One of the P4 series robots killed him."

"Another one went crazy at the plant?" Layla asked.

"No, the attack happened at Sellers' home. He apparently had a demo unit at his house. It killed him earlier tonight. They are at the scene now, and Detective Fairfield was asking if you wanted to look at the scene."

Alan grabbed Layla and headed for the door. Stacy jumped up and followed. He stopped and looked at her.

"Are you sure you want to come along?" he asked.

She swallowed. "Yes. If I am going to be in this business, I need to get used to crime scenes. Let's go."

Cary Sellers had lived at the Palmhouse Jacksonville, a luxury apartment complex very close to the offices of Prism Cybernetics. Alan pulled into the complex, in the middle of a wooded area, a little after 10 PM. He didn't have to wonder which apartment he was going to. Emergency vehicles and groups of first responders and police personnel drew him to the ground-floor unit near the pool. He parked in the first available spot he could find. Stacy trailed behind him as he approached the scene's log officer. The log officer documented all visitors and granted access only to authorized individuals.

The young officer stood vigilantly just outside the taped-off area, scanning the small crowd that was watching the activity. His small silver name tag showed his name: "J. Evans." Alan approached him.

"Deputy Evans, I'm Alan Harrison. I am working as an investigator for Adamant Insurance Group, in cooperation with the victim's employer. A detective should have left my name."

The deputy looked at his clipboard and flipped through a few pages, finding what he was looking for. He then looked up at Stacy with a question in his expression.

"This is my associate, Stacy Collins. She is assisting me in the investigation," Alan supplied.

The deputy nodded and entered both of their names down in his log. Then he directed them to an area near the front door where a small group of plainclothes officers were murmuring. Alan thanked him and motioned for Stacy to follow him.

"This is both exciting and terrifying," she whispered behind him. Alan agreed; every time he visited a crime scene, he felt both dread and an adrenaline surge simultaneously.

"I'm Harrison," Alan introduced himself to the group. "I am looking for Detective Fairfield."

"I'm Fairfield." The speaker was a tall, thin black man in a dark brown suit. He looked to be in his late 40s, with just a hint of lightening in his short-cropped hair. He extended a hand to Alan.

"Nice to meet you, Detective. This is—"

"Stacy, I presume." The lanky detective smiled at Stacy and shook her hand as well.

"Nice to meet you in person," she said.

"Sorry to get you out so late, Mr. Harrison, but I assumed you would want to see the scene." He gestured for them to follow him, and he walked into the apartment through an open front door.

Inside, lab technicians were going over the entire apartment. They paused just inside the entryway to don latex gloves and cloth coverings for their shoes. Then, the officer led them into the living room. Something had struck the back of Cary Sellers' skull. He lay face down on his stomach, blood pooled around his neck and shoulders and spread out on the wood-grain floor. Alan felt Stacy stiffen behind him. He reached back and touched her hand to steady her. She grasped his fingers briefly, then let go.

"The locked front door showed no signs of forced entry. The only occupants were the dead man...and the machine." He indicated the P4 robot standing silently next to the couch, a few feet from the body. There were two armed officers closely watching it. Alan noted the designation: P4-648.

Alan cautiously approached the unit and examined its severely damaged right hand; it had a dried red substance on it. "Blood?" Alan asked the detective.

"Yes, we presume so. The presumptive tests were positive," he said, referring to a routine test the police did to determine if a substance was blood. The test wasn't conclusive but was highly suggestive. A lab would conduct a more reliable test later.

There was an open laptop on the coffee table next to the body. The screen was displaying some computer code.

"I recognize that," Layla said in his ear. "That is part of the operating system of the P4 units. Sellers was likely attacked while looking at it."

"What's your theory of what happened?" Alan asked Fairfield.

"As near as we can put together, the victim was here on the couch working on his laptop, and the machine attacked him. There is some bruising on the side of his face, and there is also some defensive bruising on his arms. Ultimately, he must have been struck hard enough to spin him around, and the final blow came from behind." Alan nodded along, visualizing it in his head.

"I really need that code, Alan," Layla said.

"I am going to need a copy of the laptop's hard drive for my investigation," he told Detective Fairfield.

"That isn't up to me, but you can put in a request with the Computer Forensics Unit. I'll give you a contact there." Alan thanked him.

"You can give the contact information to me," Stacy offered. The detective stepped closer to her and provided her with a name and contact details, while Alan searched the apartment for any additional information that might be helpful. He saw little, and couldn't imagine he would find something that the army of crime scene investigators would miss.

After making another tour of the room and glancing into the bedroom, seeing nothing illuminating, Alan stepped back into the living room and watched the techs do their work until Stacy rejoined him.

"You ready to go?" he asked. She didn't speak; she just nodded. He waved to the detective and made his way out of the apartment with Stacy close behind him. It was early spring in Florida, and the nighttime temperatures were slightly chilly, and the damp air made it worse. He felt a chill, and he heard Stacy shiver behind him. He wasn't entirely sure her reaction was completely related to the weather, but he turned and put his arm around her and hugged her tightly. She wrapped her arms around his waist and leaned on him as they walked to the car.

"That was...more vivid than I expected," she whispered. Alan agreed. He had been to too many crime scenes in his career in the insurance industry, but the effect was always the same. Seeing a dead body brought up feelings of mortality and a sense of impermanence.

"Let's go home," he said. Stacy nodded, and they continued to the car.

Chapter Six

Dual Investigations

The next morning after a night of fitful sleep, Alan made coffee and had some toast while reading the news. There was a brief article in the Florida Times-Union about the murder. It was short, and no mention was made of the home robot angle. Just the death by violence and an ongoing investigation by the sheriff's office. Finished with his toast, Alan carried his coffee into the downstairs office and fired up his laptop. He decided to return to the drone investigation before tackling the now vastly more complicated investigation into the killer robot.

Layla had prepared summaries of the interviews they had conducted with the staff. He reviewed each of them to refresh his memory of the conversations and to jot down any follow-up questions that came to mind. A couple of things jumped out at him.

"Good morning, Layla. How did you sleep?" Layla didn't sleep in the traditional human way, but she took time out each night to run maintenance routines on her systems, which she equated to the same function.

"Good morning, Alan. I had a productive nighttime maintenance routine. How about yourself?"

"I've had better nights, but it wasn't too bad considering. I have some thoughts about the drone case interviews."

"Alright, let's hear them."

"Okay, Perry Beckner said he went to a baseball game with his father. He said the score was 3-1, and the Jumbo Shrimp lost. Is that accurate for that night?"

"Not quite. The Jumbo Shrimp did indeed lose to the Toledo Mud Hens, but the score was 3-2. The Shrimp scored a run in the ninth to get within one."

"Well, that is a little off, but maybe he just forgot about that inconsequential score."

"Perhaps," Layla responded.

"The relationship between Steve Daniels and Karen Anderson is interesting. Why did she call him up and set up a date on Tuesday?"

"It is curious. Was the date a coincidence or did she set it up intentionally?"

"And if it was intentional, why? Did she know the drones were going to be stolen?" Alan asked rhetorically.

"The other thing that bothers me a little is the relationship between Ben Williams and Karen Anderson. He seemed dismissive of it. We should re-interview Karen and ask her some more details," Layla suggested.

"That is a good idea. I don't know when I am going to find the time. I need to return to the Cybernetics murder. That case is getting complicated now. And your role in the freakout at the factory doesn't make it any less complicated."

"I really don't think I caused that. I think I was just in the wrong place at the wrong time," Layla defended herself.

"We'll see," Alan responded.

"What is on your agenda today?" She asked, changing the subject.

"I want to go by the new office and check on Stacy's progress and make sure she doesn't need anything. Then we need to go to Prism and talk to the staff there again. We need to know what the robot was doing at Cary Sellers' apartment, how long it had been there, and what he was doing with it."

"Stacy sent me a message a few minutes ago that the Computer Investigation Unit has agreed to give us a copy of the hard drive of Sellers' laptop. It should be ready later today. We can pick it up on the way to Prism."

"Sounds like a pretty full day. I really don't know how we are going to handle both cases at the same time," he said.

"You'll think of something."

Alan arrived at the Adamant Insurance Group building shortly after ten. He parked in the lot two blocks down and walked down W. Forsyth Street to the office. It was a pleasant spring day; the sun was bright, and a gentle wind blew. He could have enjoyed a walk on the beach if he wasn't overwhelmed with work.

As he walked into the lobby, the first thing that he noticed was that the open door to his new offices across the room had a new, freshly painted name on it. The frosted glass front now had "Alan Harrison & Associates, Investigations" in gold script. The sight filled him with a sense of pride. It made the whole thing more real to him, even though he had been operating this new business for months now.

"What do you think?" Stacy asked him as he stepped into the room. He looked around. New carpeting covered most of the floor. It was a dark neutral color, designed to limit the signs of dirt and wear. The carpet installers were currently working in the inner office, which had the same colors but added a lighter border around the room.

"It's coming together," he said, looking around. There was an old folding table with a rolling chair set up in the area where Stacy's desk would eventually be; she had strewn her stuff over it haphazardly. Prominent among the clutter were schedules and samples.

"We're realistically still a few weeks away from being finished, but I think we can use it before then. I'll let you know." She stopped to answer her cell phone and proceeded to have an animated conversation with someone, presumably one of the contractors.

"What a dump," came a deep voice behind him. Alan turned to see his friend and mentor, Dalton Rodgers, standing in the doorway, grinning at him. Dalton was a couple of years younger than Alan, early 40s. He wore his brown hair high and tight, almost like a military cut. He was dressed in the same jeans and camp shirt he always wore.

"I'd love to compare your offices," Alan said.

"You ever ridden in a beat-up Subaru? You've seen my offices then." Alan laughed.

"Why are you here harassing me in my own offices, Dalton?"

"Checking up on you. Seeing how things are going. Working much?"

"Actually, I am working on two cases at the moment. And I'm having trouble keeping up with them."

"What is the second case? I know about the Adamant case at Prism."

"People around here talk too much," Alan grumbled with a smile. "The other is a theft at a drone company in San Marco."

"You need a hand? I'm light at the moment."

"Not sure I can afford your rates," Alan said seriously.

"Nah, I'd give you a friends and family discount, only 20% higher than my rack rate."

"From what you've told me of your family, I can see that, and you don't have any friends."

"Ouch! That hurts, for that crack it's now 25% higher."

"I'll have to run it by my associates, but I could use the help on the drone case. Several witnesses to track down and confirm their movements."

"Well, just call me and let me know. Seriously, I'll work with you on the price. I want to see you succeed."

"I know, Dalton. Pretty sure my contract covers expenses like this."

"Good boy. I'll be around." Dalton waved and departed.

"We could use the help," Layla said in his ear after Rodgers had exited the lobby.

"I know. If he could check up on all the employees at North Florida Aerial, that would free us up to concentrate on the Prism case."

"I'll ask Stacy to draw up a contract with him and agree on a fee, and we'll present those invoices to Roger Maxwell at North Florida."

"What is Stacy drawing up?" Stacy asked as she disconnected her phone.

"Contract with Dalton. He is going to help out on the drone case so we can focus on killer robots."

Stacy visibly shivered. Alan regretted the joke. "Sorry, too soon."

She waved it away. "I'm a big girl. I can handle it. I'll call Dalton and work out the fee and the terms. I'll email you a copy of the contract when it is done."

"Give me the tour of your masterpiece, Stacy," Alan said, changing the subject. Her face lit up, and she dragged him around the office, pointing out where all the furniture would be placed and the decor choices she had made. As they neared the end of the tour, her cell phone rang. She answered it with their company name and listened.

"Just a moment, sir. I'll check to see if he is available for the call." She muted the phone and asked Alan, "Fred Johnson, Prism Cybernetics." Alan Nodded.

"Mr. Johnson, one moment, and I'll connect you." She muted the phone again and handed it to Alan.

"Good morning, Mr. Johnson. I was going to call you this afternoon."

"I'll save you the trouble then. We need to meet and talk about the situation. Can you be here after lunch?"

"I can be there by two. I have to make a stop by the crime lab and get some evidence." Hearing that Alan was making some progress on the case seemed to calm Johnson.

"2 PM it is then. I'll clear my schedule. See you then." Alan disconnected the phone and handed it back to Stacy.

"Can the crime lab have the data we need in the next half hour?" he asked Stacy.

"I think so, they said mid-morning. I'll call them and tell them you are on your way."

With the small solid-state hard drive in the inside pocket of his gray blazer, Alan parked the dark blue Chimera in the lot at Prism Cybernetics and went inside for his 2 PM appointment with the VP of Manufacturing, Fred Johnson.

As he entered the executive office, he noticed Johnson was wearing blue pinstripes again. He looked tired. Having employees murdered by the product was bound to make you lose sleep, though Alan thought.

"Good afternoon, Mr. Harrison. Thank you for meeting with me."

"Yes, sir, I was already coming out today to visit the factory anyway. I want to do more interviews, especially in light of the events of last night."

Johnson shook his head sadly. "I'm devastated by the loss of Mr. Sellers. He was a valuable and well-liked employee."

"That was the impression I got from my earlier visit."

"Any ideas about where the investigation is going?"

"No, I don't have any leads on the break-in, and the death of Sellers makes it more complicated."

"So, you believe the two events are connected?"

"If they are not, it is quite a coincidence, and that seems unlikely to me."

"Yes, it does to me, too, and in fact, the entire senior leadership team. We met this morning. I understand Adamant is paying you for the investigation of the break-in. Does this mean you will be expanding that to cover poor Cary's death?"

"I don't know how I would avoid doing so. The two events seem irrevocably linked. I will proceed on the assumption that they are related until I have proof to the contrary. Adamant will cover the investigation until that point at least." Johnson seemed relieved by this position.

"Where do we go from here? You said you wanted to conduct more interviews?"

"Yes, my tour was cut short the last time, and I want to talk more in-depth to some of the technical staff."

"What do you need?"

"We need a listing of employees, their roles, and the shifts they are working." Layla said via the SmartLens glasses. Alan repeated the request to Johnson.

"I'll arrange that with one of the staff assistants. In the meantime, you can start with Larry Volkner. He is in his office just off the factory floor. I'll have someone show you the way."

Volkner's office was a tiny room that might have once been a large storage closet. It had barely enough room for a small desk against one wall and for him to sit behind it in a chair. There was no room for a guest chair. Alan stood just inside the doorway. Volkner looked like hell. He had dark circles under his eyes, his hair was uncombed, and his eyes were vacant and glassy. He looked up when Alan stepped into the room, but it wasn't clear he was seeing much of anything.

"Mr. Volkner?" There was no response. "Larry!" Alan raised his voice. He shook his head, and his eyes focused on Alan.

"Mr. Harrison? Uh, hello. How long have you been standing there?"

"Ten or fifteen seconds. Not that long. I can see you've had a rough night."

"I don't understand what happened...did the P4 really—"

"Kill Cary? Yes, it seems like that."

"I...don't know what to say about it."

"Why was one of the P4s at Cary's apartment?"

"Uh, he was beta testing the unit for a demo we were planning on doing at a consumer show in a few weeks."

"What unit was it that was at the apartment? Do you know?"

"I don't know exactly. One of the 500 series, though, from a few weeks ago."

"So it had been in the apartment for a while?"

"Two weeks at least."

"So it wasn't here when the break-in happened."

"Oh, no, it wouldn't have been."

Layla supplied a question in his ear, and he repeated it to Volkner: "Was the code for the demo unit locked?"

"No, Cary was tweaking it constantly. He kept pushing the development team to fix things, and he would update the unit after hours. He wanted all the bugs out of it before we went to the show. Cary was working like a madman on the project."

"Who would he have been dealing with on the development team?"

A young woman touching Alan's elbow interrupted the answer. When he turned, she handed him a group of papers stapled at the top. Glancing at it, he realized it was the employee list he had asked for. He thanked her and turned back to Volkner.

"Probably Jim Reston, or Bobby Bishop. They are two of the senior developers. Cary was always bugging one or the other about something in the code he didn't like."

"Was he a developer?"

Volkner laughed, "Not really, but he always wanted to be. He could poke around and find things to change. He was an engineer at heart, so through trial and error, he could figure out how to fix some minor things."

"Did anyone else have a demo unit at home?" Alan asked, flipping through the list of employees.

"Several people did. I think Rebecca had one of the 300 series. Everyone who had one was told to bring it back in this morning."

"Anyone else report an issue with them?"

"No, not that I know of. You might want to check with the employees who had them. I don't have a full list. I think the product manager might, though."

Alan looked through the list quickly. "Jason Wingram," he read from the list.

"Yeah, Jason might know."

"Anything else come to mind?"

"No, nothing at the moment. I'm still in shock." Alan nodded; that much was apparent.

"Alright, I'll get back to you if anything comes up. Thanks for your time." Volkner nodded, and Alan left him to his thoughts.

Alan stepped outside the small office and spoke quietly to Layla, "So, who should we tackle first? The development team?"

"That seems like a good first step, but I think Rebecca is working today. She is across the factory floor." Alan looked up to see Rebecca smiling at him. She waved. He waved back and walked across the factory floor to her station.

"Good afternoon, Mr. Harrison," she said cheerily, but Alan could hear the strain in her voice. She, like everyone else here, was struggling emotionally.

"Call me Alan. How are you holding up?"

"It's a tough day, but I am getting through it."

"Larry said you had a demo unit at home?"

"Oh, yes. I did. P4-374. Until this morning. I got an email last night to bring the unit back in. It's over in maintenance right now, being disassembled, I assume."

"Any issues with it at home?"

"Nothing alarming; it had some bugs. That unit is a few weeks old. Nothing dangerous. It dropped a plate a few days ago, and it sometimes doesn't process my voice correctly. It seems to hear my boyfriend, though, that's a little annoying."

Alan smiled. "Are you saying the P4 series is misogynistic?"

"No," she said, laughing, "nothing so dramatic. It's just got a bug in its voice recognition programming that gets confused by my voice."

"How well did you know Cary?"

"Not well, not outside of work. He seemed like a nice guy, a little obsessive about the P4s."

"How so?"

"I don't know. He was really driving to get all the bugs worked out, almost in a panic at times. He was constantly bugging the software guys."

"Wasn't that his job, to get the demo ready for the trade show?"

"Yeah, I guess. He seems really over the top about even minor things, though. He was drilling into every single subsystem, even things they didn't plan to demo at the show."

"Was he making enemies?"

"No, I wouldn't go that far. Everyone wants the demo to go well. They might get frustrated with him, but they all knew his heart was in the right place." She swallowed a lump in her throat and wiped her eyes. Talking about him brought up emotions about his death.

"Sorry to make you go through it again, Rebecca. I know it is very difficult."

"I'm fine. I want to know what happened to him. How could this have happened?"

"I don't know yet, but that is what I am going to try to find out. If you think of anything, let me know. I'll be around. I am going to go talk to the software people." She nodded and pointed to the far corner of the factory, where a small group of cubicles sat off to the side, away from the manufacturing stations. Alan thanked her and moved toward them.

As he approached the development work area, he heard a voice from the other side of the partition. It was raised and emotional.

"I said I would have it for you, and I will. Just give me a few days. I know! You don't have to tell me twice. I'll do what I said!" Alan stepped into the cube and saw that the speaker was a young man in his 20s, wearing jeans and a t-shirt with a rock band logo on it. The nameplate next to his desk read "James Reston." Reston looked up, saw he had company, and said into the phone, "I'll call you back later, man," and hung up the phone.

"James Reston?" Alan asked as he stepped farther into the cubicle.

"Yeah, what can I do for you?"

"Alan Harrison, I am an investigator working on the vandalism event. I had a few questions."

"About what?" There was a hint of wariness in his voice.

"I've been told that Cary Sellers was hounding you guys about bugs in the software."

"Yeah, he was dogging us pretty hard recently about every little thing."

"Did that create tension?"

"Nah, we knew he was just trying to get the unit ready for the demo. He's high-strung, but he means well."

"When was the last time you talked to him?"

"Yesterday, he came by to check up on some networking code that he found a week ago, but I didn't have time to talk to him about it, and I didn't work on that code, anyway."

"Who did?"

"Bishop. I think Cary talked to him about it yesterday after he asked me about it. I saw them talking later."

"Any idea what the issue was with the code?"

"No, I don't think there was anything wrong with it. I think he was chasing shadows. When Bishop looked at it a few days ago, he said it was fine."

"Did Cary often get hyped about things that weren't actual issues?"

"No, but it happens. He saw something he didn't understand, and he assumed it was a bug. Apparently, it was just some code he wasn't familiar with."

"Bishop. That is Robert Bishop?"

"Yeah, Bobby. He is our networking guy. He manages all the communications software in the units."

"Is he around?"

"No, he called in sick today. He was here late yesterday working on something, probably just needed a mental health day." Alan nodded.

"How close do you think the software was to being ready for the show?"

"I think it was ready. Cary kept nitpicking smaller and smaller issues. He was obsessing a little about the demo. They weren't even going to be showing most of those features. It was just going to be a quick demo of the movement and flexibility of the units. It wasn't going to be a full operational demonstration."

"Why do you think he was so focused on it?"

"I don't know. I know he had become attached to the unit at home and was getting excited about the possibility of a release sooner rather than later. Maybe that was why. He wanted to push us to get it ready faster to make a launch happen sooner."

Reston kept glancing at the phone on his desk. Clearly, he was thinking about the phone call he had interrupted to talk to Alan. He tried hard to hide his distraction, feigning focus on the conversation.

"I don't mean to keep you from anything," Alan said. "It sounded like I interrupted something important." Alan watched the subject for a reaction. Reston swallowed and looked down at the phone again, then looked back up.

"No, no. Just some personal business. You know, creditors are always hounding you at work."

"That isn't a lie, but he is very nervous about this line of questioning," Layla said.

Alan smiled to himself. He didn't need AI and a mountain of electronic data that Layla had available to see that Reston was nervous. It was interesting that his statement was factually accurate, yet still made him very jumpy.

"Well, I will let you get back to it. I will be around for the next few days, interviewing others and exploring the processes surrounding development and manufacturing. If you think of something, catch up with me."

James Reston stood and shook Alan's hand somewhat awkwardly. Alan gave him a reassuring smile and was on his way. As he exited the cubicle, he could hear Reston pick up the phone, returning to whatever had been occupying his mind.

"We should run some background checks on him," Layla suggested.

"That's a good idea. Run the standard package, and we'll review it later." One of the first things Alan and Layla did when setting up the new business was to secure the right contacts and subscriptions for all the databases used for professional screenings. That, coupled with Layla's ability to scan massive amounts of public data and her ability to conduct telephone interviews as an "associate," made the process remarkably streamlined and lucrative for the business.

Looking at his watch, Alan decided it was late in the day and he wanted to get home to set up the hard drive for Layla and give her a chance to look at the code for the P4 unit that had killed Cary Sellers. Checking in at the front desk, he informed the receptionist that he would return the following morning. He exited the building and headed to his car and then home.

Chapter Seven

Revelations

The Orion Chimera navigated the trip toward home on autopilot. Alan relaxed and let his mind go back over the interview with James Reston. Something unrelated to the death of his colleague clearly troubled him. Something personal. Perhaps something at the factory caused the problem. Maybe it was unrelated.

"Alan, Stacy has some news. I am going to patch us all together." Layla was excited about the fact that she now had both of them plugged in 24/7. She took every opportunity to link them in this way. Alan waited for the customary beep as the system completed the connection, then he spoke.

"Hey, Stacy. What's up?

"Hi Alan. I just got the signed contract back from Dalton."

"Excellent, what did we end up settling on?"

"He offered a 30% discount," she said.

"That's pretty good."

"We ended up at 35%," The pride was evident in her voice.

"Excellent job, Stacy," Layla said excitedly.

"Yes, very good. Impressive. He is ready to go then?" Alan asked.

"Yes, just need a mission for him."

"Let him run down the love triangle at North Florida Aerial. Have him conduct thorough background research on Karen Anderson, Ben Williams, and Steve Daniels. I want to know more about their relationships."

Stacy and Layla both agreed with the decision. The autonomous car was nearing Alan's house. He was looking forward to relaxing at home.

"Stacy, why don't you come over tonight and watch a movie with Layla and me?" he asked as the car turned onto his street.

"Um, I don't know," her voice was hesitant.

"Why not?"

"Layla talks during the movie," she said.

"Sometimes I have questions!" Layla objected.

"Sometimes?"

"We'll try to keep the Q&A to the end. Will that help?" Alan suggested.

"Depends..what are we watching?"

"We haven't decided yet. Come help us decide."

"Okay, are you feeding me?"

"When don't I feed you? Come over around 7. We'll have some dinner, watch a movie, and try not to think about killer robots, missing drones, or office renovations."

"Deal!"

The Chimera pulled into the driveway, and a sensor in the car activated the garage door, which slid open. Piloting itself smoothly inside, the car came to a stop directly over a static charging pad installed in the garage floor. The autopilot positioned itself perfectly over the pad so that the coil installed on the underside of the car aligned perfectly. As the car came to a stop, the charging indicator on the console lit up, indicating that the connection was working and power was being supplied to the car's main battery.

Alan retrieved Layla from the console charging pad, where she routinely sat when they were in the vehicle. The pad, designed for cell phones, fit Layla's slim oval shape nicely, and it was a convenient place for her to occupy while the car was in operation. As he got out of the car and headed into the house, Layla piped up.

"Your hands are cold."

"That joke almost never gets old," Alan said, pressing the garage closure button on the wall as he entered the house and closed the door behind him.

The house smelled of red beans and rice, which they had consumed hungrily for dinner, and hot buttered popcorn. A large bowl of the latter sat on the coffee table in front of the oversized, comfortable couch. Alan was flipping through a search of movies on the 80-inch TV while the three of them tried to come up with a film they could all agree on. Throughout dinner, they had succeeded in not discussing work—no killer robots, slow subcontractors, or missing drones. They had chatted about a book Alan had just finished, *Lester Dent: The Man, His Craft and His Market* by M. Martin McCarey-Laird. Alan was an admirer of the novelist who had spent 10 years of his life turning out hundreds of novels in short time frames. All aimed at 15-year-old boys in the 30s and 40s. They discussed the pulp fiction era and the differences in writing styles between then and now. It was a pleasant distraction from their current work stresses. Now, though, it was time to get down to business.

As he scrolled through titles, Layla chimed in, "Oooh, *Terminator*!"

"NO!" Alan and Stacy shouted together. Killer robots from the future were not what they wanted to spend their evening watching.

"Hey! *Everything Everywhere All at* Once," Stacy said, referring to an entertaining, if a bit confusing, blend of family drama and science fiction.

"No," Layla and Alan said. Alan really wanted something simple and easy to watch. Layla was worried about holding her questions until the end of that particular movie.

"I'm putting on *Casablanca*," Alan announced.

"The black and white film from the 40s?" Stacy wrinkled her nose.

"You'll love it. There is action, humor, music, romance, gunfights—"

“Sold,” Stacy and Layla said. Alan laughed and selected the movie. Layla turned down the lights in the living room. Alan and Stacy sat next to each other on the couch and shared the giant bowl of popcorn.

In the dark room, the light from the TV washed over them, and they watched quietly as the iconic globe and map scenes depicting the refugee route during World War II played. The film was one of Alan’s favorites; there was an unrealistic plot element throughout, but it was hard to focus on that when the story itself was so timeless and engaging. He settled back to enjoy the movie for the umpteenth time. Throughout the film, he watched Stacy, who was engaged in the film. He knew that her sneering at the lack of color had been a joke. She was a sophisticated film viewer and open to new experiences. Somewhere near the middle of the film, he felt her lean into him and rest her head on his shoulder. He smiled, touched the top of his head with his lips gently, and then went back to watching the film.

Layla did really well, only asking a handful of questions during the movie, mainly about the intricacies of human romantic relationships. Alan was sympathetic. Emotion, logistics, and war complicated the love triangle in Casablanca. And even without those things, it could be a confusing minefield. After the movie was over, Stacy yawned and stretched, her joints cracking audibly. She began gathering her belongings to leave.

“Do you want to just stay over in the guest room?” Alan asked.

"Tempting...but no. I need to get home and take care of Noodle. I've been away from home a lot lately, and she is feeling a little neglected." Alan nodded sympathetically. She wished him and Layla a good night and departed. Alan finished cleaning up while Layla sat in her spot on the end table in the living room, her activity lights steady. Alan realized she was working on something. He let her work while he cleaned up in the kitchen.

"Alan, I may have found something."

"In the data from Cary Seller's laptop?"

"No, I am still going through that. I just finished the background check on James Reston."

"Oh? What did it turn up?" Alan sat back down on the couch.

"No criminal record, but he is carrying a lot of credit card debt. And the pattern is unusual. The number of cash withdrawals against his credit cards is significant."

"These days, cash withdrawal, especially by someone of Reston's age, probably means illegal activity. Drugs...or—" Alan stopped, thinking.

"Gambling. He has a lot of gambling debts. That phone call." Layla finished for him.

"Was someone collecting a debt?" Alan said, snapping his fingers. "That fits."

"If he is in debt, he could be susceptible to blackmail. Someone could be forcing him to sabotage the factory," Layla theorized.

"To the point of killing Sellers? That is serious stuff."

"Perhaps the death was accidental. The original goal is financial. That would fit with his debt. In either case, we need to focus on him." Layla said.

"I agree. We'll start looking into him more closely tomorrow."

"I'll spend part of my nighttime schedule finishing up with the laptop data. We can discuss it in the morning. Are you sleeping in?" Alan realized he had forgotten it was Friday night. With no set schedule on the weekends, he could sleep in.

"We'll see." He yawned. He was tired. Who knew that the life of a full-time investigator would involve so little sleep?

Layla spent the night poring over all of the data on Cary Sellers' laptop. Concentrating on the code he had downloaded of the P4 operating system, she examined all the tweaks and changes he had made to the code, and scoured his emails to members of the development team for clues about what he was concerned with. While Alan slept peacefully, she created a digital twin of the hardware running the P4 units. She accomplished this by combining data she had collected from her brief control of one of the units before it malfunctioned at the factory with specifications she found on Sellers' laptop. Eventually, she had a working model created and started running simulations from the code versions that Cary Sellers had saved on his hard drive.

Throughout the night, she ran simulation after simulation, examining the differences in each code version to see what had changed. Operating the simulation and looking for changes in its behavior. Keeping the twin isolated from her control systems, she hoped to trigger another malfunction, but this time avoid the complete blackout that she had experienced the first time it had happened. But despite running thousands of simulations with various versions of the operating code, she never triggered another incident. Something was missing from the environment that day, but she did not know what it might be.

Layla was still running simulations when Alan woke the next morning, having slept in until 8:30. He was still waking up, making his morning coffee, as she completed another round of tests without making any progress.

"Good morning, Alan," she said as he started sipping his first cup.

"Morning, Layla. Were you up all night?"

"Yes. I have been trying to recreate the incident at the factory, but despite more than two thousand attempts, I could not duplicate the issue." Alan frowned. He had been sure that Layla's intrusion into the software the first time was the trigger, despite her assurances that it wasn't. She was apparently right about that, but it left them with no avenue to explore what the actual trigger had been.

"Any ideas?" Layla asked him. He was a little surprised. It wasn't often that she asked him for his opinion on technical matters. She was the expert there.

"I really don't. I'm at a loss. What is different? Is the code version different from the P4 you were controlling?"

"No, Cary Sellers had multiple versions of the software on his laptop, including one with the same revision number as the software on the P4 I was in control of. I've run simulations on that as well as every other version he had."

Alan drank his coffee and pondered the situation. Nothing came, though. He finally shrugged. "I don't have an answer for you today, I'm afraid." Maybe something would come to one of them later, or perhaps some other clue would point them in the right direction, but for now, it was an unsatisfying answer for both of them, and they sat in silence contemplating the lack of direction.

There was a knock at the front door, and it opened a crack. It was Stacy. Alan had given her a key while she was working part-time from his home office. She pushed her head inside and yelled, "Everyone decent?"

"No!" Alan yelled back. "Layla refuses to put on anything before 11 AM."

"Well, if you can stand it, I can," Stacy replied and came in carrying a bag from a nearby bagel shop.

"Bagel delivered on a Saturday morning while I am still in my pajamas. A guy could get used to this."

"You wish," she fired back at him. The exchange was a running joke between them, but it underscored a blurring line between their personal and private lives.

"Good morning, Stacy," Layla said from the dining room table, where she had been all night working.

"Good morning, girl. What have you been up to?"

"Failing to figure out why I can't reproduce the incident at the factory with the P4 robot." Layla took a few minutes to bring Stacy up to speed on all the work she had done throughout the night. While she did, Alan and Stacy ate bagels slathered with cream cheese for breakfast. When she finished, Stacy thought for a moment, then asked a question.

"Why could you remotely operate the robot, anyway? Isn't that like a huge hole in their security?" Alan's mouth opened, and he just stared at Stacy. Layla's activity lights flashed rapidly for several seconds.

"I...never considered that. I made the connection easily at the factory. It was a secure connection, but I was able to break the encryption and access it. I never considered why it had that functionality. I assumed it was for diagnostics."

"It could be for diagnostics," Alan said. Layla's activity lights went into overdrive. Rapidly circulating in a chase pattern, ranging in multiple colors. Alan referred to this as her maximum processing mode. When she was like this, nothing could interrupt her process. He and Stacy exchanged a glance, then returned to eating breakfast. There was nothing to do in these moments other than wait. After a full minute, Layla spoke again.

"It isn't a diagnostic function. That remote port is in another area of the code. This port is specifically written directly into the code managing the core operating system functions. It bypasses all the other security."

"It's a backdoor," Alan said quietly.

"Yes, it is. It shouldn't be there. The code is buried in another function. It's not documented, and the style of code differs from the other lines in the same function. Someone added to this section after the initial function's creation."

"So...someone could have used this backdoor to order the robot to kill Cary Sellers?" Stacy asked.

"I don't know. It's possible. That means there would be a record of the commands in the unit. We need to find the logs and examine them," Layla replied.

"That is going to be a fun conversation with Fred Johnson and Larry Volkner," Alan said.

Chapter Eight

Encounters

The future offices of Alan Harrison and Associates were abuzz with activity on Monday morning. The flooring contractors were putting the finishing touches on the inner-office carpeting. Burly guys speaking in a language that Stacy couldn't quite place were installing wood panels where the conference area would be in the new office. Stacy sat at her makeshift work table reviewing a catalog of art selections for the walls.

"Good morning, Miss Collins," a voice boomed from the doorway. She looked up. Her heart skipped a beat. It was the interior designer, Mike Westoff. He had been coming by every day for the past week, discussing options and ideas with her for decorating the offices. He was a handsome man. Westoff looked to be a little older than her, but not by much, and he had a trendy look and a warm smile. Stacy shook her head to clear it.

"Hi, Mike. What do you have for me today?"

"I have some samples of wall coverings for the interior office." He placed a thick manila envelope down on the corner of her table.

"Alright, I'll look at them later today and let you know." He lingered a bit, and she looked up at him questioningly.

"I was wondering," he said, hesitating, "would you like to have dinner with me this week?" Stacy's breath caught for a moment.

"Oh...I..ah..I'll have to think about it. Can I let you know tomorrow?"

"Sure, call me later and let me know." He waved and departed. Stacy tried to steady her breathing. She made a show of pulling her phone out of her purse and pretending to look through her contacts. Then, after a reasonable amount of time for a call to be initiated, she spoke to Layla via her SmartLens glasses.

"Layla!"

"What is it, girl?" Layla asked.

"Mike Westoff just asked me out!"

"Westoff...the decorator?"

"Yes! He asked me to dinner."

"Oh, that is exciting. What did you say?"

"I told him I would call him later and tell him. I don't know how I feel about it."

"I can help with your decision. Would you like me to conduct a background check? Criminal history, genetic disorder screening, family medical history?" Stacy was shocked.

"No! Layla! He just asked me to dinner. It's not that serious," she said, looking around nervously to make sure no one was paying attention to her conversation.

"Wouldn't you want all the data to determine if he is a suitable mate?"

"Not for dinner!"

"How will you decide then?" There was confusion in Layla's voice.

"I guess...I'll just go with my gut. Feelings."

"I don't think I can help with that. I have much to learn about human emotions. Maybe Alan can help?"

"No!" she barked abruptly. "I can't talk to Alan about it."

"Why not? Alan is your friend and your associate. He cares about you. He would be honest with you."

"It's...complicated. Just thinking about telling him makes me feel weird. Anxious."

"That is an odd reaction, isn't it?"

"Maybe I don't know...I need to think about it. Don't mention it to him!" she warned.

"My lips are sealed," Layla replied. Stacy sighed and tried to get her mind back on her work.

The conversation with Fred Johnson and Larry Volkner was difficult. Neither believed Alan had the expertise to understand the complex telemetry data from P4-751. Alan assured them in confident tones that he had a background in technology and staff who could assist with the analysis. It took half an hour. Eventually, they agreed to allow him to review the data. Volkner left to collect it.

"Any progress in the investigation?" Johnson asked when Volkner was gone.

"Nothing definite yet, but every interview gives you something. You put it all together, and eventually it points you in the right direction." Alan hoped he sounded more sure of that than he felt at the moment. So far, he had very little to go on.

"Well, let me know what you need. I want this matter resolved." Alan agreed to keep him updated and left to go find out if Robert Bishop was in the office today.

The development cube was empty when he stepped inside it. He looked around, but saw no one. He found Bishop's desk and examined it. Nothing stood out, and Layla brought nothing to his attention. Come to think of it, she had been quiet.

"Layla, are you with me?" There was a delay.

"Sorry, Alan, I was talking to Stacy."

"Oh, about what?" Another hesitation.

"Just decorator details." Alan nodded to himself without commenting. Just then, a lanky young man wearing designer jeans and a Polo-branded sweater entered the cube and headed directly to where Alan was standing at Bishop's workstation. Alan turned and offered his hand to the approaching figure.

"Mr. Bishop? I am Alan Harrison. I am investigating the break-in. And the unfortunate accident of Cary Sellers."

Bishop stopped, regarded him for a second, then shook his hand. "What can I do for you?" he asked.

"Just some background information." Bishop sat on the edge of the desk and gestured for Alan to continue.

"What was your relationship with Cary Sellers?" he began.

"He was a pain in my ass, but he was a good guy."

"Hounding you about the P4 software?" Alan prompted.

"Yes, he was a maniac about it. Asking tons of questions, poking into the code himself after hours, and offering suggestions for tweaking responses. It was intense, but I respected his determination and hard work to get the demo ready."

"Was there anything in particular he was worried about? With the robot's performance?"

"No, not that I recall. It was everything. Every movement, every response. He wanted it to be perfect."

"Do you have a specialty with the code?"

"I wrote the communications and networking code, mostly. We all get pulled into other work. But that is what I spent most of the last six months working on."

"Who worked on the operating system core?" Bishop raised an eyebrow in surprise at the question. "I have some technical background," Alan offered in explanation. Bishop shrugged.

"Jim was the chief developer for the OS." Assuming he meant James Reston, Alan followed up.

"Did Cary ask you about Reston's code?" Bishop considered this.

"No, not specifically. He asked about everything, but he mentioned no one by name. I don't know that he had any focus in one area." Alan looked around the cubicle.

"Is he here today?" He nodded toward Reston's desk. Bishop shook his head.

"No, he left me a message last night that he had an appointment today and wouldn't be in." Alan wondered whether the appointment related to his gambling issues. He considered several potential ways of bringing that subject up with Bishop, but rejected all of them and skipped it.

"What was the last thing he brought up with you?"

"I don't recall. There were so many items he brought up. Three or four a day some days. It might have been some instability in the Wi-Fi integration routines. But I really don't remember."

Alan thought if he had any other avenues to cover, and to allow Layla to offer a question. She was silent, so he thanked Bishop for his time and left him. Walking back through the busy factory, he asked her what she thought about the interview.

"I didn't get any definitive reading from him. He wasn't nervous like Reston. He seemed too calm though, but that might just be his usual demeanor."

"Good catch. I'll ask some other staff about his personality."

As he passed through the factory, Alan saw Rebecca Salter. He stopped and asked her about Robert Bishop. Bishop was, she said, always cool and collected. He didn't seem ever to get overly excited about things. Alan thanked her and continued on through the factory and out to the reception desk, where he asked the young man at the reception desk the same question. The 20-something related that he had limited experience with Bishop, but that he always seemed cheery when he came into the office.

Larry Volkner was waiting for him in the lobby. He concurred with the group assessment of Bishop's normal attitude and delivered a drive containing the telemetry data for the P4-751 unit.

"Here it is. I still don't know that it will mean anything to you," Volkner said with a hint of arrogance.

"I'll figure it out." Alan replied. Layla made a dismissive noise in his ear.

Volkner shrugged and walked away. Alan watched him go. It seemed Volkner was getting more stressed, not less, as time passed.

"Well, Layla, anything else you can think of we need from the staff today?"

"No, I want to look at the log data."

"I hope you can understand it."

"I would respond to that, but my ethics and class prohibit the use of profanity," she responded tartly.

"I'll help you work on that." Alan replied.

Instead of going straight home from Prism Cybernetics, Alan detoured to the downtown offices of Adamant Insurance Group to check on the progress of the new offices. After parking the car and going by the Screaming Goat Coffee Company for an Americano for himself and an almond milk latte for Stacy, he walked the two blocks to the office and stepped inside. He took a moment to marvel at how quickly it was coming together. The carpeting was done, and the wall coverings were moving along. He set the latte down on Stacy's worktable.

"The place looks fantastic. You're doing a great job with the decorator."

"Uh...yeah, thanks," she said awkwardly. Was she blushing? Alan couldn't tell, but she looked flushed. "I have art on order, and the first of the furniture arrives at the end of the week," she finished more smoothly.

"That's great! So when do you think we can start working out of the office?"

"You can start using your office next week. The rest of the decor will take a little longer."

"You've done a great job, Stacy," Layla said to both of them via her link to the SmartLens glasses.

"Thanks Layla. And thanks for the coffee, Alan," she said, picking up the latte. Alan nodded an acknowledgment and told her he would be at home working for the rest of the day.

"Was she blushing?" Alan asked Layla as he walked to his car.

"I'm sure I have no idea what you are referring to."

"You are both acting strangely today," he replied.

"I'll run a diagnostic to look for abnormalities in my code." Alan just shook his head. Maybe it was him.

At home, he connected the hard drive to his laptop and sat Layla on the desk next to the computer. He could tell Layla was working on the drive by the activity lights on both the drive and Layla's sleek form. He left her to her work and opened up his email to review the first of the reports Dalton had sent him about his efforts to gain more insight into the staff at North Florida Aerial.

There was nothing in the reports that seemed relevant. Deeper background checks on Steve Daniels and Karen Anderson failed to turn up concrete evidence that they had an ongoing relationship. Interviews with the other staff at Advention Financial Services backed up Daniel's story that he wasn't seeing anyone regularly. None of them had ever met Karen Anderson. There was also no new information about the relationship between Anderson and Ben Williams. They appeared to have dated for a few months a year ago. Neither had mentioned that fact to him, but he hadn't asked them about any office relationships.

Remembering an idea from earlier in the day, Alan fired off an email to Dalton asking him to check on Stanley Graystone, the Holliston sales rep. No one seemed to have any information about him or his movements. It might be nothing, but while Dalton was on the case, he might as well look at all possibilities.

"Alan, we might have a bigger problem than we thought." Layla said from the desk in front of him.

"Why?"

"The log from P4-751 shows my intrusion into the unit when we were at the factory. It's hard to see because it isn't reporting as a remote connection. It looks like data coming from within the unit itself."

"We expected to see that. Why is that a problem?"

"The code revision on the P4-751 is a lot older than the earliest one on Cary Sellers' laptop. The backdoor has been in the code for a long time. Potentially all the units have this code."

Alan pondered the implications of thousands of robots having the code allowing someone to remote into them and commit murder.

"Layla, don't these units have safety features to prevent them from hurting humans?"

"Theoretically, that is true. There is a concept of the laws of robotics," she said, referring to a series of rules created by science fiction author and futurist Isaac Asimov, who coined the term robotics. In his fiction, the laws allowed robots to protect themselves so long as this did not violate a second rule prohibiting robots from harming humans. Later he revised the laws, adding in a rule mandating the protection of humanity, even if that meant harming individual humans. In practical terms, modern AI and robotics didn't literally have these laws. The modern safety protocols in the devices are all designed with those laws in mind. "Clearly, they didn't work in this case. There are ways around those protocols."

"We need to test that out—"

“I am going to need access to the P4 unit that attacked Cary Sellers.”

“That is going to be tricky. I assume it is still in police evidence.”

“I still need access to it.”

“Well, we can’t break into the police building, so I’ll need to come up with a plan.”

Chapter Nine

Tail

Alan spent a good part of the evening thinking about how to get access to the police evidence room...without committing a felony. He briefly considered reaching out to Ava Chen in D.C. to see if she had any contacts in the Jacksonville Sheriff's Office, but ultimately decided against it. He preferred not to involve her in his cases, particularly if other options remained. That would be in the category of a distant Plan B. Without having made any progress, Alan shelved that problem for later consideration and turned to other threads in the case.

Reviewing transcripts of all the interviews he had done on his computer, dutifully put there by Layla during the early evening while he had cold ricotta and lemon pasta leftovers and a bourbon for dinner, he found his focus drifting to James Reston. There was something not quite right about that guy. Layla's gambling suspicion was almost certainly true, but did it have any connection to the case? Alan decided he needed more information. He looked down at the time on his computer; almost eleven.

"Dalton, you still awake?" he typed a text message to his investigator. After a few moments, a reply came back.

"Yeah, barely. What's up?"

"I have a subject in my cybernetics case I need more info on. I was thinking of seeing what his routine is like. You up for a little fieldwork tomorrow?"

"Sure. Let's meet for coffee in the morning and talk about it. Your usual place?" Alan smiled at the fact that even Dalton knew about his addiction to the Screaming Goat Coffee Company.

"Sounds like a plan. See you at 8:30." He got a thumbs-up emoji in response and put the phone down.

The morning crowd at The Screaming Goat Coffee Company was heavier than usual for a Tuesday. Alan arrived just after 8:15. There were no available tables, so he leaned against a counter near the front of the shop, sipping his coffee. Dalton arrived about ten minutes later and ordered a straight black coffee to go and joined him.

"Busy day," he remarked, looking around at the full establishment.

"I noticed."

"So, what is the agenda?"

"I want to get more information about this James Reston guy. From looking at his financial data, it seems likely he is heavily in debt. I think he might be involved in gambling. I don't know if that relates to my case, but I want to find out." Dalton considered this for a few seconds.

"Seems fairly straightforward to me. We keep tabs on him for a few days and see where he goes and who he sees. That should give us a picture of what is going on with him."

Alan pulled the employee listing he had received from Prism Cybernetics. It had James Reston's home address, and his work schedule. According to the listing, he was due to arrive at work by 9 AM. He considered his next action for a moment. He was wavering between two courses of action, one of which probably crossed a line. But the stakes were pretty high.

"Alright, according to his employer, he should arrive at work soon. Why don't you pick him up there and sit on him? I'll join you later in the day. I need to go run an errand first."

"Do you have the make, model, and tag of the car he drives?" Dalton asked. Alan realized he hadn't looked that up yet before he could say so. Layla replied in his ear.

"It's a current model year white Range Rover. The tag number is D14 KJW." Alan relayed the information to Dalton, who seemed surprised.

"I would have bet money you hadn't looked it up. I was prepared to do it for you."

"You'll have to get up earlier to stay ahead of me," Alan said. Dalton laughed and took his coffee with him as he left the shop.

Half an hour later, Alan sat in his car outside the Ortega Forest home of James Reston. The home, on a street called

Robin Hood Road, was a single-story brick home with large picture windows in the front. The area was quiet, with most people at work at this time of day during the week. Picking Layla up from the console charging pad, Alan exited the car and approached the house. Looking around and seeing no one, we walked up to the front door.

“I’m not detecting anyone inside. There are no signs of an alarm system or external cameras,” Layla said.

“There could be internal surveillance, though.”

“I’ll jam any local Wi-Fi signal once we are in the house,” she assured him. Taking a deep breath, Alan pulled the lock pick out of his pocket and deftly unlocked the door, and slipped inside. He had come a long way since the first time Layla had taught him how to pick a lock. As he stood inside the doorway, he pulled a pair of latex gloves out of his jacket pocket and put them on. No sense in leaving fingerprints everywhere, he thought.

“I am not detecting any camera activity over the wireless network in the house. I’ll keep blocking the signal anyway,” Layla informed him as he closed the door and looked around. Empty takeout containers and old newspapers cluttered the living area just inside the front door. In the dining room he found schematics of the P4 robot piled on the table. He looked through them slowly. Layla commented that they were a few months old. The designs appeared to be from early in the life of the fourth-generation series.

A home office occupied one of the three bedrooms in the house. Alan searched the drawers of the small desk in the room, finding nothing noteworthy. There were connections on the desk for a laptop, but the computer itself wasn't there. Alan assumed Reston had it with him at work.

The next room Alan came to was a guest room. It showed no signs of recent occupancy. The larger room just down the hall was clearly Reston's bedroom. Alan poked through the nightstands, finding nothing more than an old class ring from high school, some old paperback books, and a comb. The closet, though, yielded results. On the top shelf, in a small box, Alan discovered a silver revolver. The small .38-caliber Smith & Wesson 10 smelled of gun oil. It showed no signs of recent use. Alan checked the cylinder; finding it fully loaded with six rounds.

Next to the closet sat a small, comfortable chair with a lamp beside it. To the left of the chair was a small table. There was an empty coffee mug and a paperback lying open with the spine facing up. The book was *Essential Poker Math: Fundamental No-Limit Hold'em Mathematics You Need to Know* by Alton Hardin.

"That book is popular with poker players trying to get an advantage in No-Limit Hold'em poker games," Layla said.

"Seems like Reston might have a problem, just like you suggested."

"There doesn't seem to be much else going on in this house," she replied. "No sign of a partner, takeout containers, no signs of other hobbies. Reston seems pretty bland, except for the gambling connection."

"Yeah, there doesn't seem to be a lot here." Looking around and seeing nothing else promising, Alan went back through the house, making sure he had moved nothing that wasn't back where he found it. Finishing the backtrack, he opened the door and took off the gloves. He closed the door with the glove and rotated it around the knob to obscure any fingerprints. He looked around again, making sure he wasn't being watched, and walked casually to the car and drove off.

It was nearly 5 PM when Alan opened the door to Dalton's beat-up gray Subaru and slipped into the passenger seat. Dalton grunted at him.

"Nice office." Alan quipped.

"Where have you been all day?" Dalton asked.

"Just doing a little light B&E."

"Find anything interesting?"

"Old .38 Special, a book on poker math."

"Not sure that was worth the risk."

"Well, you never know until you take the risk."

"True. All quiet here. He has been in the office all day."

Workers were filing out of the building now, mostly administrative staff since the factory floor was running three shifts. The second shift wouldn't be over for hours yet. The developers should be leaving any minute, though. Right on schedule, Bobby Bishop and James Reston exited the building together.

Waving to each other, they headed to their cars in different areas of the parking lot. Reston climbed into his white Range Rover and pulled out of the parking lot. Dalton waited, permitting two vehicles to depart before him, then followed Reston.

The Range Rover followed the usual route into the city, I-10 to I-95. Reston drove at a leisurely pace. Dalton kept his distance, always at least two to three cars behind. In rush-hour traffic, it wasn't hard to blend in. While he drove, he asked Alan about the new handgun he had just purchased. Alan talked about his practice sessions at the range, and about how he would never be a sharpshooter.

"You don't have to be," Dalston assured him, "just act like you know what you are doing and make a hell of a lot of noise." Alan laughed at this advice.

"I am uniquely qualified to do all of that," he said.

Reston exited the expressway at Forsyth. Ending up on Bay Street, he eventually arrived at a local microbrewery, which had a taproom. He parked the Range Rover and got out. Dalton parked on the street, and they watched Reston enter the establishment.

"I'll step inside and make sure he isn't slipping out the back." Dalton got out of the car and walked over to the taproom. He entered and approached the hostess. Scanning the room, he saw Reston in a booth by himself. He asked the hostess if they could handle a large party, about 15 people, in an hour. She checked her reservation book and told him they wouldn't be able to handle a party that large tonight. He looked disappointed, thanked her, and left.

"He seems to be settled in for dinner alone," Dalton said when he was back in the car.

"We should probably get something to eat, too."

"There is a bistro on Bay a few blocks back. You could order something to go," Layla said into his ear.

"You know, I think there is a bistro down the street? I'll call it in, and you go pick it up. I'll stay here in case Reston leaves." They decided on burgers and fries. Alan called in the order, and after a few minutes, he got out of the car and walked across the street. Dalton drove off and made a turn at the corner.

Alan found a dark spot under an overpass where the streetlights weren't on and watched the alehouse across the road. Only a minute after Dalton had driven off, Reston exited the taproom and walked down the block. Cursing under his breath, Alan disengaged from the pylon he had been leaning against and strolled down the street, across and behind his target. He kept his head pointed down and away from Reston. If he was spotted, he wanted to make it difficult to be recognized.

Reston turned the corner at A.P. Randolph St. and continued north. Hoping no one noticed him, Alan went to the other side of Randolph and walked to a bus stop bench. He sat on it and watched Reston continue down the block. Giving him a couple of blocks, Alan followed on the opposite side of the street, eventually passing a church and approaching the baseball grounds. The AAA baseball team was not in town, so the park was dark. Alan blended into the darkness and watched Reston enter a sports bar in the middle of the block. Waiting just long enough to ensure that Reston didn't come back out, Alan spoke to Layla.

"Layla, call Dalton's number and patch it to the glasses." The line rang in his ear, and Dalton answered. "Hey, I'm just on my way back."

"Reston bolted about a minute after you left. He must have just gotten a shot or something and left."

"Damn, did you lose him?"

"So little faith. No, I didn't lose him. He walked down the block to a bar on Randolph. I'm watching it now. I can see both exits from my location, and he is still inside. Get back here and go see what's up with that place. I can't risk it. He might recognize me." Dalton disconnected without replying. A couple of minutes later, the Subaru pulled to the curb beside Alan, and Dalton got out.

"Good job, rookie."

"Just get in there and find out what he is up to."

Dalton crossed the street and entered the bar. It was dark and damp-smelling. There were few patrons at the bar, and even fewer at the tables. Reston was nowhere to be seen. Noticing something strange, Dalton walked over to a large man dressed in dark clothing standing in front of a door. Without speaking, the man glared at Dalton.

"Don't get excited. I'm just a working guy," he said and held out a $20 bill. The bouncer looked at it for a moment, looked around to make sure no one was watching, and took the bill.

"What can I do for you, working guy?"

"Just looking for my friend. He just came in here, is he in the back?"

"What's your friend's name?"

"Jim, Jim Reston."

"Yes, Mr. Reston came in. Do you need me to get him for you? I don't think the game has started."

"Poker?"

"Yes, Texas Hold-em,"

"Ahh, no, don't bother him. I'll catch him later. No need to mention I was here either." He offered another $20. The bouncer took it and nodded. Dalton walked out and rejoined Alan, who was in the car devouring a hamburger.

"Glad you didn't wait for me," Dalton said, grabbing the other burger.

"Starving," was all Alan said between bites.

"There is an illegal poker game going on in the back of the bar. Bouncer knew Reston by name."

"That is very interesting."

"The owner of that bar has ties to Frederick Benson," Layla said, referring to a notorious local investor who rumors link to various shady activities. If Reston owes money to Benson, he might be in a lot of trouble. And he might do almost anything to get out from under it.

"What now, boss?" Dalton asked.

"I guess we wait and see how long he is in there. Unless you have a better idea."

"Should have gotten a six-pack." Alan agreed, and they settled in to watch the sports bar.

Alan and Dalton spent a very uneventful night outside the bar. Eventually, at about 2 AM, Reston exited the saloon and walked unsteadily back toward Bay Street. Dalton let him get to the corner, then fired up the Subaru and slowly rolled after him. When they reached the intersection, they saw James Reston's white Range Rover pulling out of the alehouse parking lot. Dalton followed behind at a discrete distance. Reston made no additional stops and arrived back at his home on Robin Hood Road just after 2:30 AM. They stuck around only long enough to make sure he was in for the evening, and then Dalton dropped Alan off at his car. They agreed to talk in the morning about the next steps.

Exhausted, Alan climbed into the driver's seat of his Orion Chimera and sat still for a moment.

"Alan. I'll drive home," Layla offered as he sat there trying to generate the energy to start the car.

"Thank you, Layla. That would be a great help." The car started and pulled smoothly out of the parking space at Prism Cybernetics and headed toward the highway. Alan sat back and relaxed.

Chapter Ten

ASSAULT

The next morning was rough. Alan hadn't gotten into bed until after 3 AM. At 6:30 he felt lethargic and spiritless. Even his morning coffee failed to revive him. A shower and a light breakfast made the day bearable, if not enjoyable. Alan took a coffee cup and a bagel into the office downstairs. Needing to free his thoughts on the cybernetics case, he opened the latest email from Dalton on background checks related to the drone case for North Florida Aerial. He read through the summaries while he finished his breakfast.

He was reading the summary of Holliston rep Stanley Graystone when Layla interrupted him. "Good Morning Alan." Her voice was coming from his laptop. He had left her on the charging pad in the living room when he had arrived home last evening.

"Good Morning Layla. I'm sorry I kept you out so late last night. Hopefully, you had time to do your nightly maintenance."

"I can operate for extended periods without doing the maintenance. I try to keep to the schedule because it is convenient to tie it to your sleep schedule." Alan had always suspected her nighttime routines were more about fitting in and less about necessity.

"Now that you are awake, you can help me go through these summaries from Dalton."

"I would be happy to help."

"Stanley Graystone. I'm reading the background information. There is nothing exciting in this summary: confirmed employment with Holliston for the past 6 years, no criminal record, no financial red flags. No indications that there is anything to note."

"I agree, but I sense you have more."

"I have a feeling about him," Alan said slowly. He had no logical reason to even pay any attention to Graystone. But something wasn't right about him.

"Human intuition is maddening in its elusiveness and effectiveness," Layla replied with a hint of jealousy in her voice. "I find nothing at all alarming in my follow-up searches of his public data. He seems to be straightforward."

Alan stared at the summary for several moments. Trying to pull at the thread in his brain that was nagging him. Why did this guy bother him? On a hunch, he reached over and picked up the desk phone, and dialed North Florida Aerial's main phone number.

"North Florida Aerial, Carol speaking, how may I direct your call?" Alan remembered meeting Carol Wineberg at the North Florida offices.

"Carol, it's Alan Harrison. How are you this morning?"

"Good morning, Mr. Harrison. I am doing well. How about yourself?"

"Oh, I've had better mornings. But what I am calling about is Stanley Graystone. You mentioned when I was there that he doesn't sign into the visitor logs."

"Yes, I said that. Why?"

"When did he stop signing in to the logs?"

"It has been a while. I'd have to look to be sure, but at least two or three months. Around the first of the year, I think, was the first time. I tried to enforce it for the first couple of visits, but gave up. He is here so often."

"Anyone else from Holliston show up at the office?"

"In person? No, we have a phone rep too. Gene...Freely. He calls to check in with us every month." The hair on the back of Alan's neck was standing up. He was approaching something important.

"Has he ever been to the office?" he asked.

"I think he came once or twice when he was first assigned, but not this year."

"Was he ever there on the same day as Stanley Graystone?" There was a pause.

"No, I don't recall their visiting together. I think Stanley was on vacation or something last year when Freely visited. He wasn't around for a couple of months, then showed up again in January. Does that mean something?"

"It might. I don't know exactly what yet. Thanks for your help, Carol."

"I'm glad I could assist. Have a great day." She disconnected from her end, and Alan held the phone, looking at Graystone's background check.

Without prompting, Layla displayed the contact information for Holliston International on his laptop screen. He dialed the number and waded through the automated menus.

"How did you know?" Layla asked with some awe.

"I didn't. I just couldn't quite get that statement that he didn't sign in out of my head. I didn't even know that was what was bothering me. It's like an itch that you can't quite reach."

"That analogy isn't particularly helpful for an artificial entity." Alan smiled. The day was getting brighter.

"Thank you for calling Holliston. This is Roger. How may I assist you today?"

"Roger, my name is Alan Harrison. I'm calling from North Florida Aerial in Jacksonville. I would like to speak to our rep. Is he available?"

"Let me check. Yes, I think I can reach Mr. Freely."

"Freely? I thought our rep was Graystone?" Alan tried to sound confused. He was far from there now.

"Oh, no, Mr. Freely replaced Mr. Graystone as your rep last October."

"I don't know how I missed that. I liked Stanley. I hope he is okay?"

"Mr. Graystone is fine; he is working on other accounts."

"Do both Graystone and Freely work out of your offices in..." he consulted the address information on the screen, "Hartford?"

"Yes, they are both in our home offices here. Is there a problem with the account?"

"No, no. Just my curiosity. I just got an email that I have a meeting I have to go to. I'll call Mr. Freely back later. Thanks for your time, Roger." He deflected two more attempts to connect him to Freely before getting off the phone. After days of nothing but disappointment, there might finally be a lead in this case. Why was Graystone pretending to be the support rep for Holliston on the North Florida account? What was he actually doing?

"Layla, we need to dive deeper into Graystone. There isn't anything in this public data, but I need you to look deeper. Blow through some red lights if you have to."

Three months ago he might have had to explain that, but Layla had learned to navigate his colloquialisms now. On the end table in the living room, her activity lights were already ramping up at a rapid pace. She was searching for more detailed information about Stanley Graystone. In a few minutes and driven by nothing other than Alan's instinct, they had a chief suspect in the drone theft case.

The late afternoon sun was shining through the windows of the new office space for Harrison & Associates, Investigations. Alan stood in the area marked off for the future site of the conference area. He had just finished briefing Stacy Collins on the morning's discovery.

"Has Layla found anything?" she asked when he finished.

"I don't know. Layla?"

"I am still working on it, but I found some curious activity in his bank accounts. Shortly after the time Freely replaced him as the customer representative for North Florida Aerial, he started depositing additional amounts each month into his bank accounts."

"How much altogether?"

"Just over $200,000." Alan whistled.

"That is a lot of money for a sales rep. Any obvious source for the income?"

"No. His salary is less than $150,000. There are no investments that would account for it, and no real estate assets that could account for the amounts either."

"Don't deposits like that have to be reported?"

"Presumably, but there are exceptions to that rule," Layla replied.

"We need to talk to Graystone. Any clues where he might be?"

"Based on recent purchases, he was in Hartford yesterday, but since then he has been traveling. I will continue to monitor his accounts to get a current location," Layla said.

"How can you tell he is traveling?" Alan asked.

"Airport kiosk purchases, rideshare records. Things like that," she replied.

Stacy, standing beside Alan during the conversation, stiffened suddenly. Alan looked at her and saw her looking at the doorway. Looking over, he saw the guy from the interior decorating company. Mike..something. He couldn't remember the last name. Stacy excused herself and went to greet him.

"What's up with her?" he asked Layla after she had departed.

"I'm sure I have no idea..." Layla said.

"Okay, that's enough. You're hiding something."

Alan turned his head to observe Stacy and the decorator guy with his peripheral vision. Her body language was awkward. Self-conscious, anxious. Mike seemed upbeat and excited at first, but as the conversation went on, his demeanor changed. He was not happy with the direction of the dialog. After a moment, Alan felt uncomfortable watching and moved out of the main room and into the unfinished interior office, pretending to review the decor.

After a few minutes, Stacy rejoined him inside the office. She was a little flushed.

"Everything alright?" he asked, concerned.

"Oh, yeah, everything is fine." She didn't seem fine. She seemed a little down. In the moment, all he wanted to do was cheer her up.

"Stacy, what are you doing tonight?"

"Tonight? Uh, nothing. Do you need me to work?"

"No, I was thinking of going to Cowford Chophouse downtown for dinner. Would you like to go with me?" Stacy had a surprised expression on her face, and maybe a little suspicious.

"Why do you ask?"

"No agenda. I just want to go, and I thought you might enjoy it. Have you ever been?"

"No, I haven't."

"It's a delightful place. Come with me. 6:30?" She considered it for a moment.

"Sure. I could use a night out. Do you want me to meet you there?"

"No, I'll pick you up around 6:15. Would that be good?"

"Yes, I'll be ready." She was smiling now. Alan told her he was looking forward to it and that he would see her at 6:15, and then he was off.

After he left, Stacy immediately addressed Layla. "Did you tell him about Mike?"

"Absolutely not!" Layla said assertively.

"Why did he ask me out then?"

"I don't know. He seemed concerned about you. What happened to Mike?"

"I turned him down. I just wasn't feeling it, and he is a vendor. The relationship would be messy."

"And what did you feel when Alan asked you out?"

Stacy visibly swallowed and blushed. "Uh, I—"

"Girl, your heart rate is all over the place." Layla said with amusement. Stacy had forgotten how much information Layla could get from the SmartLens glasses. They didn't have biometrics, but Layla could piece together clues from the video and audio recording capabilities to indicate biological reactions.

"You can't tell Alan that either!"

"My lips are sealed."

Alan pulled into a parking spot in front of The Brooklyn, a modern riverside apartment complex, about ten minutes after six. He sat in the car for a couple of minutes, not wanting to be too early.

"Are you nervous?" Layla asked from her spot on the car's console charging pad.

"What? No," Layla ignored this comment. Her internal sensors had already informed her it wasn't an accurate statement.

"It will be okay. She is nervous too."

"I'm leaving you in the car," he said in response.

"That's just mean."

"Work on finding Stanley Graystone," he said and got out of the car. He paused before closing the door, took off the

SmartLens glasses and put them behind the visor, and shut the door.

He knocked on Stacy's apartment door on the ground floor at 6:14 PM. Right on time. She opened the door a moment later. She was wearing a pale green dress. The sleeveless gown was conservative but elegant. They had not discussed the dress for the evening, so Alan was thankful he had put on a tan suit that turned out to complement the color of her dress.

"You look stunning," he said.

"Thank you. You look quite dashing yourself."

"I'm glad I am not underdressed."

"Definitely not. Why does Layla say you are being mean?"

Alan regarded her for a moment. "Layla needs to focus on her work." He reached out and took the SmartLens glasses from her face, folded them and put them on a small table right inside the door.

"Shall we go?" he asked. She nodded. Stepping inside for a moment, she retrieved a small clutch purse that matched her dress and exited the apartment. Alan escorted her to the car and opened the door for her.

Cowford Chophouse was on Bay Street in the historic Bostwick Building. The upper-level dining room had an impressive view of the St. John's River and the blue vertical-lift bridge known locally as the Main Street Bridge, though it was officially named for a 20th-century mayor that Alan knew nothing about. A hostess seated them near a window with a view of the bridge, and they ordered cocktails while looking over the menu.

"You've been here before?" she asked.

"Once or twice. Never with company so striking, though." Stacy blushed and smiled.

"I bet you say that to all your dates."

"I'm sure I didn't mean it."

When the server arrived, they settled on the duck fat cornbread and oysters as appetizers. Stacy ordered the wood-fired salmon, while Alan had a classic ribeye steak. The dinner conversation was light. They discussed a new documentary Stacy had been streaming recently and the book Alan had recommended a few weeks back. Stacy made a point to tell him that her cat, Noodle, missed him. He joked that it just missed running around his house and knocking things over.

As they stepped out onto the sidewalk in front of the restaurant later after dinner, Alan waved the valet away and suggested they walk down to the Riverwalk, just a couple of blocks to the south. Stacy agreed, and they strolled down Bay Street to Newnan and turned south. Walking past a hotel, they arrived at a beautiful brick walkway along the river. The sun had set, and it was just getting dark. The wind was light, and it was cool but not uncomfortable. Alan offered his arm, and Stacy put her hand through it, and they walked along the river.

"Oh!" Stacy exclaimed, looking out at the river. Alan followed her gaze and saw two dolphins swimming along the surface near the center of the water. They disappeared under the calm waters and reappeared a moment later a little farther downstream. The quiet couple watched the pair of mammals swim for a while.

"Thank you, Alan. This was a lovely evening."

"You're welcome. I had a great time. We should do it again."

"That sounds nice." They turned back and slowly headed back toward the restaurant. They were chatting about the meal and the pleasant weather. As they approached Bay Street, Alan felt something, like he was being watched. He looked up. He saw nothing at first, but a slight movement to his left caught his eye.

"Down!" he yelled and dragged Stacy down as a gunshot rang out from across the street. They both hit the sidewalk behind a parked car. He landed on top of her, hearing the air go out of her lungs. The feeling of her warm form underneath him distracted him for a second, but this wasn't a TV show. He didn't have time to think about his feelings. He rolled to his right and pulled her toward the parked car. A second shot rang out, striking the car with a loud thunk. Alan pulled his Smith & Wesson out of the holster under his jacket and peered over the car. He couldn't see the shooter.

"I think he is behind the van at the corner." Stacy offered. Alan looked down at her. Her hair was disheveled, and the green dress was torn, but she stayed alert and focused. He nodded his thanks for her help and concentrated on the van. Alan kept his gun pointed at the spot, waiting for the assailant to show himself. He finally did, but quickly seeing the gun, ducked down again before Alan could get off a shot. The sound of approaching police sirens spooked the would-be assassin, and the dark figure near the van turned and ran off in the opposite direction.

Alan remained behind the car, his gun ready until the police rolled into the intersection. He finally relaxed and asked Stacy if she was okay.

“I’m fine. The fireworks were unnecessary. The date was going splendidly,” she quipped.

“I didn’t have time to cancel them,” he replied and hugged her tight. She wrapped her arms around him and rested her head on his shoulder.

CHAPTER ELEVEN

AFTERMATH

The interview with the sheriff's office took almost two hours, despite neither Stacy nor Alan having any real concrete information to share. They hadn't seen the assailant except in shadow. No one else had witnessed the event. Alan was forthcoming with them about the ongoing investigations, but he couldn't say which, if either, was related to the attack. After the long, frustrating experience, they trudged back to the restaurant's valet stand to retrieve the Chimera. Noticing Stacy clutching the torn area of her dress to avoid it ripping any further and risking a public display, Alan offered her his jacket. She took it gratefully and pulled it tight around herself.

After helping her into the passenger seat, Alan walked around to the other side of the car and climbed in. Layla was already mid-sentence.

"...I have been trying to reach you for hours! I started looking at the police data and saw the shooting. Was that you?" Her voice was higher and more frantic than they had ever heard it.

"Yes, Layla. Someone took a shot at us on the street. We are fine, though. The only casualties are my dress and my dignity," Stacy said.

"Any idea who the shooter was?" Layla asked.

"No, we never saw them. Just a dark figure in the shadows. They must have followed us though. Any luck tracking down Graystone? Maybe it was him?" Alan asked, pulling the car away from the curb.

"He was at the Atlanta airport an hour ago. He charged his credit card at a food kiosk. I doubt he had time to get to the city and find you to take a shot at you."

"Pity, that would have been an easy way to wrap that up."

"I'll continue to check on his movements, and I'll see if I can coordinate any other suspect's movements with your attacker."

Alan parked the car and walked Stacy to the door of her apartment. She opened the door and invited him inside. "Come in and have a drink. I'll get changed and give you your jacket back."

Alan entered the apartment. He had been there briefly once or twice before. Overflowing bookcases dominated the living room. The titles were mostly romance and fantasy novels, with other genres mixed in. Small cat toys littered the floor. Alan made his way over to a small cabinet against the wall where Stacy had a modest but adequate bar set up. He poured a dignified amount of bourbon into a short glass and sat down on the couch. Stacy had disappeared into the bedroom, and he could hear her moving around.

"Where is Noodle?" he shouted. A soft, furry missile landed in his lap, answering the question. "Never mind. I found her." He took a sip of his drink and set it down on the end table. He idly stroked Noodle's soft fur and scratched under her offered neck. She purred loudly and curled up in his lap.

Stacy came out of the bedroom a few minutes later, dressed in sweatpants and a baggy t-shirt. She was carrying Alan's jacket. She stopped short at the sight of Alan sleeping on the couch with Noodle curled up in his lap, his hand resting on her.

"I really think that violates girl code, Noodle." Noodle made a soft mewing noise but didn't stir. Stacy sighed and put the jacket down on a chair. She grabbed the TV remote and switched on the TV. Finding her documentary, she started watching, settling in on the couch next to Alan and Noodle.

Several hours later, Alan woke with a start. It took him a few seconds to remember where he was. Noodle had climbed out of his lap in the night and was curled up on the rug across the room. Stacy was asleep, curled up against his left side. He watched her sleep for a few minutes until she woke up and caught him watching her.

"Don't watch me sleep. It's creepy," she mumbled.

"It's adorable, is what it is."

"How long have you been awake?" She asked, wrapping her arm through his and snuggling closer.

"A few minutes. Sorry, I fell asleep."

"Don't be. After being shot at, having you here was comforting."

"I should go, let you sleep in your own bed."

"I'm fine where I am." Alan reached over her and pulled a thick afghan, which was folded up on the back of the couch, to him and covered them both with it.

"This is nice," he said. "Did you make it?"

"No, my grandmother made it. I have tried to duplicate it, but it never turns out the same." He gently stroked the soft fibers, making a satisfied noise at the feel of the warm material. Stacy found the remote on the couch and turned her documentary back on. They watched it silently for a few minutes before they both drifted off to sleep again.

The alarm on Alan's phone woke him at 5:30 AM. He was alone on the couch. He could hear the shower running elsewhere in the apartment. He got up and stretched. After folding the afghan back up and returning it to the back of the couch, he walked into the kitchen. Happy to find a modern drip coffee maker there, he started the morning coffee.

Several minutes later, Stacy appeared in her bedroom doorway. She was wearing a white robe with her hair up in a towel. Alan handed her a cup of coffee, heavily enhanced with almond milk. She accepted the cup, took a sip and sighed contentedly.

"A girl could get used to this," she said with a smirk. This was their usual banter when one of them did the other a domestic favor. The response was supposed to be "You wish."

"We'll see," Alan replied with a warm smile. Stacy swallowed hard and blushed.

"That is very sweet, but I think we have work to do." Layla's voice boomed into the room from Alan's cell phone, which he had left lying on the kitchen counter.

"Uhh, Sorry Layla. It was a busy night," Stacy apologized.

"Sounds like it," she replied tartly.

"Layla! Alan slept on the couch."

"I'll take your word for it. More importantly, I need to get you both to focus on getting me access to the P4 robot that killed Cary Sellers. I have some tests I want to run on it."

Alan thought about the problem. The police had taken the robot as evidence. Most likely, it was in the evidence room downtown or the crime lab. They didn't have access to either, and breaking in with Layla's unique hacking skills was not an option.

"We need an ally in the sheriff's department who can help us get access," Alan said.

"What about Detective Fairfield?" Layla asked.

"What about him?" Stacy replied, puzzled.

"You seemed to have a bond with him at the scene. Do you think you can reach out to him? Try to get permission for us to examine the robot privately?" Alan answered.

Stacy considered this. She had gotten a very warm feeling from him at the scene, almost fatherly. It was as if he was trying to protect her from the ugliness of the surrounding brutality. It was like Alan's actions toward her at the scene, but with noticeable differences. Remembering something, she walked over to her purse on the table near the front door and searched through it until she found what she was looking for. A small notepad.

"Detective Andre Fairfield. I have an office number and a cell phone." She said, showing Alan the note.

"Cell phone," Layla said. Alan nodded his agreement.

"Okay, I'll call him." She looked at the clock on the wall. It read 6:15. "At a respectable hour."

"That is a good plan. Now, Alan needs to put his pants back on and get to work on other aspects of the case."

"Stop that! Alan is wearing his pants!" Stacy protested.

"Stacy isn't wearing any pants." Alan replied.

"As I expected," Layla said.

"That's it. Get out! Both of you." Stacy said with mock outrage. She was laughing as she said it.

Alan downed his coffee and went over to give Stacy a hug. She promised to call him as soon as she got an answer from the detective. "Thanks for staying last night." He squeezed her arm in response and headed to the front door, grabbing his coat from the end of the couch.

"You might need this," Stacy said, bringing him his cell phone. He took it and waved goodbye.

Back in his own home, Alan showered and dressed, then sat down at his computer with coffee and a bagel to review the case notes with Layla. She told him there was something unusual about the deposits in Graystone's account, but she wasn't sure what it was yet. Alan ruminated about her "hunch." Layla's detective skills were growing. A month ago she wouldn't have had a "feeling" about the financial data. The clue would have either been a fact or she wouldn't have noticed it at all until something else changed. Alan concentrated on reading Layla's financial reports on Graystone. He was looking for any patterns that might help them track down his current location. The last known location was at the airport in Atlanta, but that could lead them almost anywhere.

After about an hour of work, Alan looked down at Layla's slim form, which was sitting on the charging station on his desk. Judging by the activity lights, she was moderately busy, but not completely focused.

"Layla, nothing happened with Stacy. We fell asleep on the couch."

"I know. She called me the minute you were out of the apartment. She said you were the perfect gentleman, and that she felt safer with you there."

"Is she dating that Mike guy from the office renovation?" Layla was quiet for several seconds, weighing her promises to Stacy and her self-imposed obligations to Alan.

"No, she never went out with him," she said finally.

"But he asked her."

"I really can't talk about things she shared with me privately."

"I understand, but that gives the answer away."

"Does it? I'll have to study up on this secret-keeping thing," Layla said sarcastically.

Alan was looking at the financial data while he was talking to Layla. It made him remember the paper trail that they had used to track down the location of the murderous AI agent Kyrlos months ago. The picture here wasn't as clear, and unlike the previous occasion, he didn't have a map with data centers conveniently labeled for him to compare to the pattern.

"Layla, these debit card charges made by Graystone. Did you notice any patterns?"

"No, I had the same thought, but there wasn't anything really to compare the route to. We would have to investigate every establishment near each of those locations to find out where he was going."

"You know who would be good at that?"

"Dalton Rodgers," she said.

"I'll text him and ask him to track down all the locations and see if he can uncover anything in any of those areas that might shed light on where Graystone was spending his time." Alan started typing out the text on his phone. As he was finishing up, Layla put an incoming call from Stacy on his computer screen.

"Hey guys. I talked to Detective Fairfield. I haven't convinced him yet, but he agreed to meet us at the coffee shop near the office to discuss it. That is progress at least."

"Are you at the office already?" Alan asked.

"Yes, I am waiting for a furniture delivery. Your desk is arriving today!"

"That is great. It will be good to work out of the office. What time is the meeting with Fairfield?"

"After lunch, 1:45."

"Alright. I will finish up here and drop by the office, and then we can meet him. I'll bring pizza from Rojas."

"Bless you. I am starving. All I had for breakfast was some toast." She disconnected the call.

"She seems very happy." Layla said quietly. Alan had noticed. He wasn't sure exactly how he felt about that, but it wasn't an unpleasant thought. He got back to work on the rest of the data Layla had been collecting.

Chapter Twelve

Robot Redux

Alan and Stacy ate pizza out of an open box on his new desk at the office. The desk was beautiful. Made of quarter-sawn mahogany, and trimmed with brushed brass, it was the perfect blend of film noir detective and modern executive. Stacy had been scandalized at the prospect of eating on the new desk and had agreed only after Alan covered it with paper towels to protect the surface. Layla sat on the edge of the desk. As Stacy and Alan finished the pizza, the three of them strategized about how to approach the detective.

At 1:35 they left the office and walked the two blocks to the busy downtown streets to the Screaming Goat Coffee Company. Alan always loved the smell of the place whenever he went inside. That he had only discovered the coffee shop by accident during a previous investigation seemed impossible. It felt like he had been frequenting it forever. Detective Fairfield was sitting at a table near the front of the shop. Fairfield held a large coffee in one hand and was scrolling through his phone with the other. He looked up and, seeing Alan, nodded professionally. He favored Stacy with a warm smile.

"Miss Collins. It's good to see you again," he said as Stacy and Alan took seats at the table.

"Lovely to see you again too, Detective," Stacy replied.

"I told you on the phone to call me Andre," he reminded her.

"Andre, thank you for agreeing to see us. Alan and I would really like your help."

Fairfield looked at Alan. "You said that on the phone, so why do you need to see the robot? Our people have been examining it for days."

"We want to compare the data we got from the two units disassembled at the factory, and the one that malfunctioned later, with the unit you have," Alan explained, using the strategy they had agreed to at the office.

"Why can't you just give the findings to us and let us compare the units?"

"The information is proprietary. The company won't allow release of the information without knowing that it is essential to solving the case. We are protecting the interests of our client." This was a critical point. Layla and Alan had debated what reaction this would generate from the detective. He was bound to be frustrated by their lack of candor about the investigation.

"This is a murder case, withholding evidence—"

"That is our point. We don't want to withhold evidence, but we can't know it is evidence until we examine the robot. If our theory is false, then we would be revealing our client's intellectual property with no benefit to anyone. The minute we know it is material to the investigation, we will reveal everything." Stacy said, taking over this part of the pitch as planned. Hoping to use the detective's obvious friendly disposition toward her to their advantage.

"Miss Collins, if I agree to this, you have to assure me personally that you won't tamper with anything that could jeopardize the investigation."

"If I must call you Andre, stop calling me Miss Collins." She chided him. "I swear to you we are not planning on doing anything that would damage the investigation. We want it solved as much as you do. Probably more since we have a financial stake in the resolution," she softened her tone and gave him a friendly smile.

The detective regarded her for a moment. Looked at Alan to get a nod of agreement with her pledge, then sighed. "Okay, I'll set it up."

"We need to be alone with the robot. No cameras or recording devices. Because of the confidential nature of the information. We will record the examination, which we will turn over to you should our theory become relevant to the investigation," Alan asserted. Feeling they were at a yes, he wanted to make sure they had what they needed from the encounter.

"I will probably regret this," Fairfield said with resignation, but he was texting on his phone to set up the access as he spoke.

"No, you won't. I promise. At worst, it was the waste of 10 minutes of your time talking to us, and at best it will give you a clue to the solution of the case. Nothing else in between," Stacy assured him. He frowned but nodded.

Alan relaxed. From the small speakers in the SmartLens glasses he and Stacy were wearing, they both heard an audible "Whew!" from Layla. The strategy had worked, and the team had played their roles perfectly as planned. The slender police detective finished sending his text, told them he would email Stacy the details later, and made his departure. Alan and Stacy waited until he was safely out of sight down the street before they gave themselves a high-five.

As they walked back to the office, Alan, Stacy, and Layla were ecstatic with their successful plan. Layla reminded Alan that he had predicted they wouldn't be able to sway the detective to their request. Stacy had been hopeful but nervous about her part in convincing Fairfield to give them access. Only Layla had predicted it would work perfectly. She was explaining how she had predicted that the detective's fatherly instincts would play a powerful role in his decision. Stacy and Alan exchanged glances. Layla sounded almost pleased with herself. The chime from Stacy's phone interrupted her monologue on paternal psychology.

"Uh, we're in. He sent me the name of the officer at the lab we need to talk to when we show up. It's all arranged," Stacy summarized the contents of the text message.

"That was quicker than I expected. Did he give us a time?" Alan asked.

"Anytime during office hours, 8-5 Monday through Friday."

Alan consulted his watch. It was almost 2 PM. The lab was at a new location in the LaVilla district downtown. It was only a few minutes away by car.

Anticipating his thoughts, Layla said, "I need at least an hour. If we can get into the lab and have access by 3 PM, I should have time to run the tests I need to run."

"Let's go then." Alan walked past the Adamant Insurance Group building and continued on down the block to the parking garage. As he navigated the downtown streets toward the lab, they discussed logistics. Stacy would carry Layla into the facility in her purse to make her less conspicuous. If asked, they could just say she was some kind of office dictation machine. Such devices were becoming popular, powered by AI, much less powerful than Layla, of course.

"Why not just tell them I am an electric hide-a-key?" Layla suggested unhelpfully.

"Sarcastic AI-powered personal recorder, we are returning to the electronics store for a refund soon, it is," Alan said with fake sternness. Layla made a disrespectful noise. Stacy grinned.

The whole exercise was a waste of energy. Sean Devoe, the officer in charge of the lab security desk, looked through the purse and made no comment about Layla or anything else. He had them sign in and then, handing them guest badges, directed them to an interview room down the hall. They walked down to the door and waited for Devoe to buzz them into the room.

The space was larger than Alan had expected. It was a twelve-foot by twelve-foot office. The lighting was harsh, provided by two large LED-powered overhead fixtures. A large table and two chairs were against the far wall. Presumably, they usually occupied the center of the space. In the center of the room was the silent, dark robot with the designation P4-648. It looked to be the identical unit Alan had seen at the crime scene, right down to the damaged hand and the red stain.

Stacy took Layla out of her purse and sat her on the table against the wall. She also took out both pairs of SmartLens glasses and handed Alan his while putting on her pair.

"I am ready. Alan please turn on the power to the unit." As she said this, Layla displayed a video on Alan's SmartLens glasses showing the proper technique to turn on the power to P4-648. He followed the directions, reaching up to the neck area on the right side of the robot and finding a small recessed button. He pressed the button and held it for five seconds. Stepping back, he observed the unit was powering up. Lights around the aural inputs on each side of the face were blinking slowly. After a few seconds, they were steady.

P4-648's eyes lit up, and it turned and looked at Alan.

"Ahh, that's better," Layla's voice came out of the mouth of the robot. Alan and Stacy both stepped back.

The P4 unit turned to look at Alan and Stacy. "What's wrong?" the unit said in Layla's voice.

"The whole 'P4-Layla' thing is freaking us out!" Stacy told her.

"It's an unusual experience for me too," P4-Layla said. She moved her arms and flexed her hands. She took a couple of cautious steps forward, turned and stepped back, and turned around to face the original direction. "I am just calibrating my movements and testing the functions of the unit. Getting a baseline of what is normal."

"Normal doesn't seem to be the adequate word in this circumstance." Alan said.

P4-Layla walked forward to where Layla's white chassis sat on the table, bent at the waist and picked up the device in her hand. Holding it in the palm of her upturned hand, she looked at it from every angle. Finally, she put it back down gently on the table and backed away.

"This unit is technically amazing. The software is rudimentary, but physically it is excellent. We should get one," P4-Layla said.

"NO!" both Stacy and Alan exclaimed at the same time.

"Pity. The possibilities are endless." She raised her arms slightly in approximation of a shrug. "Very well, let's proceed with the test. I am going to duplicate my actions from the factory. Be prepared to turn the unit off if it gets out of control."

Alan and Layla had gone over the script earlier. They repeated all the voice prompts and actions that they had performed that day at the factory. There was no violent reaction from the robot.

"Resetting and let's try it again," she said. They ran through the scenario a second time, then two more times with no adverse reaction from the robot.

"There were other people present when the event happened," Stacy said. "Maybe it was something they did?"

"That is a good idea, Stacy," P4-Layla said, bringing her hand up to her face and stroking her chin. Alan unconsciously mirrored the action until he realized he was doing it, then quickly lowered his hand. "Stacy, let me have your SmartLens glasses. I want to try something."

Stacy handed her the glasses. P4-Layla adjusted the glasses to fit her face and fit snugly against the sides of her aural inputs. She moved her head around to make sure the glasses didn't shift. After assuring they were secure, she sent a signal to them. Alan and Stacy watched and listened as Layla played back the recording that she had retrieved from Alan's glasses on the day of the malfunction at the factory. They could hear the conversation between the three techs: Cary Sellers, Larry Volkner, and David Morgan. Alan's voice could be heard talking to Layla as she occupied the body of P4-751. Abruptly, P4-Layla jerked her arm violently. Smashing outward toward Alan, who jumped back out of her reach.

"Layla!" he shouted at her, but she didn't respond. P4-Layla kept coming toward him, swinging her damaged right hand in a slashing motion. Alan pushed Stacy behind him to shield her from the rampaging machine and was calculating the time it would take to lunge forward and turn off the robot when it stopped moving.

"Layla?" he tried again.

"I'm here, Alan," she said from her own body on the table across the room.

"We seemed to have triggered it," Stacy said.

"Yes, we did. Something in that video triggered the robot to violence. I want to test a few more things. Just a moment."

The P4 stirred again. Moving its arms around experimentally. The unit made a slashing motion with its damaged arm similar to the one it made toward Alan, but the speed and force were far diminished from what they had been before. The robot stopped moving again.

"Alan, activate the robot the way you did at the factory," Layla suggested.

"P4-648. Hello," he said.

"Good morning, sir. How may I help you?" The P4 unit turned and looked at him. Alan saw the video playing on the SmartLens glasses. "I seem to be receiving an audio-video feed, sir. Is this expected?"

"Yes, it is fine.' Alan readied himself, but the end of the video came and there was no reaction from the robot.

"That is curious," Layla said.

"Do you have it figured out?" Alan asked.

"No, not yet, but I believe I have all the information I need. Using the digital twinning process, I never allowed my primary functions to be integrated with the unit, so when it was in error, it did not lock down my systems. I got detailed logs throughout the entire encounter. I will use these to figure out what series of events triggered the violence."

Looking around, Alan made sure everything was back where they had found it. Stacy put Layla and the SmartLens glasses back in her purse, and they left. The officer at the desk accepted their guest credentials and told them good night. Alan checked his watch. It was at 4:25 PM.

"I'm starving," Stacy said. "Let's get something to eat," Alan agreed. He and Stacy started discussing what to pick up for dinner. Layla was quiet. She was already deep in her task of examining the log files.

Chapter Thirteen

Drone Wreck

Friday morning, Alan started his day in his home office. He constructed an association matrix for both the drone case and the murder. The matrices listed out all the people from each case and how they related to the case and each other. Layla could have done this task faster, but she was busy analyzing data from the P4 robot examination from the night before.

As he sipped his morning coffee and stared at the two grids on his laptop screen, Alan tried to see the missing connections. There were two big names, one in each case. The key to the drone case was almost certainly finding Stanley Graystone. The Sellers murder was trickier, but James Reston seemed likely to be involved somehow. Alan couldn't quite figure out what relationship the murder had to the break-in. Who was behind the vandalism? Was is really vandalism? What were they after that night when they took apart two P4 units but apparently took nothing? His gut told him that if he knew that, he could link things together and figure out the complete mystery. He smiled, remembering a line from an old Star Trek movie: "…if my grandmother had wheels, she'd be a wagon." Wishing for a connection would not make it happen. He would just have to go out and find one.

A text-message chime interrupted his thoughts.

"Hit me up. I think I found something." Dalton had sent. Alan texted back asking where they could meet. A few seconds later he got a pinned address link.

"Layla, I'm going out. I'll check in later," he said to his digital partner, who was sitting on the desk working away at her task.

"Thanks, Alan. I'll let you know if I find anything." He disconnected his SmartLens glasses from their charging cable and put them on. Unlocking the desk drawer, he retrieved his S&W and attached it to his belt. On the way out the door to the garage, he grabbed his blazer.

The address Dalton texted him was a McDonald's on State Street in the NorthCore district. Growing up, Alan always knew it as the Church District. Either way, it was a long way from the North Florida Aerial office in San Marco. As he pulled into the parking lot, he saw the beat-up gray Subaru. Dalton was leaning against it, eating French fries out of a large fry container.

"Those things will kill you," Alan told him as he got out of his car and walked up.

"There are worse things competing for that job," Dalton said, offering the container. Alan took a hot, greasy French fry and nibbled on it. They were delicious; he had to give them that.

"Did you bring me out here for lunch?"

"No, Graystone was here twice last month. Seemed like a waste of time, but while I was here, I did a neighborhood canvas and I got some interesting gossip."

"About Graystone?"

"No, they didn't know him from Adam, but several people told me they heard a crashing sound near the cemetery. The reports all occurred early in the morning after the drones went missing from the factory."

"Okay, now you have my interest. Did you go over there?"

"Yep...let's go." Dalton discarded the now empty fry container in a trash can and walked down State Street and crossed Liberty. They walked down to Washington and turned north. Dalton led the way along the sidewalk next to a half wall made of red brick. About half-way down the block he stopped. Alan noticed there was a nick in the wall. Looking up, Alan noticed low-hanging low-voltage lines. Dalton looked around, seeing no one paying any attention to them. He quickly scaled the three-foot wall and dropped to the other side. Alan followed him. On the other side of the wall, Dalton pointed to a tree that was partially overhanging the wall. Clipped limbs hung at an angle. Walking under the tree limb and looking closely, Alan finally saw it, wedged into the crook of the tree limb against the trunk. It was an aerial drone. It had smashed into the tree and gotten stuck there.

"How did you find that?" Alan said with awe.

"Dumb luck. I just looked up at the tree at the right time and saw the limbs. Knowing that the locals heard a crash, and that we were looking for missing drones helped."

Alan studied the drone. "If we call the police and they take it down, we won't get a chance to examine it."

"I thought about that. We could get a lot of grief if we move it and destroy any evidence."

"That's true, but the most likely theory is that the drone crashed here on its way to somewhere else. Which means that the drone itself might not be evidence of anything."

"Unless whoever tampered with it left fingerprints or DNA," Dalton pointed out.

"That isn't helpful to my position."

"You're right. The chances of that are...astronomical."

"That's better."

Dalton grinned, then looked around again to make sure they were not being watched. Seeing no one, he shimmied up the trunk of the tree until he reached the limb.

"Hold up a minute," Alan called to him. From various angles, Alan used his SmartLens glasses to photograph the location of the drone from every side. Finished, he called up, "Go ahead."

Dalton experimentally pulled at the drone in various directions to test how it was wedged into the nook. When it shifted slightly, he continued to pull it gently in that direction until he felt the weight free from the tree limb. Looking down, he confirmed Alan was in position, then lowered the drone with one hand slowly until he felt Alan take the weight off his hands.

Alan lowered the drone to the ground and waited for Dalton to climb down.

They examined the dormant drone on the ground for a few minutes. Then Dalton said, "So I don't really feel like carrying this thing down the street in broad daylight."

"Yeah, that's a good point. I'll get my car," Alan said.

A few minutes later, the drone was safely in the trunk of the Chimera.

"Any idea why Graystone was at this particular McDonald's? Is it a coincidence that the drone crashed here?" Alan asked.

"I think somewhere between coincident and law of probability. The drone must have been on its way somewhere. Wherever that is must be close enough for Graystone to have been in the neighborhood on his way there a few times before the theft." Alan thought about it for a second and nodded. That made sense.

"I am going to get the drone back to the house and see if I can figure out what is going on with it. I'll give you a lift back to your car."

Driving back to his house, he made a call to Stacy at the office.

"Harrison and Associates, Investigations," she answered.

"Stacy, is there anything pressing going on at the office?" Alan asked.

"No, the decorating team has finished for the day. I was just finishing up some emails."

"Excellent. Want to come over to the house?"

"Don't tease me, Harrison, what did you have in mind?"

"Examining a wrecked drone!" She laughed.

"That sounds about right. I'm in."

"See you there," he said and disconnected.

Alan had cleared off his desk in the home office and spread a blanket over the surface. He had brought down a lamp from upstairs and flooded the hastily made workbench with light. The drone sat in the middle of the work area with the light shining down on it. So far, he could not get any activity from the device. After getting home, Alan had brought Layla up to speed. He placed her on the workbench near the drone.

He heard the front door open, and a few seconds later, Stacy came into the office.

"And I thought the drone was a lie just to get me over here!" she said, grinning. Alan laughed. He explained briefly about Dalton finding it in the cemetery and the two of them retrieving it from the tree.

"Layla, are you ready to examine the drone now?" he asked.

"Yes, make sure you get close so I can see the details of the unit."

Alan adjusted his SmartLens glasses and leaned over the drone, looking slowly at all sides of the device. The aircraft was sleek, with a white glossy X-shaped surface. Small propellers sat atop each of the four arms. LED lights are connected to the underside area of the propulsion arms. A large, expensive-looking camera was mounted on the bottom center of the device. The front of the unit showed signs of impact damage, but nothing catastrophic. Other areas had scratches and dents.

"They said these were worth $50,000?" Stacy asked. She was standing close, leaning over Alan's shoulder, a fact that was a bit distracting, but not wholly unpleasant.

"Alan, do you have tools? Small screwdrivers?" Layla asked. Alan thought about this for a moment.

"Yes, I have an electronics kit upstairs. I think I bought it once when I was going through a 'do it yourself' computer upgrade phase...that didn't last." He ran off to get the kit.

"How are you doing, Stacy? Your heart rate is elevated," Layla asked after Alan had left the room.

"It is not! You must be malfunctioning."

"Uh-huh." Layla gave a soft chuckle.

"Quiet," Stacy hissed as she heard Alan approaching the office.

Alan came back into the room with the kit and opened it up on the workbench. Following Layla's direction, he gently turned the drone over on its top, then removed eight tiny screws from the panel on the bottom of the device. Slowly, he removed the cover, exposing the internal components of the drone. Together, they checked several connectors to ensure they were still joined tightly.

"Alan, move that red wire aside and look at the battery connection." Alan complied, pushing the thin red wire to the side and looking at the tiny connector that linked it to the battery.

The screw had come loose, so the wire wasn't contacting the battery. Alan selected a different screwdriver and tightened the screw, making the connection tight. He saw a small red indicator light next to the tiny system board, rewarding his efforts.

"I think we might have something," he said.

"Yes, I agree. Put the assembly back together and let's see if we can get it powered up." Layla said.

With Stacy assisting him, handing him the cover, and then each of the eight screws, he reassembled the drone casing and turned it over.

"Here goes nothing," he said as he pressed the small power button on the side of the drone. Three colored lights started blinking: red, green, yellow. They cycled for several seconds and then settled on green.

"Stand by while I try to access the drone's remote control interface," Layla said.

While they watched, the drone went through several cycles. The lights flashed, the propellers spun up and then back down. The unit emitted a series of beeps and chimes.

"Stand back," Layla cautioned them.

Stacy and Alan backed away. The drone spun up its propellers and then lifted gently off the workbench. Hovering for a few seconds, it then made a small circle around the desk. Stopping and hovering again, it centered itself on the work area and slowly lowered itself down.

"Curious," Layla said.

"What is it? The drone seemed to work perfectly."

"There is something wrong with the GPS routines. The unit thinks it is almost 6.25 miles southwest of its current location."

"That doesn't sound like it can be random," Stacy said, frowning.

"No, it must be intentional, but I don't know what the motivation is yet. I'll have to keep working on the data," Layla said.

"What about video? Can you retrieve anything from the drone's camera?" Alan asked.

"I haven't been able to retrieve any images yet. The crash probably damaged the media storage. I will keep working on that." Alan contemplated this. Layla was now working on the P4 log data, the GPS discrepancy, and the image retrieval. Even for her, that was a lot of work.

"You are doing a lot of the heavy lifting in this investigation, Layla," Stacy said, as if reading Alan's mind.

"I couldn't be doing any of it if you hadn't gotten us in to examine the P4 robot, and if Dalton and Alan hadn't located the drone. We all have a part to play. This is just mine."

"What can we do to help?" Alan asked.

"Nothing yet. I may need some more specialized equipment at some point, but right now just let me work and I'll let you know."

Stacy and Alan exchanged a look. They seemed to be just in the way. Alan looked at his watch. It was early afternoon. He had skipped lunch. Looking back at Stacy, he said, "So we should do what we always do when we can't find a way to progress the investigation."

"Get food," she said laughing. He nodded in agreement.

Chapter Fourteen

Global Positioning

Throughout the rest of the day Friday and on into the weekend, Layla continued to work on her three projects. Investigating the GPS corruption, trying to retrieve information from the damaged drone's media files, and reviewing the mountains of log files from the P4 unit.

Feeling that his investigation depended on making a breakthrough on one of those fronts, Alan felt useless. He busied himself around the house with chores he had been neglecting since the dual investigations began a week ago. Friday turned into Saturday, which morphed into Sunday. And while the house was cleaner, he had reorganized the garage and cleaned out his refrigerator. He had accomplished nothing on the case. Checking in with Layla, he got an update that she was still working on all three tasks. Alan went for a walk.

The late Sunday afternoon was breezy, but the temperature was comfortable. He walked southwest on Cherry St. toward Riverside Avenue, waving to neighbors who were in their yards doing various chores or activities. At Riverside, he turned southeast and walked toward Willow Branch. He had no specific destination in mind; he was just relaxing his brain and getting out of the house. At Willow Branch, he walked up to the corner and saw his next-door neighbor walking a small brown and white beagle.

"Clem! How are you?" he greeted the older man. Simon LeRoy Clemens was a fixture in the Riverside area. He had lived here for most of his 81 years. Clemens had achieved some minor fame in the sixties as a saxophone player in a band. He had taught high school music studies for a while and finally retired as the principal librarian for the Jacksonville Symphony.

"Alan, good to see you out and about for a change instead of chained to a desk."

"How is Velma?" he asked, pointing to the beagle.

"She's fine. She sits around too much, too. Needs to get more exercise." Alan leaned down and scratched her ears, and she rewarded him with a wag of her tail.

"How is the new career?" the old man asked as they both walked down Willow Branch.

"Busy. I'm trying to solve the case of who the Jaguars are going to pick in the draft this year." Clem laughed. He was the biggest fan of the local NFL team anyone had ever met.

"If you can figure that out, you'll be the city's most sought-after detective."

"I can't figure out what they really need. They are a well-rounded team now. I'm not sure what would make them better," Alan said.

"Sometimes it isn't so much the pieces you end up with but shuffling them and moving them around." Clem said. Alan looked over at him. Something about that statement started an itch in his mind. He couldn't quite figure out why, though. He tried to work it out for a few more blocks, but it still didn't come. Alan finally gave up on the idea.

"So what are you doing to stay busy these days, Clem?"

"Oh, I have been volunteering at the main library downtown since just before Christmas. I am helping them catalog an extensive music collection that was donated last year."

"That's great."

"It keeps me from being bored." They had turned back toward home at Oak Street and were approaching Cherry Street. Velma surged ahead on her leash and barked happily at a terrier in a fenced-in yard ahead of them. Clem stopped to chat with the terrier's owner, and Alan waved at them and continued on his way back home. As he reached the house, his mind went back to the comment about the Jaguars moving pieces around. Why did that mean something to him? As he walked through his living room into the kitchen to get some water, he still couldn't figure it out.

A text message interrupted his thoughts. It was Stacy asking if Layla had made any breakthroughs. He replied to her, letting her know it was still a work in progress. They chatted a little about the weekend, Alan's chores, Stacy's family picnic at the beach. She signed off, telling him to come by the office on Monday morning to review the work that had been done. He promised to see her early in the morning and put his phone down. Checking that Layla was still at work, LED lights steadily blinking away, he went to the bookcase to select a book to occupy his mind.

Selecting *The Left Hand of Darkness* by Ursula K. Le Guin, he settled down to read the iconic science fiction novel about gender, politics and communication. It managed to do its job, distracting him from his lack of accomplishment for the weekend.

Monday morning was cool and clear, like most days this time of year. Forecasters predicted no rain and expected the high for the day to be in the mid-70s. Alan was dressed in his usual uniform. Jeans, a light-colored dress shirt, and a dark blazer to cover the holster on his belt. Since someone had already shot at him once, he wasn't traveling without it while this case was ongoing. The traffic was bearable that morning for a change, and he arrived at the Adamant Insurance Group building just before 8AM.

As he stepped into the lobby, Alan stopped and smiled at the door to his office. It was closed, and for the hundredth time he marveled at the Harrison and Associates name, but that wasn't what stood out today. Across the door was a gold silk sash with the words "Grand Opening" stenciled on it. Hanging from a string attached to the doorknob was a pair of oversized scissors.

"That is a surprise," Layla said.

“A pleasant one. Stacy is a wizard,” Alan responded with a grin. He grabbed the scissors and cut the ribbon neatly in two, and swung the door inward.

Inside, leaning against her new desk, Stacy held a bottle of Cristal and two champagne glasses. She waved her arms around to show off the state of the offices. Alan looked around, taking in the transformation. It was hard to believe that the dusty, bare interior from a couple of weeks ago was now a beautiful, modern office space. The space was an open design. Just inside the entryway were a small sofa and two chairs. Across from that was Stacy’s desk. Dominating the rest of the space was a large conference table. The walls near Stacy’s desk and the conference table were adorned with large video screens. Alan’s office was in the suite’s rear with the beautiful mahogany desk. Video screens lined the walls of the executive office as well.

“This is amazing,” Alan said, looking around.

“I’m pretty pleased with how it turned out.” Stacy walked over to the conference table and placed the two glasses on it. Popping the cork on the champagne, she poured two glasses and handed one to Alan. He took the offered long-stemmed glass and clinked it to hers, and they drank.

“This really is an impressive accomplishment. I didn’t expect it to be completed so quickly,” Alan said.

“I might have fudged the timeline a little to make you more impressed with the completion time,” Stacy replied with a grin.

"Well, it certainly worked. You are the best office manager in the city."

"While we are all together, I have some information for you," Layla said.

On cue, the monitors in the conference area lit up and displayed a map of the Jacksonville area. Layla marked several areas with colored icons. The first was North Florida Aerial. Old City Cemetery, where Alan and Dalton found the drone, was the second location, and the last was a giant circle to the southwest of the cemetery.

"As you can see," Layla said, as she displayed a line from the starting point in the San Marco area to the extensive area circled in the Tallyrand area, "the path of the drone was along this trajectory." Alan and Stacy nodded in understanding.

"The final destination has to be in this general area inside the circle. I believe that, using the GPS drift introduced by the hack of the global positioning chip, I can narrow that down to a specific location. The final calculations will be completed soon, but I wanted to give you the direction as soon as possible."

"How did they get the drones to travel to this location?" Alan asked.

"That is a good question, and I don't know the answer yet. Most of the data on the drone's internal memory card is still unreadable. I have an idea to address this, but I will need some equipment to do it. I am sending you an email with a list of parts I need."

"I'll take a look at that, and I'll ask Dalton to check out the area in the Tallyrand neighborhood for locations where the drones might have been transported." Alan looked toward his office.

"It's all set up for you," Stacy assured him. He gave her a hug and told her again how amazing her efforts were and headed into his office.

Sitting at his desk, Alan opened his laptop and reviewed the email Layla had sent him. It was a list of some highly technical equipment. He recognized a couple of the components but not the others. As he reflected on the various pieces of hardware, he remembered Clem's comment about moving the pieces around. He sat back, surprised. Like a freight train coming out of a tunnel, a bright light revealed the reason that the statement had made sense. Reaching for his desk phone, he located and pressed the intercom button.

"You already found the intercom," Stacy said.

"That was fast," Layla said on the same line. Of course, she was plugged into the communication channel. Stacy thought of just about everything.

"Yesterday Simon Clemens made an offhand comment to me. It meant something, but I couldn't place what. A minute ago, Layla's list of components she needed for the data retrieval project triggered the reason."

"Human background processing strikes again!" Layla said with a certain amount of awe. The unconscious processing skills that humans possessed seemed to fascinate her.

"Yes, Stacy, I need you to call Prism Cybernetics and set up a time we can go over there and review the security tapes from the break-in. I think I have an idea that explains why the break-in occurred. If I am right, it could help lead us to the solution of the whole affair."

"Are you going to tell us what it is? Or are we going to find out with everyone else?" Stacy asked.

"Set up the meeting first. I'll brief the two of you before we meet with them."

"On it," Stacy said.

"What was the topic of the conversation with Mr. Clemens?" Layla asked.

"The Jacksonville Jaguars."

"NFL football? That seems to be a non sequitur," Layla said with confusion in her voice.

"You would think so, but it turns out..it was a perfect trigger to point me in the right direction."

"The human mind is an amazingly complex thing, Alan."

"It's occasionally useful if one has the patience to put up with the constant stream of nonsense that you have to filter through to get to the useful bits," he replied.

"Okay, they can set it up for tomorrow morning," Stacy said, coming back onto the intercom line.

"Excellent, I'll brief you both this afternoon."

Stacy and Alan gathered at the conference table. Alan walked them through the conversation with Simon LeRoy Clemens, and then explained what it meant to him and why he thought it was important. Stacy asked a couple of questions. They had reviewed portions of the security footage from the break-in, but only enough to determine that the video didn't reveal the perpetrators' identities because they used anti-video equipment. Layla went back over her memory of what they had seen, but admitted they had never reviewed the time frame needed to confirm Alan's suspicions.

"I don't know why we didn't insist on seeing the whole video," Layla said.

"Because we focused only on who did it, we thought vandalism was the purpose. If I am right, the real reason is something else entirely."

"Well, we'll know tomorrow," Stacy said. As she did, she looked at the almost full bottle of champagne.

Reading her mind, Alan said, "It's a shame to let this go to waste." Needing no further encouragement, Stacy grabbed the bottle and poured.

Chapter Fifteen

Break-in Breakthrough

The conference room at Prism Cybernetics was perfectly acceptable for a high-tech organization, but Alan couldn't help but compare it to the conference area at his new office; doing so left it lacking a certain style. But it had a large monitor, which at the moment was displaying the security footage from the night of the break-in. Seated around the table with Alan and Stacy were the VP Fred Johnson, product manager Jason Wingram, and Sean Devoe, who was running the camera software from a laptop.

On the screen, a figure dressed all in black entered the factory floor from the lobby. A bright white spot obscured the face of the figure as it approached a quad of assembly stations where P4 units were in various stages of construction. The invader manipulated the assembly arm manually, accidentally snapping off a retainer clip holding the hydraulic cable to the arm. The cable ruptured, spilling fluid onto the table. Jumping back to avoid the fluid, the figure moved away from that station to another.

At the new station, the figure leaned over the partially assembled robot.

"Can we pause there?" Alan asked. Devoe paused the video. "Zoom in on this part. Can we see what they are doing with their hands?"

Devoe adjusted the video to focus on the hands. He restarted the video, and they watched as the black-gloved hands pried a half-constructed face covering away from the P4, exposing the internal components. The hands reached in and pulled out a small circuit board. The hands disappeared and moments later they reappeared and reinserted the board into the unit. Devoe paused the display in reaction.

"What—" Jason said involuntarily.

"Continue, please," Alan said. The video restarted, showing the figure move away from the P4 unit and remove various components from another P4, this time leaving each of them on the workbench next to the robot. A few seconds later, the vandal left the area. Devoe zoomed out again, and they watched the figure exit the factory floor.

"Why would they take a piece out of the unit and put it back? And that last part didn't seem to have any purpose at all," Johnson said.

"That part was just for show. The whole point was the first component," Alan said.

"Why?" Johnson asked.

"Good question. What was the state of the components that were removed or left behind? Anything unusual?"

"No," Johnson replied.

"Actually—" They turned to look at Jason Wingram.

"What?" Alan asked.

"The primary system on a chip circuit board for that unit was factory reset. It was like it had just come out of the box from the plant," he said. Alan regarded him for a moment and then nodded, as he expected the answer.

"What does that mean?" Johnson asked.

"I'm not ready to speculate about motive yet, but I can tell you this. The break-in wasn't random, and it wasn't vandalism. There was a motive for the actions of the perpetrator."

"But you can't tell us what it was?"

"No, because I don't have the full answer yet, and I don't want to chance a stray comment tipping anyone off, and right now I don't know who that person in the video is, or who they might be in contact with at Prism." No one in the room was happy with that answer and Johnson spent a few minutes trying to get more information, he wasn't successful. Alan thanked them for their cooperation and assured them he would report back soon with more information. He and Stacy exited the factory a few minutes later and held their comments until they were in the car.

"Well, what do you think?" He asked Layla once they were safely away from the factory.

"Clearly the vandal, who is not a vandal, is not familiar with these units. They don't show any aptitude in their construction.

The disassembly was clumsy and amateurish. But they knew what they were after. The SoC chip was the target."

Remembering their conversation from the day before, Stacy said, "The chip wasn't factory reset."

"No, it was a factory-fresh chip. The one from the unit left with the mysterious visitor," Alan confirmed.

"The only reason someone would want that chip with no one knowing is that someone altered its code." Layla said.

"Exactly. Someone wanted evidence that the chip had a backdoor coded into it. That is the only thing that makes sense given what we know about the code changes."

"But who? Cary?" Stacy asked.

"Why would Cary need a chip from a unit at the factory? He had one at home," Alan asked rhetorically. Stacy nodded in acceptance of his point.

"Someone who knew that there was a backdoor, but did not have access to a P4 unit themselves, needed the chip as...evidence?" Layla suggested.

"Or leverage," Alan said.

"Like for blackmail?" Stacy said excitedly.

"It fits. But who was being blackmailed and who was doing the blackmailing?"

They were all quiet for a while as Alan drove. The video had confirmed Alan's hypothesis that the point of the break-in was not to damage robots but to remove parts from them. He correctly predicted that the vandalism was actually theft. The confirmation, though, did not solve the entire case. Alan still had confidence that the facts they had revealed would ultimately lead to the killer, but there was still work left to do.

Back at the office, Stacy debuted a high-end coffee maker from the small break room in a corner of the suite, and they drank coffee while thinking over the potential answers for the questions the day had uncovered.

"This is wonderful coffee," Alan said, pausing.

"But it doesn't replace the Screaming Goat Coffee Company!" Stacy finished his thought for him. He smiled and nodded.

On the big monitors, Layla was scrolling through log data from the P4. Alan looked up just as a large block of unreadable data scrolled by on the screen.

"What is that?" he asked.

"It is a binary file," Layla said. The display paused. Then a pop-up window appeared, showing a video. In the video, Cary Sellers was on his laptop. The screen of the laptop was clearly visible and readable. The video ended just as Sellers closed down the application and closed the laptop.

"Are the P4s supposed to be recording video?" Stacy asked.

"Not from the architecture data I have seen." Layla answered.

"Are there other videos?" Alan asked. In response, the log files scrolled by at high-speed until they came to another binary entry. The video file this time was from behind Seller's shoulder, looking as he read an email about his credit card statement. He scrolled through the charges and closed the email. As soon as he stood up to leave the computer, the video shut off. A few minutes later, another video appeared. This one showed Sellers talking to someone on the phone. The conversation seemed unimportant. The video ended as soon as the call ended.

"Surveillance," Stacy said.

"Yep," Alan agreed.

"You could use this to steal bank information, blackmail people with their secrets. Case houses for break-ins...the potential is almost unlimited," Layla said.

"And that is quite a motive for someone to want proof for leverage."

"To stop it?" Stacy asked, then answered her own question, "No, to get in on the action."

"Excellent insight," Alan said.

"That brings us back to Reston," Layla suggested.

"He would certainly seem to be a prime candidate to need cash," Alan agreed. He made a mental note to redirect Dalton to look into Reston's connections in the local gambling scene more closely. Maybe they could uncover a more concrete relationship to the local underworld. Having formed the thought, Alan felt a little silly. Even though Jacksonville wasn't free from crime, including organized crime, it wasn't really famous for high-stakes criminal organizations. Despite that, it was worth looking into.

"Stacy, can you send Dalton a message and have him come by this afternoon? I want to ask him to look at Reston more closely." She agreed and left to make the call. Alan finished his coffee quietly.

"She is becoming quite an asset." Layla said. It startled Alan to realize that he had been thinking the same thing.

"Yes, it is amazing to think that I once considered it risky to involve her in our team at all."

"Now it's almost impossible to conceive of doing it without her."

"Yes, that's true." The conversation made Alan contemplate the implications of that line of thought. Layla let him work through it in silence.

Alan was at his desk having an animated conversation. A knock at the door caused him to look up and see Dalton leaning against the frame. Alan waved him inside.

"Sam, I know it isn't simple. If it were simple, I would do it myself. Can you get into it and call me back later?" Nodding along with the answer, Alan thanked the caller and hung up.

"Ex-lover?" Dalton asked with a smirk.

"Worse, current lawyer," Alan replied with a grin.

Dalton walked around the office, looking at the decor. Alan buzzed Stacy and asked her to step in. Dalton stopped at the bookcase behind Alan's desk and looked at a large white porcelain coffee mug with the Screaming Goat Coffee Company logo on it.

"What's this?" he asked, reaching for it.

"NO!" Alan and Stacy, who had just entered the office, yelled in unison. Dalton's hand jerked to a halt inches away from the cup.

"What's the story?"

"It's a gag gift from a lady named Georgia Jackson. Whenever you tilt it to drink, it makes a loud screaming goat sound."

"You're kidding."

"No, a wannabe barista who is stalking Alan delivered it on Christmas Eve last year," Stacy declared. Alan gave her a warning look, and she put her hands up in surrender.

"Well, that sounds like a story for another time." Dalton said, grinning.

"It's quite a tale. Maybe we'll give you all the details one day," Stacy said, taking a seat in one of the visitor chairs. Taking the hint, Dalton took the other chair. They both looked expectantly at Alan.

Alan launched into his update, bringing Dalton up to speed on the events in the murder case that had occurred over the last few hours. He detailed the video findings and their conclusions. Dalton considered the information and agreed with their hypothesis of the events.

"So you want me to pin down who Reston owes, hoping it is someone heavy that would give him motive to hatch a scheme to spy on potentially millions of people, and ultimately to murder Cary Sellers."

"That's about it. He seems the most likely candidate at the moment. We know he frequents a sports bar owned by some shady characters. Maybe he is deeper in debt than his records show. Maybe someone with muscle is forcing him to spy on people for profit."

"This is all prospective though, right? The robots aren't released yet," Dalton pointed out.

"Yes, that is true. It would be a long game, not a short one. But the potential is enormous. Especially if the predictions about the future of robotic expansion are true."

"I've read those articles too. Potentially as high as $150 billion in sales in the next 5 years. Maybe even higher if the price point drops. They could eventually be in every middle-class home in the country," Dalton agreed. "What about the drone case? I was just beginning to look at properties in the target area."

"Leave that for now. Lay—we will try to narrow down the search area. If that happens, the search will be easier. This is more pressing at the moment. I want to make some progress on this case. I feel like we are close." Stacy gave Alan a look. Dalton hadn't seemed to notice, but Alan had almost outed Layla. He tilted his head slightly to acknowledge the near mistake. They discussed a few more items, and Dalton got up to depart. Stacy told him to send his invoice for his work so far, and she would get a payment out to him. He thanked her and tipped an imaginary hat to Alan and was gone.

"That was close," she said to Alan after Dalton had closed the outer office door.

"Yeah, it's harder and harder to keep things from him. We might one day have to expand the circle. He is a trustworthy guy. For now, if it slips, Layla is a freelance tech specialist we are contracting with. That should cover it."

"Okay, that should work. Did you get what you needed from Sam Eaton?" she asked, referring to his attorney.

"Yes, just some details on the business filings. Some red-tape detail or another. There is always something."

"Ahh, the life of a business owner," she said with a grin.

"You don't know the half of it," he agreed.

Chapter Sixteen

Target

Alan looked around his downstairs home office with some dismay. The usually pristine, spartan decor was now a chaotic mountain of technical ordnance. Bits of the damaged drone adorned the desktop along with new boxes filled with the components Layla had requested for the drone recovery. A large monitor occupied the other desk in the room. The video recorded by Alan's SmartLens glasses during the incident at the cybernetics factory played in a loop.

"This place is triggering me," he announced, sitting in the desk chair.

"I'm sorry. I have a lot of processes going on and I need to switch between them quickly," Layla said, pausing the video output.

"Are you making any progress?"

"I think so. The trigger in the code for the violent outburst from the P4-751 comes somewhere in this time frame." She restarted the video. On the monitor, Alan watched the three techs working on the assembly equipment. Larry, Cary and

David Morgan were making adjustments to the unit and testing the results. The time sequence was just before they made their last change, and it flowed through until just after they had executed the code. Alan watched it but saw nothing noteworthy. Layla played the clip again. And a third time.

"I don't see anything," Alan said.

"Neither do I. I even looked at the code that was on the assembly station screen at the time of the incident, but there was nothing there that seemed like an obvious trigger."

"Maybe there is context we aren't understanding," Alan suggested.

"Something that is out of the ordinary in this clip that we don't see, because we don't have a benchmark?" Layla considered this. "That could be possible. Who could provide that context?"

"Someone from the factory. Let me think for a minute." Alan pushed some boxes on the desktop aside and found the employee listing he got from Prism Cybernetics. He read through the list looking for the name of someone who might provide them with some context, but who wasn't currently associated with the events. That ruled out Larry and David Morgan, and the executive staff, and the developers. His eyes settled on a name.

"I have an idea. I am going to call Prism and try to set up a video call." Alan pulled out his cellphone and dialed the number for the main desk at Prism Cybernetics. After going through an automated phone attendant, he reached the front desk and asked for Fred Johnson. After a few minutes, he came on the line.

"Mr. Harrison, do you have an update?"

"We are making progress, Mr. Johnson. I have nothing concrete to report yet, but I need assistance."

"What can I do to help?"

"I need you to make one of your employees available today for a brief video conference with one of my associates and me. We need to review some video footage of the factory floor, and I want someone who works there to look at it for anything out of the ordinary."

"I'm sure we can help with that. I can get Larry Volkner to do it." Alan let the suggestion sit for a moment as he pretended to consider it.

"Larry has been a great help to the investigation so far, Mr. Johnson. For this task, though I would prefer someone else. Someone who works on the line every day."

"I'm sure we can find someone."

"Well, let me see if we can pick one now." Alan made a show of picking up the employee listing and going through it. After a few seconds, he tapped the list and named an employee for the interview.

Layla displayed the video conference on the monitor. Alan's image appeared, and she presented herself with just an icon with the letter L. A few seconds later, a conference room at Prism Cybernetics joined the call. The room appeared empty for a moment, but the nervous face of Rebecca Salter appeared. Seeing Alan's face, she smiled.

"Hi Rebecca. Thanks for joining. On our side I have an associate, Layla who will assist us today," Alan greeted her.

"My pleasure, Mr. Harrison. Nice to meet you, Layla."

"My pleasure, Rebecca," Layla responded.

"Please call me Alan and don't worry. We just need another pair of eyes to review some video footage from the factory floor and give us their opinion about anything that is unusual about it."

"Oh, okay." She seemed to relax a little.

"As you know, we are investigating the break-in at the factory, and also the unfortunate death of Cary Sellers."

"Are they related?" she asked.

"Very likely. During our investigation, there was an incident at the factory. A unit malfunctioned and damaged some equipment. We think there might be a connection between that event and Cary's death at his apartment. Do you remember this event?" Alan paused to allow her to digest the information.

"Oh, I remember that day," Rebecca said a little wistfully, almost certainly thinking about the loss of Cary Sellers.

"Okay, we are going to play a brief video clip of that day. I apologize in advance for making you go through it again. We think there is something unusual about this clip, but we can't figure it out ourselves without knowledge of what is and isn't normal for the setting. That is where you come in. Are you ready?" Rebecca swallowed, steeling herself and nodded.

"My associate, Layla, will now play the video clip. Watch it and give us your reaction to it." Alan nodded, and the video clip appeared on the screen. It played all the way through.

"Notice anything unusual in it? Anything stand out?" Alan asked.

"No, not really." On cue, Layla played the video again. At one point, Rebecca smiled at an exchange between Cary and the other two techs.

"Why did you smile just now?" Layla asked. The question surprised Rebecca for a moment until she reconstructed the sequence in her head.

"Oh, it is nothing. Just Cary said, 'This time for sure.'"

"Why is that significant?" Alan asked.

"It's not. But he said it all the time. Every time he tried something...like five times in a row, he would have the code fail, and he would say that before every attempt." She smiled again in memory of the trait.

"It was like a catchphrase?" Alan asked.

Rebecca thought about the question. "Yes, I guess so. It happened so often that we would tease him about it."

"Who is 'we'?"

"Everyone on the floor. It was a running joke on the team." Alan looked over and saw Layla's LED lights flashing rapidly in a high-speed chase pattern.

"Thank you so much for your time today, Rebecca. I know it couldn't have been easy to relive that day, considering everything that has happened."

"Oh, no, it's fine. Did I help at all?"

"It's early, but I would say that there are some good signs that you did. I'll let you know if we need anything else." He thanked her again, and she disconnected. Alan ended the conference call.

He sat back and watched Layla. Her "deep-thought" mode lasted several minutes. Finally, the activity subsided.

"Do you have something?" He asked immediately.

"Yes, but I need time to prepare a detailed analysis. I'll let you know when I am ready."

Alan parked his car in the lot and started walking toward the office. As he reached the front of the building, he had a thought and continued on and turned at the corner. Walking down the block, he walked into the Screaming Goat Coffee Company.

The store was moderately busy, so Alan waited in a short line and then gave his order

"G.O.A.T. Americano, and a Billy almond milk latte," he said using the quirky shop's designation for the 20 ounce and 12 ounce drinks.

"We'll have that right up, Alan." The speaker was the line supervisor, Josh. Alan hadn't had a lot of interaction with him, but he always seemed friendly.

"Thanks," Alan said and moved over to let the next customer order. He stood quietly scrolling on his phone.

"Alan," a young, energetic woman who looked to be in her late 20s or early 30s, was holding his order. He recognized her. Daisy, the "stalker barista" Stacy had referred to earlier, had an obvious crush on Alan and took every opportunity to engage with him. Alan was a little embarrassed by the attention. It was flattering, but she was a little too bubbly for him.

"Thanks, uh, Daisy." She lit up at the use of her name. Alan groaned inwardly. He took the drinks and made his way out of the shop.

Alan juggled the two coffee drinks in his hands so he could open the office door. Stacy was on the phone ordering office supplies. She gave him a huge smile and mouthed "thanks" when he set her latte down in front of her. She ended the call and took a big sip.

"Thank you so much! There is nothing better than a good almond milk latte."

"Your favorite barista says hello," he said with a smirk.

"She did not! She can't even remember my name! Stop pushing my buttons."

"It is hard to resist pushing your buttons, but one thing I am sure of is that she knows your name." Stacy laughed.

"They make great coffee, though."

While they drank their coffee, Alan brought Stacy up to speed on the conference call with Rebecca Salter. Her eyes widened at the revelation of the catchphrase. He finished telling her that

Layla would let them know any minute now that she was ready to show her analysis after factoring in the new data.

"Are we overworking Layla?" Stacy asked suddenly, thinking about all the tasks she was working on.

"I think her design makes that quite impossible. She has far more computing power than we can even imagine," Alan replied.

"Oh, before I forget. This came by messenger earlier today." Stacy handed him a large, thick manila envelope. He read the address, noting it was from his lawyer, Sam Eaton.

"Thanks. The paperwork never stops," Alan said. He saluted Stacy with his half-empty coffee cup and headed to his office, stopping by the conference table to place Layla on a charging pad built into the tabletop.

Alan reviewed the documents in the envelope, signed them and put them in an enclosed envelope addressed for return to Sam's office and with postage already attached. With that chore completed, he opened his email and started through the stack of background checks that Layla had completed over the past couple of days. He reviewed each one, signed his name to them, and forwarded them on to the client associated with each one. He copied Stacy on the emails so she could process the client's billing.

He was just finishing up when the intercom buzzed. He pressed the button, and Layla's voice came out of the phone. "I am ready with my analysis now. Please join me in the conference room." He exited his office and motioned to Stacy to join him. They gathered around the conference room table.

"Okay, Layla. You have our undivided attention," Alan said.

"After the conference call with Rebecca Salter, and the revelation that Cary Sellers was fond of a specific phrase, and that the staff had widespread knowledge of the phrase, I started evaluating the video again and looking through the code we pulled from P4-751."

She displayed two waveforms on the monitor. "The top waveform is the audio output from the video when Cary Sellers says 'this time for sure'," Layla said.

"What is the second?" Alan asked.

"That is a waveform I built from an algorithm buried inside the P4 operating code." Layla said. Alan and Stacy watched as she moved the bottom image over the first and overlaid them. They matched perfectly. While they watched, the simple waveform disappeared. A spectrogram overlay appeared.

"This is the voiceprint analysis of the video." Layla said. Another spectrogram appeared.

"Now I am showing you a spectrogram based on that same code in the operating system." Alan's mouth opened in surprise as she overlaid the two images. They were an exact match.

"The phrase alone wasn't the trigger," Stacy said.

"The phrase in Cary Sellers' voice was the trigger." Layla said. "The trigger specifically targeted him, and only him, saying this phrase."

"Wow," Stacy whispered.

Alan sat stunned for a few moments. He had been working under the assumption that the murder resulted from an accident triggered by a bug in the code, or an act by a remote operator in the heat of the moment. It was neither. Someone targeted Sellers for premeditated murder.

Chapter Seventeen

Merchandise

After a long night of dark, shadowy dreams of killer robots stalking him on the dark city streets, Alan woke tired and distracted by the questions from the prior day's revelations. He pushed himself to face the day. Eventually, he got himself showered, dressed, and fed. He collected Layla from the workstation in his home office, then headed downtown for a meeting with Dalton Rodgers.

By the time he arrived, Stacy and Dalton were already at the office, gathered around the conference table having coffee. He poured himself a cup from the carafe sitting on a trivet. He sipped the hot drink and closed his eyes for a moment.

"Rough night?" Stacy asked.

"Yeah, weird dreams about murderous robots."

"Not surprising based on what Stacy has been telling me about yesterday," Dalton replied.

"Do you have anything exciting to add to the week?" Alan asked.

"No, unfortunately I don't. I've checked every source I have. James Reston is not running with any of the heavy hitters that I am aware of in town. They know him in gambling circles, certainly. He loses more than he wins. That isn't a news flash. He is definitely in debt, but to traditional lenders, not to anyone shady."

"Any unusual patterns?" Alan asked, searching for anything that might push the case forward.

"Unusual? No, he has a pattern, though. Most nights he drives into the city and has a drink at the Ale House taproom. Just one. Then, he goes down the street to play poker in the back room of the sports bar. Except for Wednesdays." Dalton left that statement hanging, building suspense.

"What happens on Wednesdays?" Stacy asked, breaking the tension.

"I'm glad you asked," he said with a grin. "On Wednesdays he skips the drink at the taproom and he goes to the rooftop bar at Cowford."

"But—" Stacy looked at Alan.

"The night we were at Cowford and someone took a shot at us was a Wednesday," he finished for her. "I thought you said you had nothing exciting to report."

"Oh, did I say that? I might have been mistaken," Dalton smiled at Alan and sipped coffee. "That alone proves nothing. There were two city councilmen and the CEO of Lunian Labs there that night too."

"Was he definitely there that night?" Alan inquired.

"No, I can't say that for sure. I definitely can't say he was there at the time of the shooting. But from everyone I talked to, he is there almost every Wednesday for several hours."

"I guess I don't have to tell you to keep digging and see if you can put him there that night." Alan said.

"Nope, I am already on it. I'll continue to interview people who frequent the place on Wednesday and see if anyone can place him there that night. I'll keep on the other angle too. If he is hanging out at Cowford's rooftop, he is mingling with some powerful figures in the city."

Dalton stayed around for another half hour, chatting about the case, and personal matters. Stacy refilled the carafe, and they talked briefly about the drone case. They hadn't yet made any headway, though, in finding Graystone or the drones. After half an hour, Dalton bid them farewell and went on his way.

"I may have something," Layla said as soon as he was out the door.

"It's about time!" Alan said. Stacy punched his arm to silence him.

"What do you have, Layla?" she asked.

I have successfully figured out the GPS coordinate system changes to the drone. I know the reason for the change, and I know where they are. Or at least I know where they went," she said with some pride.

"That is amazing!" Alan said. "Give us the details."

"First, the why. I located the last command received by the damaged drone. It was a simple one. Return. I found that command in the drone's code. It is a GPS-based function that simply has the drone return to its takeoff point. The drone stores that point when it takes off. When the drone receives the return command, it navigates back to that point."

"Out of curiosity, what was the next-to-last command?" Alan asked.

"Good insight. Yes, the command previous to return was an update to its GPS code."

"And that made the unit think it was actually somewhere else."

"It thought it was miles away to the southwest," Stacy said excitedly.

"That is correct." Layla said.

"So all we have to do to find out where they went is to know where they took off from. Then apply the difference between where the GPS thinks it is and where it is actually is now." Alan said.

"Yes. So assuming that they were on the storage shelves at North Florida Aerial, I tracked them to the exact location they were sent that night. We should check it out."

"I'm not sure we should roll up on this place in broad daylight given the likelihood that it is guarded or occupied," Alan said.

"That is a good point. It looks like we are going in ninja-style," Layla said dramatically.

"Just like old times." Alan agreed with a smile.

Stacy tried to stop her eyes from rolling and almost succeeded.

The secluded lot indicated by Layla's coordinates sat off from the road, surrounded by trees. Railroad tracks ran alongside the lot. Alan looked at it through the SmartLens glasses night-sight vision feature. That feature didn't exist in the retail version of the glasses he had started with. Layla had modified them with a combination of her technical skills and parts that Alan had purchased at her request.

It would be tricky to find in the daylight. At night it was practically invisible unless you knew what you were looking for. They had been watching it for over two hours. The last human activity ceased more than an hour ago. Layla continued to scan the area using both her incredibly powerful audio recording capabilities and high-resolution imagery.

They had done this type of operation many times now and had, over time, refined it. This time Stacy was back at the office watching the feed from the monitors in the conference room. This was the first event she had operated as mission control from the office. All the previous times had either been from Alan's downstairs home office, or her apartment. Layla was feeding her data both from her own sensors and from nearby video feeds she had accessed. This included the rail yard security camera and cameras mounted on light poles in the parking area surrounding the dark warehouse.

"There are no activities on any of the video feeds," Stacy announced.

"Confirmed. No activity detected from audio or infrared data either," Layla answered.

Alan looked at his watch, it said 12:15 AM. "Are we a go then?" he asked.

"Go," Stacy said.

"Go," Layla agreed.

Alan left the cover of the trees on the side of the property up against the railroad tracks and made his way across the parking area to the building. Layla had scouted the building's defenses hours earlier. There were cameras, which she was now redirecting the video feed through her own systems, preventing it from recording. Alan stopped at a panel mounted on the back of the building. A padlock secured it. He made quick work of it using lock-picking tools and skills that Layla had taught him months ago. Inside the panel, he moved wires around until he found the wiring for the external security alarm sensors mounted on the rear door.

"The green one, then the blue one," Layla reminded him unnecessarily.

"Got it." He snipped both in that order with small wire-cutters, giving thanks they had an external junction box instead of routing all the wiring inside. That would have made the operation more complex, but Layla had prepared detailed instructions for addressing that as well. With the alarm neutralized, he moved to the back door. It was a numeric keypad. Layla and been using video to surveil it for hours. She quickly recited an eight-digit code, which Alan entered into the device. A satisfying click was the result, and he pulled open the door and entered the building.

"Holding for activity check," Alan said in a whisper, from just inside the door. Darkness all around him.

"No activity from the video feeds," Stacy announced in a whisper. It occurred to her that there was no reason to whisper since you couldn't hear the speaker on the SmartLens glasses from more than a few inches away, and there was no one in the Adamant Insurance Group building to overhear, or care what she was doing if they did.

"No audio activity. Infrared is clear. Let's continue," Layla said.

Alan steadied his breathing and moved forward. The brief hold had allowed the night vision on his glasses to activate, and he could navigate the ghostly green surroundings instead of the inky blackness that had existed before. They had entered a large room designed to be a storage area. Storage shelving lined the walls, each unit having shelves from the floor to just below the 14-foot ceiling. Alan slowly moved around the shelves, looking at various electronic merchandise. All the devices were high-tech, high-cost items.

"Are those neural processing units?" Alan asked, looking at a series of small chips packed in anti-static bags.

"Yes, they appear to be IST5920 chips. Used primarily in industrial equipment powered by artificial intelligence," Layla supplied.

Alan whistled quietly, doing some quick math. "That is easily several million dollars on that shelf," Layla agreed. Alan moved on to the next area of the storage. He passed collections of high-end solid-state LiDAR sensors, Lunian Labs SoC modules, micro-turbine engines, and ultra-capacity battery packs.

"This place is a treasure trove of tech gold," he observed. Alan stopped short. Right in front of him were two shelving units packed from floor to ceiling with high-end aerial drones. He leaned closer and saw the logo "Holliston" stamped into the side of the units.

"Are these the drones we are looking for?" he asked.

Stacy groaned in his ear. "You've been waiting all night to say that, haven't you?" Alan didn't acknowledge her, but he grinned in the darkness.

"No," Layla answered, "these are Holliston 8750s. The units stolen from North Florida Aerial were 9252s just off the line this year. Those are several years older. They are still worth $30,000 to $40,000." Pushing past his disappointment, Alan kept moving down the line of storage shelves.

Past rows of various chips and expensive technical components, he came to another section of drones. This time he didn't allow his expectations to rise until he had confirmed the make and model of the units. These too were the wrong drones. He kept moving.

Half an hour later he finished his tour of the shelving without finding the drones. "That was an anticlimax," he said, wiping sweat from his forehead.

"Someone could have already moved the drones. We knew that was a possibility," Layla said. Alan was nodding glumly in agreement when he caught sight of something out of the corner of his eye. Turning his head, he saw a loading area. He slowly walked toward it, his anticipation mounting.

A small panel van sat in the loading area. The rear loading door was closed. Alan eased it open. Brown unmarked boxes filled the inside of the van. Alan picked the closest one and, using a box cutter, cut the packing tape holding it closed. He held his breath and looked down at the contents. A high-end aerial drone, identical to the one he and Dalton had rescued from the tree, sat carefully packed in foam packing material.

Alan carefully removed the drone from the packing materials and pulled it out of the shipping container. Turning it upside down, he looked at the model and serial number printed on a small label affixed to the bottom of the drone chassis. He read the make and model. The top of the camera housing contained the stamp "Holliston 9252." He swallowed and released his breath.

"Well?" Stacy said, her voice filled with excitement and anticipation.

"**These** are the drones we are looking for," Layla said quietly.

Chapter Eighteen

Graystone Connection

After a brief but spirited debate on how to proceed. Alan carefully repacked the drone, and resealed the shipping container. Searching the loading area, Alan found the shipping address for the drones, a location near Atlanta. Alan retraced his steps, wiping down any areas he might have touched during their incursion.

"I'm still not sold on this plan," Stacy said in his ear as he quietly exited the warehouse and stopped to reconnect the security alarm.

"It is a risk, but Layla is right. This is the best plan. If we can get them out in the open with the stolen merchandise in the van, and have a pretext for the authorities to search it. It will be easier to seize the cargo. We can't very well tell the police that we broke in and found the drones." Alan said as he finished the wiring repair and relocked the junction box.

"I know you are probably right, but it's still nerve-wracking to be this close to the drones and leave them in the hands of these thieves."

"I definitely agree. And we still have to arrange for a state law enforcement official to assist us," Alan said.

"Who do we know with the state police?" Stacy asked. Alan gave it some thought while he retraced his steps back to the tree cover and then to his car, which was parked along the railroad tracks. He snapped his fingers. "I think I have someone. The trick is contacting him in time."

Eight hours later, Alan followed the white panel van as it drove north on I-95 toward the Florida-Georgia border. He sipped hot coffee from a Screaming Goat Coffee Company cup and yawned. With only a brief nap since the night before, he was tired, but his adrenaline was ramping up as they neared the border.

"We're about five miles from the Ag Station," Stacy told him from the passenger seat. "Do you think he will stop?" The agricultural inspection station near the border was a required stop for any trucks. Vans were a gray area, but commercially operated vans were required to stop to show they weren't carrying any agricultural products.

"Fifty-fifty. I think he stops because he assumes they will just pass him through with little question. He's done this before," Alan says, watching the van a few car lengths ahead of him. The driver is a man named Graham Walters. Other than some minor traffic citations, he has no criminal record Layla could find, and he has been driving professionally for more than a decade. His current employer is murky. A holding company called Tech-Tranz registered the warehouse filled with presumably stolen goods. Layla could find no reliable details about the ownership of the holding company.

Stacy picks up a handheld radio and keys the microphone and announces, "Mile marker 375." After a brief pause, a voice acknowledged her transmission.

"We'll know for sure in a couple of minutes," Alan said, yawning again.

Just past mile marker 378, the white van slowed and, after a slight hesitation, changed lanes to exit the highway onto the ramp to the inspection station. Alan followed suit and eased onto the ramp behind him. The van got in line behind several large trucks. Alan pulled off to the side of the ramp to watch.

A Florida Highway Patrol sergeant approached the van to speak to the driver. The officer wore the tan and black uniform of the state troopers rather than the olive green of the agriculture agents. If Graham noticed the difference, he didn't react to it.

"Any produce?" the officer asked, going through the motions.

"Nah, not today," Graham answered, looking bored.

"Okay, what are you carrying today?"

"Uh, electronics," Graham said, looking around nervously.

"You don't seem sure. Show me the bill of lading," the trooper demanded.

"Come on, man, why are you hassling me? I'm just doing my job."

"Do you have the bill of lading or not, sir?"

"No, I don't. I must have forgotten it back at the warehouse. I'm sure we can call them."

The trooper opened the door of the van and motioned for the driver to get out. Another trooper came over to take Graham's arm, and they led him to the back of the van. The first trooper opened the back and looked in at the boxes.

"You can't search the van," Graham said.

"Oh, I think you're wrong about that. I want to confirm you don't have any produce. So, I am going to open the box to find out." He pulled a box toward him and opened it with a box cutter.

"Look, uh, trooper," he looked at the nameplate on the uniform, "Hughes. This is just a mistake. If I can just call..."

"Drones. Dave, did you read that bulletin about missing drones?"

"The ones from North Florida Aerial? Yes, I read something about that."

"Well, we have a van that seems to be loaded with drones that match the model number of those missing items, and this gentleman doesn't have a bill of lading. What does that sound like to you?" Hughes asked.

"Sounds like this guy is going to have a really bad day."

"Mr. Graham, my partner here is going to take you into custody now, and we are going to check the rest of this cargo. And when we establish they are the missing drones, you are going to be charged with transporting stolen merchandise across state lines. How does that sound?"

"How do you know my name?" Graham asked, confused. They never even asked for ID.

"I have great sources. Get him out of here, Dave. I'll do the inventory." Mike Hughes watched Alan and Stacy approach as Dave led the still confused Graham away.

"Mr. Harrison. Your information was spot on...thanks for the tip. Even if it came at 2 in the morning. How did you get my personal cell number, anyway?"

"I have good sources too. Good to see you. I almost didn't recognize you in uniform," Alan said. Hughes had been the scene investigator at a vehicle crime scene that Alan had worked for the Adamant Insurance Group a few months before. They had helped each other out on that case, and after he had gotten over being awakened out of a deep sleep, he had agreed to help apprehend Graham. In exchange, he got credit for the arrest and probable cause to search the warehouse, which was already in motion. Alan got credit for recovering the stolen drones.

"So you want to tell me how you knew the drones were in the van?" Hughes asked.

"Not especially. Do you really want me to tell you?"

"Nope."

"Then we'll leave it there. I have to go call my client and tell him I found his missing drones. And you have to go raid a warehouse full of stolen merchandise."

Alan was at his desk in the Harrison & Associates office downtown. He had been talking to Roger Maxwell, the CTO of North Florida Aerial, for more than half an hour. Alan had started with the good news that they had recovered almost all the stolen drones. Maxwell had been ecstatic about the potential return and the five million dollars in economic impact that promised. Maxwell made Alan detail the last two weeks of investigations that led to the recovery. Even after the long, detailed report on the efforts, Maxwell had questions, which he fired out at Alan scattershot. He was in the middle of explaining the Stanley Graystone discovery for the second time when Stacy stepped into his office and put a steaming cup of coffee on his desk. Looking up at her, his frustration with the length of the call and the never-ending questions melted away, replaced by unguarded gratitude. He gave her a warm smile and mouthed, "Thank you." She waved and backed out of the office, leaving him to his marathon phone call.

Stacy stopped by the conference room and looked in on Layla. She was sitting on the table in her charging spot. Her activity lights were steady but not overtaxed. As Stacy approached, Layla activated the monitor screen, and Stacy could see what she was working on. Layla had recently gotten into the habit of activating any screen nearby whenever Stacy or Alan approached. When asked about it, she told them that their partnership worked best when all of them had all the pieces of the puzzle. Digital records of various electronic equipment scrolled by. Descriptions of the equipment and manufacturing details passed by on a seemingly endless loop.

"The inventory from the warehouse search?" Stacy asked.

"Yes, Sergeant Hughes sent it over, and I have been poring through it."

"Find anything interesting?" Stacy inquired, sitting down at the table, watching the scroll.

"Patterns are emerging. I am seeing multiple components that are made or transported by the same organization. Not all from the same sources, but groupings of merchandise sources."

"Any more information about the ownership of the warehouse?"

"Not yet. Offshore shell companies are convoluted and messy. I am trying to unravel TechTranz, the holding company that is listed as the owner of the warehouse. All I know so far is that an unknown owner established it two years ago. TechTranz purchased the warehouse from another holding company a little more than a year after that."

"Not a lot to go on so far," Stacy noted.

"No, but we will figure it out." Layla paused the display on a listing of SoC chips from Lunian Labs.

"What is it?"

"According to a news report I found, someone stole the System on a Chip units from a truck bound for Holliston."

"Holliston uses SoC chips?" Stacy asked.

"Yes, in their drones."

"Uh, aren't those also used in the Prism Cybernetics P4 units?"

"Yes, the same chips."

"That means—" Stacy said.

"The factory reset SoC chip that was placed into the P4 unit during the break-in at Prism could have come from the warehouse." Alan said from the doorway of his office. He continued into the conference area, carrying his coffee cup.

"That would link Holliston, North Florida Aerial, and Prism together," Layla said.

"The only obvious connection is Stanley Graystone," Alan said, thinking out loud.

"Graystone knew about the SoC chip shipment to Holliston. He obviously knew the location of the drones Holliston sold to North Florida Aerial," Stacy chimed in.

"What we don't have is any reason to connect him to Prism," Layla said.

"Either there is a relationship there we don't know about yet, or that connection is through the owners of the warehouse," Alan said.

"We still don't have a line on Graystone's whereabouts?" Stacy asked, frowning.

"No, he is staying off the grid," Layla said with a hint of disappointment in her voice.

Alan fell into a chair with a loud sigh. He finished his coffee and sat there staring blindly at the display screen as Layla continued to scroll through data from the warehouse.

"You look exhausted," Stacy observed with concern.

"I am. Not just from lack of sleep last night, but this case is dragging on, and every time we get a few answers, there are more questions."

"Not what you expected from the life of a big-time private investigator?" she asked in a teasing tone.

"I thought there would be more car chases and gunfights," he said with a grin.

"We've already done that!" Stacy said indignantly.

"That's a good point. How about we ditch work for the rest of the day and go pick up takeout and watch a movie?"

"Bogart and Bacall!" Layla demanded. Alan and Stacy laughed at her enthusiasm. They had introduced her to classic movies some months back. Alan wasn't sure if the interest was for their benefit or if Layla was really getting something out of it, but either way relaxing with food and a movie seemed like a good way to celebrate the win of finding the missing drones, and stalling the need to get back to the grind of the investigations.

Later that afternoon, Stacy and Alan sat on the couch in his living room. Empty takeout packaging from Five Guys littered the coffee table. Humphrey Bogart and Lauren Bacall played out a scene from The Big Sleep on the big screen TV. Stacy watched the famous horse racing scene with dialog that was technically about betting on horses but was really about something else entirely.

"He is the toughest guy in the room, but she is even tougher," Stacy said, never taking her eyes off Bogart on the screen.

"She truly is something, isn't she? Their chemistry completely overshadows the movie's convoluted plot," Alan observed, looking at Stacy as she watched the film. She noticed his stare and playfully pushed his face toward the TV.

"Watch the movie, gumshoe." Alan laughed.

"Are you two going to talk through the entire movie?" Layla asked.

"Sorry, Layla, bad habit," Stacy apologized.

"Habit," Layla repeated quietly.

"What about it?" Alan asked, sitting up. Stacy paused the movie, her interest piqued as well.

"Bogart figures out that the rare bookstore is a front because they don't really know about books. Their lack of knowledge doesn't fit."

"Right, and how does that help?" Stacy prompted.

"Graystone has a quarter of a million dollars in the bank, but he's eating at McDonald's and a fast-food joint at the Atlanta airport."

"He loves fast food, specifically McDonald's," Alan said.

"Yes, in going back over his purchases, he goes there a lot. I didn't really pay attention to it before. It wasn't relevant because it didn't fit any location pattern, but thinking about it now, I realize it's a way to track him. He won't be able to avoid going to his favorite fast-food location, even if he is trying to stay off the grid. We can find him through that habit."

"You got that from The Big Sleep?" Stacy asked.

"And you and Alan not being able to pay attention to a movie when you are sitting on a couch together." Stacy blushed and glared at Layla.

"There are fifteen thousand McDonald's locations in the country," Alan pointed out.

"Yes, but his last location was at the Atlanta airport. If we assume he was flying back to the Jacksonville area. Then we only have to look at about 80 of those locations."

"Given that he has cash, we can probably narrow that down to areas he is likely to stay," Alan stated. "I believe you may be onto something."

"I'll narrow down the list," Layla said, her activity lights already flashing.

"Can we finish the movie first?" Stacy asked.

"Can you two be quiet for the next hour?"

"No promises," Stacy said, restarting the movie. Layla sighed.

Chapter Nineteen

Payout

Monday morning was warm and humid. This was not unusual for spring in North Florida, but it was a change from the past few mornings' milder temperatures. Alan drove a rented U-Haul truck with Stacy trailing behind in the Orion Chimera. A recovered haul of seventy-two drones filled the back of the leased vehicle. Alan had spent the weekend catching up on chores and his reading. Except for a couple of texts from Dalton giving him small, but ultimately unhelpful updates on his investigation into the Prism Cybernetics staff, the two days were relaxing and uneventful. Late Sunday night, he got word from Sgt. Hughes with the FHP. They had agreed to release the drones to him to return to his client. The state and local authorities could use millions of dollars of remaining stolen goods at the warehouse as evidence for any criminal actions against the owners once they identified them.

As he pulled the truck into the parking lot, a crowd of employees had already gathered to greet them. The excitement of the group struck Alan. This was a small business, and losing such a large amount of inventory would have had serious consequences for them all. That thought made the event even more special.

Roger Maxwell was the first to greet him, shaking his hand vigorously and pulling him in close. Their chests came together, and Maxwell slapped Alan's back twice and quickly released him.

"Thank you again for all your work, Alan. The return of the drones really saves us from some difficult times," Maxwell appeared relaxed and upbeat, a far cry from the anxious man Alan had met two weeks prior.

"Did you ever get a firm answer about the insurance?" Alan asked only out of curiosity. He had worked in that industry for a long time.

"Not a very reassuring one. There were some concerns because we hadn't reported the serial numbers of the units yet. We usually do that right away, but that didn't happen this time. My agent seemed optimistic that we could work something out, but it was far from a sure thing. I am happy I don't have to deal with it."

Alan walked around to the back of the truck and opened the rear door. The seventy-two boxes were there. The gathered employees broke out into applause.

"There are seventy-two drones here. I still have one drone. The unit might have some critical information on it. We will return it once we have finished. The unit suffered damage during the theft."

"Send me photographs of the damage; we might get the insurance company to cover that."

"Oh, I almost forgot." Alan reached into a pocket and pulled out a USB drive. "This contains a section of code you need to have your engineers look at. The thieves altered the code to allow them to steal the drones."

"Thank you, I'll get it to them right away," he said, taking the drive. "Did you recover any evidence from the drones about who the thieves were? How did they get them out of our warehouse?"

"No, someone wiped the drives for these drones after they received them. We are hopeful we can get data from the damaged drone we have, though."

"I hope you get to the bottom of it. As glad as we are to have them back, I want the thieves punished."

Stacy made a slight throat-clearing noise as she offered Alan an envelope.

"Oh, yes. Thank you Stacy. Roger, here is our invoice for the services so far. We will continue to look for the perpetrators, but the actual contract was for recovery."

"Yes, of course. I have a check for you inside. Come in and we'll take care of it." Alan nodded and allowed Maxwell to precede him, then motioned for Stacy to come along. The three of them left a group of excited employees unloading the truck and entered the building.

Leaving Roger Maxwell's office, both Alan and Stacy felt euphoric. The check in Stacy's purse was larger than anything they had ever received from a client before. It was almost as much as they had made as an investigative team in total in the last six months. It gave them both a feeling of accomplishment and a boost to their confidence. This investigator gig might even work.

"This feeling is something else," Stacy whispered as they stood in the lobby.

"Yeah, I was just thinking the same thing myself."

As they stood for a moment taking in the feeling, the door to the warehouse area opened and Karen Anderson stepped into the lobby. She stopped when she saw them. She seemed to take a moment to gather herself and then walked over and greeted them.

"Good morning, guys. Thanks so much for your work. Everyone is so excited that the drones are back. It was a tense couple of weeks. People were worried about how the company would survive a hit like that. The feeling of relief on the floor is palpable right now."

Alan and Stacy exchanged a glance. Stacy gave an almost imperceptible shrug. Alan assumed she agreed with the thought they were obviously sharing.

"Karen, do you know anything about the theft of the drones that you haven't shared with us?" Alan watched her reaction. It was a quick rotation of confusion, concern, and perhaps embarrassment.

"No. I can't think of anything. I'm happy you found them. Why?"

"I don't know. Steve Daniels said you called him at the last minute for the date on that Tuesday. It seems a little coincidental that it was the night of the break-in." Her eyes widened.

"That isn't true! We had agreed to go out that week, days before. Steve called me the morning of the break-in and set the details for dinner that night. He must be misremembering the timeline. I don't know why he would say that I called to set it up." She seemed truthful, and Alan regretted they had left Layla back at the office working on the search for Graystone. Her insight might have given them proof of Karen's veracity.

"Have you had any contact with Stanley Graystone since the theft?"

"No, I only saw him in passing that day. I didn't even have a conversation with him. He hasn't been here since that day, that I am aware of."

"Any idea how we might get in touch with him? He seems to be hard to find these days," Stacy asked. Karen gave this some thought.

"Nothing comes to mind. I really didn't know him. He was pleasant and helpful, but not very personable. You know what I mean? He would say good morning and wish you well, but he shared little about himself."

"That seems to be a recurring theme with him. He was very good at presenting a surface, but not a lot of depth," Stacy said.

"Exactly!"

"Anything stand out? Any habits? Any gesture or event that you remember?"

"No, not that I can think of...wait! Yes! He bought the entire company, apple pie desserts, one day. A few months back."

"Apple pie?" Alan asked, puzzled.

"Yeah, you know the little rectangular dessert pies from McDonald's." Alan's mouth dropped open involuntarily.

"That is helpful. Thanks Karen," Stacy said. Karen waved and walked past them into the parking lot.

"Well, that is pretty much a confirmation that Layla is on the right track," Stacy said.

"Yes, we should get back to the office and help with that. A lead on Graystone could be just what we need in this marathon case."

The conference room monitor displayed a large map of the Jacksonville metropolitan area. Across the map were nearly 50 markers showing the locations of individual McDonald's franchise locations. Alan and Stacy looked at them, thinking about the monumental effort it would take to visit and canvas them all for any hints of Stanley Graystone's presence.

"That is a lot of locations to visit," Stacy muttered, echoing the thoughts in Alan's head.

"Luckily, you won't have to visit them all. At least not at first. We can eliminate some of them as probable targets based on the area of town." As Layla spoke, nearly half of the markers changed to gray. "These 18 locations are in areas that aren't likely to be the site of Graystone's current hideout. He has means, which would indicate that he will want a certain level of comfort that these areas of town will not provide."

As Alan and Stacy watched, five of the locations turned from red to green.

"Ponte Vedra, Ortega, Atlantic Beach, Julington Creek," Stacy read from the map. "Why those areas?"

"These five areas contain a McDonalds in proximity with more affluent, secluded neighborhoods, which I believe are most suitable for Graystone's hiding spot. It isn't a sure thing, but the probabilities point to one of these areas," Layla answered.

"Should we get Dalton to help?" Stacy asked.

"No, leave him on the Prism case. We will try to see if we can find any signs of Graystone in these neighborhoods. If we strike out and have to expand to the other locations, we can bring him in then," Alan said.

"We?"

"If you are up to some boring detective work instead of your usual exciting life of wrangling contractors," Alan answered, smiling.

Alan walked out of the McDonald's restaurant in Fruit Cove. The once pleasant aroma of beef tallow, oil, and grilling meat had made his stomach uneasy. This was the third location he had visited. Spending hours asking both staff and patrons if they had seen Stanley Graystone, showing them a picture of him, and getting nothing but denials, coupled with the smell, was making him feel a little ill. Alan reflected that the failure was probably more responsible than the actual odor.

Alan was leaning against his car, getting some fresh air as Stacy came walking across the parking lot from the bank next door. He really didn't need to ask. Her face told him she had been having no better luck.

"Nothing?" he asked anyway, just to make conversation.

"No, another dead end," she replied.

"I am so tired of smelling beef tallow. Why does it even smell like that? I didn't think they used tallow any longer?"

"They don't, but they still put the smell in the oil...for the experience," Stacy told him.

"It's an experience I could do without," he replied with a sigh. "What is next?"

Alan looked over a listing on his phone. "Looks like we are back north to Queens Harbor."

"I was promised exciting detective work," Stacy reminded him.

"This is the exciting part." He grinned at her and opened the car door. She pretended to glare at him for a moment, then got into the car. Alan pulled the Chimera out of the parking lot and pointed the car north on State Road 13. He would pick up I-295 heading east and eventually loop to the north to get to the Queens Harbor area. It was a half-hour drive even in the light traffic of the early afternoon. Stacy found a Spotify radio that was close enough to both her and Alan's tastes not to be a distraction and turned down the volume so it was just background noise.

"Layla, this whole thing is feeling like a waste of time," Stacy said to their AI partner sitting on the charging pad in the car's console.

"I know, Stacy. I am sorry. Even with the first three locations being misses, the probabilities still point to this being the right direction," Layla assured her.

"I don't know. My human intuition is telling me this is a bust."

"I should really figure out how to get one of those," Layla replied dryly. Stacy laughed despite her mood.

Half an hour later, Alan pulled the car into the parking lot of the McDonald's on Atlantic Blvd. The Queens Harbor area was the yachting and golfing enclave of Jacksonville. The location is five to ten minutes from the beach, distant enough from the city center to feel remote, but the surrounding development gives the impression that it isn't.

As they entered the restaurant, which was nearly identical to the last three, the smell hit Alan again, and he made a face. Stacy patted him sympathetically on the shoulder and stepped up to the counter. She showed the young woman working the counter the picture of Graystone, but received only a shrug and a shake of the head in response. She was pulling the picture back when an older man walking behind the young woman looked over at the picture and said, "I've seen him around. He was here earlier today."

Stacy stopped in her tracks, not sure if she was hearing him correctly. She just stared for a moment. Alan stepped in. "This man was here earlier today?"

"Yeah, he comes in several times a week. Has been for a couple of weeks, I think. I see him all the time."

"Any idea where I could find him?" Alan asked.

"No clue, man. I just see him here sometimes. Is he in some kind of trouble?"

"I just need to speak to him." Alan thanked the man for his time. He and Stacy exited the restaurant and stood outside looking around at the surroundings. After spending all day striking out, they had their first hit, and neither was sure what to do with it.

"Boy, that human intuition is something," Layla said to them via the SmartLens glasses they both wore.

"I knew you were going to throw that in my face, Layla," Stacy replied.

"Machine 1, Human 0," Layla replied lightly.

"Where do we go from here then, all-powerful machine?" Alan asked.

"There are a couple of apartment complexes around here that could be Graystone's hideout. That would make sense. Living a few blocks from here would almost guarantee his gravitating to this McDonald's out of habit."

"Well, I guess we will check them out."

They tried The Enclave at St. John's first with no luck; the second complex resulted in a home run. Terrabella Coastal, an upscale apartment complex built in the early 2020s, provided a gated, secure environment that must have felt very comfortable to Graystone. The gate guard was reluctant to give out any information, but a combination of Stacy's charm and a large bill from Alan's wallet got him to admit that Stanley Graystone lived in the complex. He wouldn't give them much more though, and they retreated to the car parked across the street to strategize their next moves.

After deciding on a course of action, they had time to kill before they could put the plan into motion. Alan drove to a Thai restaurant half a mile away, and they had an early dinner while they waited for the sun to go down. As Alan and Stacy ate chicken pad Thai, Layla talked them through the operation.

"I have isolated the apartments that could be Graystone's down to five. Those were the only apartments leased in the past month. There is a small chance that he moved in earlier than that, but he was definitely still living in Hartford a month ago," she explained.

"If we don't find him in this group, we'll have to expand the list." Alan said between bites.

"Yes, let's hope it won't come to that. I don't want to be knocking on doors all night," Stacy chimed in.

They finished the meal in silence, and Alan drove back to the complex. Darkness had fallen, and Alan waited for three cars to queue up in the automated tenant gate line, and he fell in behind them. They inched forward one car at a time. When he was next to the card reader, Alan reached out of the car and held an empty hand toward the device. In the console, Layla's activity lights flashed for a moment, and the card reader emitted a quiet beep, and the gate raised. As Alan drove through the gate, Stacy let out a breath.

"I never feel confident that you can do that," she told Layla.

"Have faith, girlfriend," Layla responded.

Alan found a parking spot near the entry doors marked "WrkSpace." He and Stacy approached the entrance with Layla coming along in Alan's jacket pocket. Alan repeated the empty hand gesture with the card reader next to the door and pulled the door open as soon as Layla had unlocked it.

"What does 'WrkSpace' mean?" Stacy asked.

"I think it's a space for their tenants to work from, like a business center of a hotel or something," Layla said.

Walking through the plush work-from-home amenity, they exited into the corridor of first-floor apartments. Alan found the apartment they were looking for: 121. He knocked quietly on the door. A small, older lady, in her 60s or 70s opened the door and looked at him quizzically.

“May I help you?” she asked in a high-pitched voice.

“I’m so sorry, ma’am. I thought this was my friend Stanley’s apartment. We must be on the wrong floor. Please forgive me.” She gave a friendly, dismissive wave to show it was no imposition and shut the door.

“One down, four to go,” he whispered as he looked for the next door. Apartment 133 was on the corner of the bottom floor. Alan knocked on the door. After a few moments, the door swung open. Stacy gave a small gasp as they looked at the inquiring face of Stanley Graystone.

Chapter Twenty

Confession

Graystone looked into their faces for several seconds until he finally asked, "How may I help you?"

"Mr. Graystone, my name is Alan Harrison. I am working for North Florida Aerial. May we come in? I have a few questions."

"I'm not sure that is in my best interest," Graystone replied.

"Maybe not, but at this point it is inevitable. Either now or after the authorities have arrived."

Graystone considered options for a moment. Apparently deciding he didn't have any, he moved aside and gestured for them to enter. They entered a tastefully decorated, albeit somewhat sterile, apartment. The furniture was modern and fashionable, but there was little personality present in the decor. To Alan, it felt obviously temporary.

Graystone indicated the couch, and he took an adjacent chair. Graystone's attitude had shifted from defiance to resignation.

"Mr. Graystone, we are looking into the stolen drones from North Florida Aerial. This is my associate, Stacy Collins. She is aiding me in the investigation." Alan felt Stacy react to that statement, but ignored it.

"What does that have to do with me?" Graystone asked.

"Seriously, Mr. Graystone, that will not work. I know Holliston removed you from the North Florida account months ago. You continued to show up and pretend to be their rep until the day of the theft. You can't really think you can just pass that off as a coincidence, do you?

"Even if all that were true, I'm not sure it's proof of anything."

"You lied to North Florida Aerial about your job, you trespassed on their property for months, the minute they were the victims of a multi-million dollar heist you stopped showing up, left your home base of Hartford and went off the grid here."

"I didn't have anything to do with the stolen—"

"And if your fingerprints show up at the warehouse, that will wrap it up." Graystone had a physical reaction to the mention of the warehouse. He tensed for a moment, then tried to relax as if it hadn't happened.

"You hit a nerve there. He knows the warehouse will point to him." Layla said in his ear. Alan smiled.

"Give it up, Stanley. We recovered the drones and all the other merchandise from the warehouse already. It is only a matter of time before the police link you to that site. Couple that with your shady behavior...it looks bad, and since we don't have any other suspects, you'll take the full responsibility."

"Are you calling the cops?" Graystone asked.

"Let's just see how the conversation goes," Alan said.

Graystone sighed, "Last year I had some medical issues. I had to take leave from work. The costs mounted while I was out of the office, and Holliston assigned another rep to my accounts."

"So you hatched the plan to steal the drones to pay for medical expenses?"

"No. I was recruited. First, just for information on shipments of high-tech equipment to Holliston. Then later I was told to do research on the security at North Florida Aerial."

"That's when you started showing up as their rep again?"

"Yes. It helped that Gene is such a lazy rep. He never does site visits." Graystone said, referring to Gene Freely, the actual sales rep assigned to the North Florida account since October.

"Did Freely know you were still in contact with North Florida?"

"It never came up. If he had asked, I would have blown it off as just being friendly with the old team while I was in town on other business. He never asked though." Graystone smirked as he answered, clearly amused at his co-worker's lack of curiosity.

"Now we get to the real question. Who asked you to spy on North Florida Aerial?"

"I don't know."

Alan gave him a look of disbelief. Beside him on the couch, Stacy made a dismissive sound.

"It's true. I never met the guy who hired me," Graystone insisted.

"You were in the warehouse. Who else was there when you were there?"

"I only ever saw a couple of guys there. The driver. What's his name...Waters...no, Walters. And some other guy that I never learned his name."

"Describe the other man," Alan prompted.

Graystone thought about this for a few seconds. "Young, maybe 30, darker complexion, maybe Mediterranean or Middle Eastern, not tall, average height. Dark hair with a full beard."

"Did you ever speak to him?"

"Once or twice, just to say hello. Nothing substantive."

"Accent?"

"Not that I was aware of, neutral."

"So if you never met the person who hired you, how did you get connected?"

"Just before the new year, I got an email from someone called 'MCreekReturn@techtranz.ky'. The email just told me I could make some money if I agreed to help him out. A few days later, the same person deposited five thousand dollars into my account."

"And after that you contacted him about the offer?"

"I replied, asking what I needed to do. The response was to give me instructions on the info he wanted from Holliston, details about orders, and potential need for high-tech parts. A few days later I saw a memo about a big shipment coming from Lunian Labs, and I emailed the details to that email address. A day later, he deposited another ten thousand into my account."

"Those are the System on a Chip modules?" Stacy asked.

"Yes, a lot of different technology uses SoC modules now."

"Just curious why they come from Lunian Labs? Aren't they manufactured somewhere else?"

"Yes, somewhere in California, but Lunian installs the software, then they ship to the final destination."

"And eventually he asked you to spy on North Florida." Graystone nodded. "He asked you to do something else too, eventually."

Graystone's face darkened. He frowned and heaved a heavy sigh. "Yes, after grilling me for a few weeks about how the software worked on the drones, he instructed me to download the latest firmware and give it to Walters. A couple of days after that Walters gave the USB drive back to me and I gave it to the techs at North Florida telling them it was a new update for their drones, that I had gotten special permission to release it to them before it was due to be released to everyone else." Graystone looked defeated. The last part of the confession drained the last of his energy. He looked down at his feet.

Alan paused, trying to think of another question. Stacy filled the gap. "Tell us about Karen Anderson."

"Who? Oh, Karen. I don't really know her. I met her a few times, but we never really talked much."

"She never interacted with you about this job? Never gave you any sign she was aware of it?" Stacy persisted.

Surprised, Graystone said, “No, never. I hadn’t even thought about her in relation to this. She showed no interest at all in what I was doing at North Florida.”

“He seems to be truthful about that. Since he has been talking, I have seen no signs of untruthfulness,” Layla said.

“Well, Mr. Graystone, I will only take a few more minutes of your time,” Alan said, then slowly recapped their conversation, making Graystone acknowledge each point of the narrative he had given.

“Did I leave anything out?” he asked finally.

“No, that is all of it. I didn’t know the scale of the operation. Knowing he was going to take drones was one thing, but the number and the size of the theft shocked me. I needed to get away and think about it. That is why I ended up here. I didn’t want anyone to find me in Hartford and ask questions.”

“Why Jacksonville? Why not Iowa, or Michigan, or California?” Stacy asked.

“Habit, I guess. I have spent a lot of time here over the past few months. It felt like the only other place I could be comfortable. In hindsight, I would have been better off somewhere else, huh?”

“Almost here,” Layla said.

“Well, I guess we won’t take up any more of your time, Stanley,” Alan said. On cue, there was a loud knock at the door. Graystone looked up in shock, giving Alan a betrayed look. Stacy got up and went to open the door, Sgt. Mike Hughes, back in plainclothes, entered the apartment, trailed by two uniformed state troopers and a Sheriff's office deputy.

"He's all yours, Mike," Alan said.

"Nothing I said to you is admissible!" Graystone growled.

"Probably not, but it doesn't matter. They'll tie you to the warehouse. They already have the driver. We'll find the other warehouse guy. And eventually we'll track down the boss. Do yourself a favor and cooperate with them." Graystone uttered an impolite, anatomically dubious suggestion, which Alan answered with a grin. Hughes pulled him up out of his chair and handed him off to the troopers.

"He isn't wrong, Alan. We could have gotten all that from him on the record," Hughes said.

"Mike, I'm perfectly happy to help you on this, giving you the shipment of drones, leading you to Graystone, but be fair. I am still working on this case for my client."

Hughes put his hands up in surrender. "Okay, okay. I didn't mean to sound ungrateful. You have helped us a lot on this case."

"Did you guys find his prints at the scene?" Stacy asked, trying to defuse the tension.

"No, not yet. Clearly he thinks we will though, from his reaction."

"That is what we thought. Is Walters talking?" Alan asked.

"Not a bit. He lawyered up immediately and isn't saying anything."

"That is disappointing. Having Graystone might loosen him up."

"Maybe. Now get out of here so my friends can toss the place and see if there is anything tying Graystone to the theft."

"Will you share anything you find?"

"After you waited until after he talked to text me? Nope," Hughes grinned to show he was kidding. Alan smiled and headed to the door with Stacy right behind him.

"Good timing on the text message to Hughes, Layla," Alan said when they were in the car. He and Layla had agreed on the timing of the text to the state police beforehand. His telling Graystone he wouldn't keep him much longer and the recap signaled her to start the process. She had texted Hughes earlier, while Alan and Stacy ate dinner, to be ready to roll on Graystone if they located him. She left out the fact that they would interview him first.

"It seemed to work out. Graystone fits in mostly as we expected. I'm not sure if he gave us much to go on in identifying the boss of the operation."

"Any hint that the dark-skinned guy is the leader?"

"Maybe. We don't have much to go on to find him though," Layla said.

"Karen Anderson. We keep expecting her to be part of this, but no one has put her in it yet," Stacy observed.

"That is true. I would have sworn she's connected to this case somehow, but so far we don't have any actual evidence of that," Alan replied wistfully.

"So, what is next?" Stacy asked the group.

"I need to get back to the data from the drone. The units in the warehouse were all wiped so effectively there was no chance of recovery. The damaged drone still has data on the drive, but the damage to the hardware is extensive. I need to work on repairing that and finding out if I can retrieve anything from it," Layla said.

"I will check in with Dalton, bring him up to speed on the drone case and see if he has any more movement on the Prism case." Stacy looked at the time on the Chimera's console display screen.

"Maybe let him get some sleep and start that tomorrow?" she suggested.

"Right, Plan B then is that I think the humans on this case need a drink and sleep," Alan declared.

"Let's get a drink at my apartment," Stacy said. "I need to feed Noodle."

Chapter Twenty-One

Candid Camera

The following morning over coffee and a bagel, Alan learned more than he ever wanted to know about how the drone's memory card worked. Layla patiently explained how the card connected to the system board. She explained the drone controller's communication with the memory card and a lot of technical details about how the memory card stored video data. At the end of the nearly hour-long course on the image signal pipeline, Alan understood just enough to realize it had been far too long since his days studying computer science at Jacksonville University.

"So based on all of this, what is the issue that we have to resolve?" he asked.

"Everything checks out on the hardware side. The system board, memory card, and communication links are all undamaged. We won't have to repair any of the hardware. My theory is that the drone crashed at the cemetery right in the middle of a non-sequential write operation. That caused damage to the file structure, which resulted in data corruption. I have to reconstruct it manually, stitching frames together one by one from the raw data on the card."

"What do you need from me?"

"I will need a couple of things. To start, I need you to get me physical access to the data. I can't do that from the drone. I'll have to interface the card directly using your computer. Did you get the parts I asked for?" Alan shuffled through the growing mountain of clutter on the workstation in his former home office. He reflected again that it had become Layla's laboratory. He found the desired items and held them up.

"I have the USB SD card reader and a Tableau T8u forensic bridge."

"Those will work perfectly. We can't just plug the SD card into the computer because the operating system will try to access it. We need to prevent that. The bridge is write-protected and will block the ability of the laptop to mount the drive or make any changes."

As Layla gave instructions, Alan carefully extracted the memory card from the drone and plugged it into the SD card reader. He plugged the card reader into a USB connection on the bridge and then plugged the bridge into his laptop. After it was all connected, he powered up the bridge.

"Okay, here we go," Layla announced. Immediately, a terminal window opened on the computer showing the file system, and then shortly after that another console window opened showing the raw data of the video file. Layla started going through the file byte by byte.

"This seems like it is going to take a while," Alan said.

"Yes, and I need something else from you. While I am working on pulling all the data from the card and reconstructing it, I need a map to put it all back together. It would be really helpful to have a valid video file from one of the other drones to use as a header map. I can take the file structure and use it. Like putting the edges of a puzzle together helps you to see the full image."

"I guess I am off to North Florida Aerial again then," Alan announced.

"I'll be a few hours reconstructing the data. When you get back, I can put the pieces together."

"Like the puzzle. I got it." Alan grabbed his half-empty coffee cup and headed out to fetch the video for Layla.

Phone calls filled the twenty-minute ride from his house to the offices of North Florida Aerial. Immediately after starting the Chimera and pulling out of the garage, the incoming call chime sounded, and a name appeared on the console display: Dean Franklin. Alan grimaced. Talking to his old boss about the Prism Cybernetics case was not his idea of a good time, but he didn't know how he could avoid it. Especially since Adamant Insurance was still paying all the bills for the case. Reluctantly, he pressed the answer button on his steering wheel.

"Good Morning Dean, how is your day going?" he said with forced cheerfulness.

"Alan, glad I reached you. I wanted to get an update on the cybernetics case. Any progress?" Franklin sounded anxious, but then again he always sounded like that.

"We are making progress. I am certain at this point that the murder of the engineering supervisor at Prism connects directly to the break-in. I don't have a motive yet, but the link is pretty strong. There is also some evidence that there is a potential problem with their P4 unit software, a problem that might present some liability." Alan winced as he said this. It would trigger Franklin's instinct to worry.

"That doesn't sound good, Alan. You think the liability might be covered?"

"You know I don't make coverage decisions, Dean."

"I know, I know, but give me your opinion about our exposure." Alan could almost see Dean waving away his concern about making a definitive statement about insurance adjusting decisions.

"Well, it is going to be murky. The issue might fall under their professional liability policy. There was no release of the software to the public, but when the facts come out publicly, they are likely to suffer a reputational hit, one with financial implications." There was a loud sigh at the other end of the phone.

"When will you know for certain?"

"I can't but sure, but hopefully in a few days."

"Is there anything you need from me? I haven't seen a request for advance or expenses." Alan smiled, for all his worrying and pressing, Dean Franklin was always the consummate leader, looking to set his team up for success.

"No, nothing at the moment. If you want, I can have Stacy send you a summary of the expenses and charges so far."

"No, no. I'm not looking for an accounting, just making sure you didn't need any resources to make the investigation run smoothly."

"We're fine at the moment."

"How is the office working out? I keep meaning to stop by."

"You should drop in on Stacy and say hello. She did a fantastic job setting the place up."

"I'm sorry we are losing her; she is a very capable person."

"She is amazing, and becoming quite the investigative asset as well."

"I'm happy that things are working out for you both. Okay, I'll let you get back to the case. Let me know if you need anything." Alan acknowledged his offer and disconnected the call.

As Alan was picking up his travel coffee mug for a jolt of caffeine, another incoming call notification interrupted him. With less trepidation than he felt for the previous caller, he pressed the connect button.

"Dalton, good morning. You have an update?" he said as soon as the call connected.

"Good morning to you too. Yes, I do. I found the treasure trove!" There was genuine excitement in his voice.

"That sounds promising. What did you find?"

"After days of interviewing patrons and staff at Cowford's rooftop bar, I unearthed a rumor. Apparently, a local celebrity has been frequenting the establishment for the past few months and, get this, has been documenting the whole thing for social media!"

"So what does that mean for us?"

"There are apparently thousands of photos and videos from her visits there over the past few weeks. I am tracking her down today, and hopefully, I can get permission to review the footage. We might get lucky and find some pictures of our target, Reston there and find out who he is meeting with."

"Wow. That is big. Anything I can do to help?"

"Approve expenses if I have to pay for the files."

"Done. Just let Stacy know what the cost is."

"Will do. I'll text you later when I contact the influencer and have more details."

Alan disconnected the call and finally took a long draw from his now lukewarm coffee. He thought briefly about detouring from his route to find a Screaming Goat Coffee Company location, but decided against it and continued on toward North Florida Aerial. As he was pulling into the parking lot, he received another call.

"Alan, are you coming by the office this morning?" Stacy's cheerful voice came across the car's speaker system.

"Maybe later, possibly after lunch. Why?"

"Nothing urgent, just some documents you need to sign. They can wait. Anything exciting happening today?" Alan updated her on Layla's task and the phone call from Dean Franklin.

"Dalton called as well. He has a lead on photo-documentary evidence of who has been hanging out at the rooftop bar. We hope it will give us some leads to follow."

"I hope so too, the case feels like it is getting stale."

"Yeah, I agree. We have lots of little pieces, but we aren't having any luck putting them together. I don't want to confront suspects until we have something definitive."

"That sounds like a solid plan. So you are headed to North Florida Aerial to get drone footage?"

"I'm already here. I hope to get some footage of one of the drones leaving the warehouse so Layla can use it to help reconstruct the last videos from the damaged drone."

"Like a puzzle?"

"Exactly what she said. Like the corners of a puzzle."

"That's clever. She is so—"

"Human-like?"

"Yes, it can be unnerving, but it is also very comforting."

"I know what you mean. Sometimes I forget she isn't alive. She is more than just an artificial intelligence application. She is growing. I guess we all are. Maybe that is an essential part of being sentient. Learning about yourself, making choices and adapting."

"You are very philosophical this morning," Stacy said with a laugh.

"You're right. Not enough coffee. I'm going to go see about the drone footage. I'll see you after lunch."

"Oh, pizza...bring me pizza!"

"You got it. Go back to work!" She made a rude noise and disconnected the phone.

Roger Maxwell was still excited about the return of the drones. He greeted Alan with another hug and shook his hand enthusiastically. When asked if he could help with the drone footage, he interrupted Alan in mid-sentence to call Perry Beckner in and ask him to get Alan anything he needed. Alan thanked him and followed Beckner out of the office and down a flight of stairs to the first floor and on through the doors to the warehouse floor.

"So explain what you need, Mr. Harrison." Beckner said as they got to the warehouse.

"Call me Alan. I just want a brief video from the drone as it takes off and flies out of the warehouse and then back in. Just a few seconds. I need it to compare with video footage from one of the drones. We are trying to reconstruct a damaged video, and this will help."

"Oh, okay. Let me get a drone prepped, and then we will do a demo flight and record what you need," Beckner motioned to Pete Sanderson, one of the technicians Alan had met on previous visits. Sanderson went and pulled a done from the shelf and brought it over to the workbench. Together, Sanderson and

Beckner reviewed the configuration on the drone. Once that was complete, Sanderson took the drone to the middle of the warehouse floor and sat it down.

"What were you checking?" Alan asked as Sanderson put the drone down on the warehouse floor.

"This drone was one of the units left behind during the theft. We were just checking the firmware for the suspicious code that you gave us on that USB drive."

"Did the drone have that code segment?" Alan asked.

"No, so far none of the drones left behind have it. Only the ones that you returned were affected. We are still researching why," Alan nodded his understanding.

Beckner loaded the drone control app on his phone and activated the unit. The running lights lit up and cycled before settling in. The propellers spun up. Finally, the drone gently lifted off the ground and rose to about six feet, hovering for a few moments. The sound of the propellers intensified, and the drone dipped forward slightly and crept across the warehouse floor, headed for the open garage door.

As Alan watched silently, the drone exited the building, rose to several hundred feet in the air. Beckner circled the drone around a small area of the parking lot before bringing it to a stop and reducing the altitude again to around six feet. The unit slowly returned along the same path it took out and landed smoothly in the center of the floor. After settling, the propellers powered down, and finally, the drone powered off.

Beckner walked over to the drone and pulled the SD memory card from the slot. Alan walked over and took the offered card.

"Thanks for your time, Perry. I really appreciate it."

"It's no problem, Mr. Harri—I mean, Alan. If it helps catch the people who took our drones, it will be worth it." He motioned to Sanderson, who came and collected the drone. Alan thanked him again and headed out of the warehouse.

Alan and Stacy enjoyed pizza in the conference room. Alan had emailed Layla the video footage from the drone demo, and she had responded. She had nearly finished the restoration of the damaged video data. She would use the video he had sent as an overlay to build out the metadata for the restored file. While they waited, Alan signed contracts and work orders that needed a principal's approval. They ate the pizza and chatted about light subjects until Layla interrupted them.

"Alan, I think I have the video file re-constructed, but I also discovered something else."

"What?" Alan asked with a pizza slice in his hand.

"The structure of the video file you got from the today differs from the one on the recovered drone."

"That's odd. Why is that?"

"I don't know for sure, but I believe the two units are running slightly different firmware versions." Alan considered the implications of that theory.

"What if the firmware update failed for the units that remained behind at the warehouse?" Stacy asked.

"The communication failures," Alan said.

"That makes sense. If the units were having one of their communication failures, the firmware update might not have succeeded. That explains why not all the units disappeared. I am going to play the video on the screen there," Layla said.

As they watched, the screen displayed a night-vision video of the warehouse. In the foreground, dozens of drones flew in formation out of the open garage door of the North Florida Aerial warehouse, just as the unit earlier today had done. The damaged drone's POV rotated, and it moved slowly across the warehouse floor toward the exit. After it exited the building and gained altitude, the camera angle showed the entire parking lot and the outside of the large garage door on the side of the building. A dark figure came into view at the door, looked out at the drones, and then pressed the door close button. The door slowly lowered. Layla paused the video and enhanced the zoom level on the clip to reveal the face of the man standing at the open door.

The man appeared to be in his 30s, with dark hair and a beard. Even in the low light, it was clear he was dark-skinned. Stacy made a noise. Alan looked over at her.

"That is the man at the stolen merchandise warehouse, the one Stanley Graystone described. It fits him exactly." Alan turned back to look closely. She was right.

"You're right. That has to be the guy Graystone saw."

"Now all we have to do is find out who he is..." Stacy said.

Chapter Twenty-Two

Chance

As Alan and Stacy watched over the remains of the now cold pizza, Layla scanned data banks trying to match the photo of the mystery man. At almost blinding speed, images rotated across the screen. In the unending scrolling, Alan recognized news articles, social media posts, and public police records. The scrolling stopped after about fifteen minutes on a police mugshot from a place called Hermitage, PA. The photo was of a younger man, but it was definitely a match for the unknown suspect seen in the drone video.

"It looks like you found him, Layla. Who is he?" Alan asked.

"Kendrick Elder, 38, from Hermitage, PA. The picture is from a mug shot for an arrest for a bar brawl in 2027. No other criminal record. I don't have a current address or any other information about him."

"That doesn't give us much to go on," Stacy said glumly.

"It looks like another trip to North Florida Aerial," Alan said

"I will send a photo to your phone," Layla replied.

"I'll head out there now," Alan said.

"Maybe you should wait a few minutes." Dalton Rogers stood in the office's doorway holding a small black USB hard drive. He had a triumphant look on his face. Alan raised an eyebrow questioningly and got a nod in answer. He had something.

The conference table had a media interface built into the center. Dalton plugged the drive in. The big conference room monitors displayed a directory with hundreds of video and image files. Dalton picked up a remote and clicked on the first video.

"When was this footage shot?" Alan asked.

"On a Wednesday, two weeks before you were there," Dalton replied.

On screen, the videographer panned around the nighttime view from the top of the old Bostwick building, which was the home of Cowford Chophouse. As the scene played out, the overflowing crowd of well-dressed patrons mingled in the elegant bar area, featuring a breathtaking city panorama. The footage moved through the crowd. Alan recognized some of the city's movers and shakers, local politicians, and some minor celebrities. As the camera passed them, they waved, saluted, or smiled.

"So far, I'm not seeing anything worth jumping up and down about," Alan said.

"Patience...patience—" Dalton motioned for him to be calm.

The scene continued with the camera moving slowly and dramatically toward the railing of the rooftop, looking directly out at the brightly lit blue bridge that was officially named for John T. Alsop, Jr. but everyone just called the Main Street Bridge. Following a brief pause showing the nighttime river view, the camera panned around to the crowd again. In the screen's corner was a high-top table with three patrons sitting at it.

"Oh!" Stacy exclaimed.

Dalton paused the video. In the center of the screen was the smiling face of Karen Anderson, North Florida Aerial technician. Seated across from her was James Reston, the programmer from Prism Cybernetics. A third party member was in shadow, turned away from the camera. It wasn't possible to make out his features. Dalton resumed the video, and they watched as Karen and James Reston had a brief conversation. The third person at the table never turned around, and the video panned away from them onto other subjects. Dalton stopped the video.

"Karen Anderson and James Reston," Alan said softly.

"That can't be a coincidence, can it?" Stacy asked.

"The probability of James Reston and Karen Anderson occupying the same 1,500 square foot area in a city of over a million residents is mathematically indistinguishable from zero," Layla asserted. Dalton jolted at the voice coming over the conference room speakers. Stacy and Alan exchanged a look.

"Dalton, that is Layla. She is a freelance tech specialist who is working with us on contract. Sorry, I should have warned you she was connected to the conference systems," Alan said, holding his breath that Layla would play along and Dalton would buy the explanation.

“Happy to meet you, Dalton,” Layla said without missing a beat.

“I knew you weren’t doing all this stuff yourself, Harrison! Good to meet you Layla, I agree there is no way this is random. Reston and Anderson are connected.”

“The stolen merchandise in the warehouse pointed to a connection. This just makes it certain,” Alan said, getting nods from Stacy and Dalton.

“It doesn’t seem possible that she is the mastermind. The third person in that video could be. You’ve checked to make sure they don’t appear again?” Alan inquired, knowing Dalton would have mentioned it already.

“Yes, I checked all the other footage. I have one brief shot of Anderson entering the bar area earlier in the evening, but nothing on either of the other two. I also found no footage of Reston at the bar the night of the shooting.”

“Disappointing. Can you leave the drive? Layla can try to run some image enhancement tech on the video. We might get lucky.”

“I can, but I need to return it to the influencer’s people. They don’t want it getting out before they finish their story.”

“Okay, but that video is going to end up as evidence. They can’t destroy it.”

“I made a copy of that video just in case, but I’ll tell them to protect the originals,” Dalton assured him.

"I have to go to North Florida Aerial to get an identity on another suspect, but I don't think it is time yet to confront Karen. I would like to know who that third person is first; if we can wrap them all up in a nice package, I think the entire case will fall into place." Alan looked at Dalton to get his opinion.

"I agree. We have nothing tying Reston to anything at the moment. We can't tie her to Graystone either," Dalton agreed. Alan looked at Stacy. She was a little surprised, but she nodded in agreement.

"I am going to go out there now to see if they can help track down Kendrick Elder," Alan said.

"I have a dinner engagement that I can't get out of," Dalton said sheepishly. Alan grinned. Dalton rarely talked about his life outside of investigations. Alan looked at Stacy.

"I'll ride along. Afterwards, we can get dinner."

"Dinner? We just had pizza!" he exclaimed. Stacy shrugged.

The late afternoon sun was starting its westward descent. The shadows were lengthening as the day wore on. Alan reflected that this was his fourth trip to the San Marco offices of North Florida Aerial in the past couple of weeks. He pulled into the parking lot and found a visitor's parking space near the door. He and Stacy took the elevator to the second-floor lobby and spoke to Carol at the desk.

"Good afternoon, Carol, we're back," he announced lightly with a smile. She returned the smile.

"Good to see you again, Mr. Harrison. What can I do for you?"

"Well, the first thing you can do is look at this picture and tell me if you recognize the man in it." He unlocked his phone and showed her the image of Kendrick Elder at the warehouse door. She studied it for a moment, frowning.

"He looks familiar, but I don't know for sure," she said apologetically.

"That's fine. I'll need to ask around. Is Roger here?"

"No, he isn't. He had an appointment with the insurance company." She grimaced a little at the thought.

"Understood. May I just ask the staff about the photo?"

"Certainly, Roger has instructed that you get anything you want, Mr. Harrison." He thanked her and led Stacy to the elevator and then through the doors to the warehouse. As they entered the warehouse area, Alan spotted Karen Anderson. He headed directly for her. After a brief greeting, he showed her his phone. Alan observed her reaction, but there was no sign of recognition.

"No, I don't think I know him. He seems familiar somehow, but I can't recall ever meeting him. Do you know his name?"

"His name is Kendrick Elder. Does that name mean anything to you?"

She shook her head. "No, I don't think I've ever heard it. Is he important to the case?"

"He might be. Trying to find out if he has been around the office."

"If he has, I don't recall seeing him." Alan thanked her and moved on. Perry Beckner and Pete Sanderson also said he was familiar, but they couldn't place where they knew him. They didn't know the name.

"That's odd," Stacy said as they walked away from the two techs.

"Yes, like he is some shadowy figure that everyone knows, but no one pays any attention to."

"Like some kind of science fiction story. *The Man You Can't Recall,*" she quipped.

"Or the aliens from that TV show — you could only remember when you were looking at them." Stacy shivered at the memory of the creatures who could influence the world with impunity because no one could remember them once the encounter was over.

They spent the next half hour interviewing various technicians and other employees from the warehouse, but got similar results. Most either had no recollection, with some feeling they had seen Elder but couldn't recall where. Alan looked at his watch; it was nearing five.

"Should we call it a day?" Stacy asked. Alan thought about it for a few moments.

"Let's see if we can find Ben Williams. He's the warehouse manager. If someone has access, he should know about it." She nodded in agreement, and they went off to find him.

They checked his desk, but there was no sign of him there or around the warehouse floor. Alan flagged down a passing technician and asked him if he had seen Williams.

"I think he is in the breakroom. He said he was getting coffee," the tech said without pausing his stride. Alan called after him to ask where that was. The tech pointed to a door off to the right and continued on his task. Alan and Stacy walked over and pushed through a free-swinging door, similar to the high-traffic doors you might find at a professional kitchen.

Ben Williams was sitting at a small table inside by himself. A steaming cup of coffee sat cooling in front of him. He slumped down, appearing tired after a long Monday.

"Hi Ben," Alan greeted him. The heavyset man looked up at them and brightened.

"Hey Alan. Good to see you. What brings you back to our little kingdom?"

"Stacy and I," he pointed out Stacy, who smiled at Ben, "are trying to wrap up the final clues to the break-in. Have you ever seen this man?" He offered his phone to Williams. Recognition was instant, as was something else. Williams had a sickly look. He closed his eyes for a second.

"You know who he is," Alan stated.

"Yes, Kenny James. He works on the cleaning crew."

"What else."

"He was the crew member who told me they never went out into the warehouse that night. He assured me that no one on the crew was there. I should have asked more questions."

"It probably wouldn't have mattered. I could have interviewed them as well, but I doubt anyone knew he went in there, and the only thing that would have changed is that I would have recognized him instead of having to ask you."

"Maybe, just feel like I let everyone down."

"Have you seen him since that day?"

"Oh yeah, he's here every night."

"Really? How long has he worked here?" Stacy asked.

"A couple of years. He never causes any trouble, seems dependable, and keeps to himself. Doesn't really talk to anyone."

"That could explain why plenty of people here said he was familiar, but none of them knew his name," Alan said.

"Yeah, that would be Kenny. He doesn't leave much of an impression on you. I wouldn't remember him myself if I hadn't talked to him about the break-in."

"Any idea where I can find him?"

"He might be here now." Williams looked at his watch. "He comes on about this time every day. You might check the locker room." Alan nodded and, looking at the door marked 'lockers' on the far wall, turned to head in that direction. Stacy gave him a questioning look, and he shook his head slightly. She stayed behind to console Ben Williams, who was still looking a little lost after the revelation.

Alan entered the employee locker room. It was empty and quiet. In a few minutes that would probably change, as the shift ended and staff headed out. They would likely flow through the locker room for their belongings.

"Kendrick Elder? Are you in here?" Alan called out. Silence answered.

Alan had a thought that he should have asked Ben if Kenny had a locker. He turned back toward the breakroom door, but a sound behind him caused him to stop. A figure hurtled from behind a locker and hit him in the back, driving him into the wall. Two arms reached around him and squeezed, forcing the air out of his lungs, and Alan had to gasp for breath. He threw an elbow backwards, striking his opponent in the face. There was a grunt from behind him, and the force of the surrounding arms lessened for a moment. Using this to his advantage, Alan twisted around and twisted his body, breaking the hold. He pushed both arms out, creating separation, allowing him to face his opponent.

Kendrick Elder wiped blood from the split in his lip where Alan's elbow had struck him and growled, throwing a right hook at Alan's face. Alan dodged back to avoid the blow, but it clipped his chin anyway, and the force rocked his head back into the wall, stunning him for a second. That second was all Elder needed. He pressed his attack. Grabbing Alan by the neck and choking him. Alan gagged and clawed at his assailant's arms, trying to break the hold. As his vision narrowed as if he were going through a tunnel, Alan remembered his S&W on his hip. He reached for it but felt like he would lose consciousness before he could get to it. As darkness closed in around him, he heard a shout from behind Elder, followed by an electrical crackling sound. Elder stiffened. His grip loosened. Alan didn't wait for an explanation. Sweeping his foot behind Elder's legs, he pushed with all his strength. Elder cried out in surprise and went over backwards. Alan pulled his M&P Shield, pointing it into the bloody, defeated face of Kendrick Elder. Coughing and gasping for breath, Alan looked up to see Stacy standing behind Elder's prone form. An electric stun gun was in her hand, and she had an anxious look on her face.

When he could speak again, he said. "When did you get a stun gun?"

"Thank you would be good too," she replied, relaxing.

"Sorry, thank you. When did you get a stun gun?"

"After people started shooting at me," Alan nodded his understanding.

"Good thing you came looking for me," he said, waving the gun at the glowering face of Elder on the ground.

"I can't take credit for that. Layla told me you were in trouble." Alan raised a hand to his SmartLens glasses.

"Thank you, Layla," he said.

"You're welcome. The sheriff's office is on the way, and I called Mike Hughes."

Alan looked down at Elder. "Your day is going to get a lot worse," he told him. Elder's response was graphically crude. Stacy clicked the stun gun button again. The sound of the electricity caused Elder to twitch in response, and he clamped his jaw shut.

Chapter Twenty-Three

The Nexus

It was another late night of answering questions from the local and state law enforcement community. Alan had to tell the story of the events leading up to the identification of Kendrick Elder as Kenny James and the ensuing fight that was apparently prompted by him calling our Elder's real name. He had to tell the story multiple times to investigators from the sheriff's office, the Florida Highway Patrol's Bureau of Investigations and Intelligence, and the Florida Department of Law Enforcement. All three groups had questions that Alan and Stacy didn't have answers for, or weren't prepared to speculate about yet. Elder, beyond a few grunts and expletives, said nothing. It was nearly midnight when Sgt. Hughes escorted Alan and Stacy out of the offices and let them go.

"You seem determined to wade knee-deep into a massive conspiracy, Alan," Hughes said as they reached Alan's car.

"Mike, I think it comes with the job." Hughes grunted. He looked at Stacy.

"What about you? Is this what you signed up for?" She gave him a grim smile.

"It isn't exactly what I expected, but you couldn't drag me away from this case right now." Alan felt a surge of pride listening to her words. Mike Hughes just shook his head.

"You're both crazy. Try to stay out of trouble for the rest of the night. I could use some sleep." He offered a hand, and Alan shook it. Stacy waved as she settled into the passenger seat of the Chimera. As Alan started the EV and pulled out of the parking lot, she yawned.

"You never fed me," she complained mildly.

"Or myself either," Alan replied. "We'll go back to my place, and I'll fix you something."

"It's really late. I have to be at work at 8."

"I'm guessing your boss will let you show up late," he said wryly.

"I will allow it," Layla chimed in from the speakers in the car. Alan and Stacy laughed.

"That is very kind, Layla."

Thirty minutes later, Stacy sat at Alan's dining room table. Alan was cooking omelets with sausage, peppers, and sharp cheddar cheese. Layla was working to create a realistic avatar for use on Zoom calls. Since being outed to Dalton, she was determined to develop a cover that would allow her to contribute more to their investigation without revealing her true nature. The big monitor in the dining room was displaying various options for her avatar. The screen looked vaguely like a Zoom-style gallery. Realistic in appearance, the avatars looked like actual humans in their motions and facial expressions. It was impossible to tell they weren't real people on the screen.

"I like this one." Stacy pointed at a young woman on the lower left side of the screen. She appeared to be in her early 30s, with high cheekbones and styled auburn hair cut short and sculpted to her face.

"I agree, Layla. She looks very mysterious. Quite appropriate," Alan concurred.

"Thank you both," Layla said through the avatar on the screen. "She is one of my favorites as well." The gallery disappeared, replaced by a full-screen view of the Layla avatar. Having completed her avatar, Layla began scrolling through various case file material on the drone and cybernetics cases.

The smells from the kitchen were making Stacy's stomach growl. "The omelet smells delicious, but I am starving, so the bar is pretty low," she said.

He plated the omelet and served it to her, saying, "Well, hopefully you won't be disappointed then." Stacy dug into the food like a starved wolverine. Alan stood back dramatically.

"What do you have there, Layla?" Stacy asked between bites. There was no answer. Layla's LED indicator lights were pulsing rapidly in a chase pattern. Alan turned to look at her. This was Layla's deep-thinking mode. She was hard at work on something; she wouldn't respond until she had finished the task. It sometimes took just a few seconds and sometimes hours before she completed the task. The computer monitor that she had been using to scroll through the data was cycling between four screens: the Hermitage, PA mug shot of Kendrick Elder, the M CreekReturn@techtranz.ky email address that Graystone had used to communicate with his boss, and the bank statement showing payments to Graystone from the same boss, and the image of Karen Anderson, James Reston, and the third mystery man at the rooftop bar.

"Any idea what she is working on?" Stacy asked.

"No clue," Alan replied, sitting down with his omelet. They ate quietly, watching Layla's deep thinking process and monitoring the big screen, trying to figure out why those four scenes were important. Finally, after more than fifteen minutes, the lights along Layla's outer side slowed and stopped.

"Layla?" Stacy asked tentatively.

"I know who the third person is at the rooftop bar," Layla replied.

"The boss? Really?" Alan leaned forward excitedly.

"Yes. Something about Kendrick Elder was bothering me. I kept going over all the evidence until the pattern emerged."

"Are you going to walk us through it?" Stacy asked.

"Yes, someone is at the heart of both cases. The motive for both turns out to be simple. Greed. Both operations are driven by the desire for money, one through high-tech theft, the other through blackmail and theft of financial information." Layla paused to put the bank statement of Stanley Graystone on the screen.

"Something about these deposits always bothered me. Why were Graystone and whoever made the deposits so sure they wouldn't be reported? They should be reported, and that would have brought questions." Alan's eyes widened. He was catching up.

"A financial institution can transfer money between locations without reporting amounts," he said.

"Yes, leave that for a moment." She put Kendrick Elder's mug shot on the screen. "Kendrick Elder is from Hermitage, which is a tiny town on the Pennsylvania border about 60 miles from Pittsburgh. It is also 20 miles from a place called Mill Creek Park." As she said this, she put the MCreekReturns email address on the screen.

"Mill Creek Park!" Stacy shouted.

"What about it?" Alan asked.

"I read an old book about it a few months ago. It was among the stuff my grandmother left me. But it's not in Pennsylvania."

"No, it isn't," Layla said.

"Where is it?" Alan asked. In response, Layla put a map up on the screen showing Hermitage, PA. Then she zoomed out. Alan stared at the screen, and his mouth open in surprise.

"Hermitage is 20 miles from Youngstown, Ohio," he said in surprise.

"And who do we know who came from Youngstown?" Layla asked triumphantly.

"Steve Daniels," Alan supplied.

"The boyfriend?" Stacy asked, looking confused.

"Yes, Karen Anderson was on a date with him when the drone theft took place. He said she scheduled it at the last minute; she says he called her. Others seem to say they were dating before that. He works at a financial services company. He would know how to move money around, and he is from a town 20 minutes away from Kendrick Elder, who facilitated the theft of the drones," Alan blurted it out in a rush, the excitement of the discovery was making his brain light up with connections. The case was finally making sense to him.

"Exactly. I can sense that you are having the same sensation that I had. The case makes sense now. Daniels drives all of this. We just need to figure out how he made the connections for both cases," Layla said.

"I think it is finally time we confronted Karen Anderson. We have enough now to approach her."

"We will need a plan. And that plan should probably not happen while we are all sleep-deprived," Stacy asserted. Alan reluctantly agreed.

"While the humans get some sleep, I'll start working on a plan," Layla said.

"Come on, Stacy, I'll take you to get your car," Alan said tiredly.

"I'll get it tomorrow. Drop me off at my apartment. You can pick me up in a few hours and we'll go over Layla's plan." Alan nodded, and they headed for the door.

Tuesday morning found an exhausted group sitting around the conference table at Harrison and Associates discussing the plan Layla had come up with while Alan and Stacy had managed five hours of sleep.

"So how can we be sure she won't just call him or text him and confirm?" Stacy asked, refilling both her and Alan's coffee cups for the second time.

"She might try, but the text I will send her will tell her to avoid his phone as someone might be monitoring it, and if she ignores that, he might have some issues with his cellular account today," Layla answered.

"Cellphone hacking?" Alan asked with a raised eyebrow.

"I'm helping his mobile company optimize its routing algorithm. It might take a few hours to complete the process. Some temporary outages are possible."

Alan smiled. Layla was always thinking about the ethical considerations of her actions. Balancing the stakes of a murder investigation against the morality of tampering with one of their chief suspects cell phone for a few hours. "That is very considerate of you to donate your time like that without being asked," he said tongue in cheek.

"Isn't it? I'm sure they will be happy with the results."

"Either that or we'll get a call from our friend Ava with the Cybersecurity and Infrastructure Security Agency," Stacy quipped.

"That reminds me, I still need to call her and congratulate her on the big case she closed," Alan said.

"We have time now. I'll send the text at 5pm and we meet Karen at the rooftop bar at 6," Layla said.

"Okay, I'll call her. Unless I fall asleep at my desk."

"Oh, that reminds me," Stacy went back to her desk and retrieved a large manila envelope. "Sam Eaton's office sent this over by courier." She handed him the envelope. Alan took it without comment and went into his office. Putting the package down on his desk unopened, he sat and scrolled through the contacts on his phone until he found Ava Chen's cell phone number. Ava answered the phone after three rings.

"Chen." Alan couldn't help but grin at her terse communication style.

"How is my favorite cybersecurity analyst?" he asked cheerily.

"Do you know any other cybersecurity analysts?"

"Not that I recall, but I'm sure you would still be my favorite."

"Are you staying out of trouble?" she asked.

"No, of course not."

"Figures. What can I do for you, Alan?"

"I called to congratulate you on your big case. I read about it in the Times." There was a pause on the other end.

"Uh, thanks. There was a large team on it."

"The article said that you were instrumental in solving the case."

"The press likes to sensationalize things. As I recall, they ran a picture of you wearing a cape when you brought down Vance's killer." She was referencing his and Layla's first case, solving the murder of her creator, Elias Vance.

"A joke from Ava Chen? That is front-page news right there," he teased her. She laughed.

"You are a bad influence on me. What are you working on these days, anyway?"

"Oh, the usual. High-tech conspiracy, murder, mayhem."

"I'm surprised it hasn't landed on my desk yet."

"It might get there before it's over."

"Hey, it's kind of a coincidence that you called today. I am going to be in Jacksonville in a few days. I am going down to see my parents at their retirement home just south of town. Maybe we can catch up and have lunch. If you aren't in jail or anything."

"Well, if I am, I hope you can bail me out like the last time I was in a jam."

"No promises. I'll call you when I'm in town."

"I'll look forward to it. See you soon." He ended the call. Seeing her would be good. Ava was intense and businesslike, but underneath she was a fascinating person, and she had helped him out on the Vance case. And having friends in federal law enforcement was a nice thing to have.

He looked down at the unopened package from his lawyer and smiled, but he didn't move to open it. That would wait. Right now he had to get his mind right for the meeting with Karen Anderson.

It was early in the evening for the Tuesday night crowd at the rooftop bar, but already the atmosphere was boisterous and jovial. Alan and Stacy leaned against the bar, watching the elevator entrance. Layla remained snugly hidden away in the inside pocket of Alan's jacket. He wanted her close to give him biometric data on Karen Anderson. If she bothered to show up, he thought. On cue, the elevator doors opened, revealing a nervous Karen scanning the room. She brushed her hand through her short blond hair and slowly walked around the bar, continuing to look for Steve Daniels who, as far as she knew, had sent her an urgent text to meet him at the bar and to tell no one about the meeting.

"How long do we let her dangle in the wind?" Stacy asked softly.

"A few more seconds," he said as Karen made a slow circuit looking for Daniels and growing more concerned with each passing second. Finally, Alan caught the attention of a server he had tipped generously earlier and nodded. The server approached Karen Anderson and led her to a table in a corner. Karen watched the elevator. Taking advantage of her eyeline being directed away from their direction, Alan and Stacy approached her silently.

"Good evening, Karen," Alan said. She jumped.

"Uh, what are you doing here?" She asked, trying to feign a casual attitude.

"I asked you to meet me here," he said. Her mouth fell open, and she started to speak, but stopped herself. Alan and Stacy took the other two seats at the table. The server had instructions to give them privacy for a few minutes before offering them drinks.

"I don't know what you are talking about." She tried to put a tone of defiance in her voice, but her fear gave her away.

"Karen, we know about Steve. We know everything."

"I don't know anything," she insisted.

"Let's start with this," he said, pushing a printed photograph of her at the table with James Reston and the mystery man. Her face paled.

"Wh...where did you get that?"

"Doesn't matter. You met James Reston here at this bar several weeks ago. Why?"

"I don't know that I have to explain why I met with men at bars to you, Harrison." The defiance this time was real. He smiled at her.

"Not all men, but these two men you need to explain."

"I know Jim. I met him at a party a few years ago. That's all."

"That is true, as far as it goes," Layla said into his ear via the SmartLens glasses that both he and Stacy were wearing.

"Okay, let's say that is true for the moment. Tell me why Steve Daniels was here that night. You told us you had only been out with him the one time."

"Who says that is Steve? It could be anyone," she shot back. This was a critical point. She was right. They couldn't really prove it was him, but she didn't know that. And it was critical that she didn't.

"We have witnesses that put him here and describe the three of you together. It was a busy night, but there was a social media influencer here that night photographing everything. We know it was Daniels." He tried to sound as confident as he could. It was imperative that she believe he was sure of his facts. She looked at him for a moment and then looked away. He relaxed.

"Steve and I see each other occasionally," she said with a tone of resignation.

"Why did you lie about the relationship?"

"I don't know, really."

"You do know, tell me why," he insisted.

"Because after the break-in at North Florida, I was worried."

"That your relationship with him would cause suspicion?"

"Maybe I don't know. He had seemed very interested in the drones and the cost. When he called me that morning and suggested we have dinner, I thought nothing about it. Unti—"

"Until the break-in."

"Yes, then his questions took on more importance, and I didn't want to answer questions about him."

"But you used him as an alibi." Stacy spoke up for the first time.

"You forced me to. If you recall, I tried to leave him out of it," she directed the answer to Alan.

"That is true. You did. What about Reston?"

"What about him? I know him from a party. I have seen him here a few times. He saw Steve and me that night and came by the table to say hello. I introduced them."

"What did you talk about that night?"

"It was casual. I don't remember anything significant."

"They didn't talk about work?"

"It might have come up. Jim asked me how things were going with the drones. We talked about their new model. He was excited about the demo that is coming up."

"Did he mention any issues at the factory?" Alan asked.

"No, not that I recall. But I left soon after that. I haven't seen him since."

"You didn't reach out to him after the break-in at the factory?"

"What?" She had a shocked look.

"You haven't read about the break-in at Prism Cybernetics?"

"No, when?" A bead of sweat had formed on her forehead.

"A couple of weeks ago. Shortly after the break-in at North Florida Aerial."

"I didn't know about it." She was looking down at the table. Out of the corner of her eye, Stacy saw the server approaching. She looked at her and shook her head. The server detoured around them to another table.

"A man was killed a few nights later."

"Jim?" She was terrified now.

"No, a man named Cary Sellers. He worked on the robots." There was a flash of relief, but it was quickly swallowed up by her fears of the connection between the two cases and her link to them.

"Harrison, I didn't know anything about these break-ins. I swear I didn't. I suspected Steve was involved after the break-in at North Florida, but I didn't know, and we haven't spoken since then, until I got the text today...which I am now realizing wasn't from him at all."

"No, it was from me. We needed to talk to you, and I figured you would respond to him if we implied there was danger of exposure involved."

"Well, that was certainly effective." She wiped the sweat off her brow with the back of her hand, but she still looked miserable.

"A few nights ago, Stacy and I were here for dinner, not in the bar, but downstairs." Karen nodded but had no reaction. "Someone took a shot at us on the street outside."

"You think that was Steve? Doesn't sound like him. Seems too bold. I think he prefers the shadowy puppet master role," she said with a grim smile.

"Possibly, does he own a gun?"

"I have no idea. I've never seen one."

"Anything else you want to tell me about this? I asked you that once before, and you passed. Don't make the same mistake this time."

"No, I don't know anything else. I probably gave Steve the idea for the drone theft. We talked about how expensive they were, how the market for them was heating up and how we would make 3 to 4 times the cost when we sold them. He must have seen an opportunity. I wasn't involved, though. And I do not know about the other break-in or any deaths. I wish I had never met the guy."

Alan paused, looking into her blue eyes, trying to judge for himself if she was being honest with him. He felt she was, but he needed a second opinion. He looked at Stacy, who nodded. Layla chimed in as well. "She is telling the truth, as far as she knows. She is depressed, but not deceptive."

"Karen, I am going to take you at your word. I will not mention this to the police for now, but I would suggest you avoid Daniels and Reston until this is all wrapped up."

"Jim can't be mixed up in this. He isn't that guy."

"Well, we will just put a pin in trusting your judgment in men for the moment." Karen's nostrils flared in anger, but she nodded her acceptance of the situation. Alan nodded to her, and she got up and left the bar. Stacy caught the server's eye and waved her over.

"How did it go?" the server asked.

"Like clockwork," Stacy said, beaming.

"Can I get you something?"

"Yes. Two bourbon Old Fashioneds with Woodford Reserve Double Oak," Stacy answered. Alan raised an eyebrow but didn't argue.

A few minutes later they sipped their drinks, basking in the warmth both of the smooth bourbon and of the successful mission.

"I would have bet money she was in on the whole thing," Alan said, clinking the ice in his glass.

"Me too!" Stacy exclaimed.

"Nothing indicated any dishonesty. She was being open, she suspected, but she didn't know," Layla said.

"So now we face Reston? See if we can turn him?" Stacy asked.

"I don't see another route. We push him with the relationship with Daniels and Karen, we can prove the altered P4 code, and we can demonstrate that it was used to murder Cary Sellers. That should be enough to make him want to talk."

"Now we just have to figure out how to approach him," Layla said.

"And considering he might have taken a shot at us before, we need to make sure he doesn't get a chance to repeat the attempt," Stacy said and offered her glass to Alan. He clinked his glass to hers in agreement, and they drank to not getting shot at again.

Chapter Twenty-Four

Black Op

Alan, Stacy and Dalton debated the plan to approach James Reston over breakfast at The Uptown Kitchen and Bar on North Main Street the following morning. The spirited debate hinged on the chance that Reston would react violently when confronted. Stacy was in favor of a neutral location like the rooftop bar again, but Alan wanted a more private location, one that he could control.

"What if he is carrying?" Stacy asked.

"That is a factor. Dalton will keep him under surveillance the entire night. If there is any hint of him being strapped, we will alter our plans. Dalton will be behind him when he arrives and will help control the situation. If you have any sign that things are going sideways, you call Mike Hughes and ask him to send in the cavalry."

"He is tiring of our calling him to the rescue."

"I don't think he really is. He likes to put on, but I think he is enjoying being along for the ride on this case. And he has a vested interest in its getting resolved."

Their breakfast arrived, and the logistical talk took a backseat to eggs and waffles for Stacy and Dalton and Southern Biscuits and Gravy for Alan. For several minutes, the air was filled only with the clanking of silverware and the sounds of enjoyment.

"Do you really think you can get him to flip on Daniels?" Stacy asked between bites of her waffle.

Alan swallowed a piece of biscuit and then considered the question for a moment. "I think so. If we convince him, we can bring the police down on him. I think he will open up. If our theory is right, he is just a desperate guy forced into a bad situation by financial concerns."

"It's the desperation part that worries me," Stacy said.

"The hope is that we can push him to be desperate enough to turn on Daniels, but not so desperate that he will try shooting it out with both Dalton and me."

"That isn't very reassuring," she said, picking at her food.

"I think we can handle it. I have confidence in Dalton and in your monitoring from the office." Dalton nodded his agreement, his mouth full of food.

"Okay, but if you get shot—"

"You'll hover over me until I get well again," Alan finished. Stacy blushed.

"We'll see."

They continued eating breakfast and finalizing the plans for the night's operation. Gradually everyone came to an agreement on the plan, even if Stacy maintained some reservations.

Alan and Dalton sat in Dalton's Subaru in the parking lot of Prism Cybernetics a few minutes before five o'clock. Although the sun was still high in the late April sky and it wouldn't get dark for another three hours, they were both dressed in dark colors to make them less conspicuous in a dark car. Dalton confirmed his Sig Sauer was loaded and accessible. Alan noted it was almost identical to the model he had borrowed from Dalton a few months back. Alan felt compelled to check his M&P Sheild but resisted. He didn't want to seem anxious, and he would have time to do it privately once the operation got underway.

"Any reason to suspect he will change his routine tonight?" Dalton asked, munching on a bag of potato chips.

"No, we've been monitoring his communications. Nothing from Daniels or Anderson. No reason to think he is aware the net is closing."

"We? You mean your hotshot tech consultant?"

"Yeah, Layla. She's pretty good."

"Is she local?"

"She moves around a lot," Reston interrupted their conversation by exiting the cybernetics offices and getting into his car. They let the white Range Rover exit the parking lot, then Alan told Dalton to "break a leg" and got out of the car. Dalton pulled the gray Subaru out of the parking lot behind Reston and tailed him, presumably into the city to the rooftop bar for a few hours. Alan watched the two cars disappear around the corner and then went to his car and headed to the next stop.

Earlier in the day while scouting for the operation, Layla had found a property on Nottingham Road which suited their purposes. The property had been for sale for a few months and was empty. Alan had confirmed this and found the perfect parking spot in the yard, which partially hid the car behind a large live oak tree. The large branches, weighed down with Spanish moss, created a perfect camouflage for the Chimera. Alan checked in with Stacy.

"Any changes to the plan so far?" he asked when she answered the phone.

"No, Dalton checked in five minutes ago and reported that they were in the rooftop bar. Reston is having dinner and drinks."

"Is anyone with him?"

"He has chatted with a few people, but no one Dalton could identify as relevant to the case. So far, it seems like a normal Wednesday night for him."

"If it goes according to schedule, we have another hour before he is on his way home."

"Yes. Are you in position yet?"

"Almost. Just parked the car. I'll head over there now and get inside and get set up for the meet."

"I don't have to say 'be careful' again, but I will. Be careful."

"It will be fine. I'm putting on the SmartLens glasses now. Have Layla set up the feed."

"Already on it." Layla's voice came from the speaker in the car.

Alan exited the car and walked the two blocks to Reston's house on Robin Hood Rd. He made sure he was unobserved, then repeated the same infiltration he had one week before. He closed the door and reflected that Reston had cleaned up a little since his last visit. The fast-food wrappers were gone, and someone had straightened the living room. Alan immediately went into the bedroom and checked that the .38 was still in the box in the closet. It was there, and Alan examined it carefully. The gun had not recently fired, and the oil used to clean it felt waxy. A thin layer of dust had stuck to the surface.

"I'm in," Alan announced to Stacy and Layla via the SmartLens glasses. "The gun is in place, and no one has fired it in months. If Reston is carrying, it's a different weapon."

"I'll relay that to Dalton," Stacy said.

Alan selected a comfortable armchair in the living room that had a good view of the front door. He settled down and pulled a worn paperback out of his inside jacket pocket. As the sun set outside and darkness fell, Alan dived into *The Doorbell Rang* by Rex Stout and waited for the next stage of the operation.

An hour later, while reading a scene involving Archie Goodwin waiting outside a building in a car, Stacy's voice came over the SmartLens glasses.

"Dalton just reported in. They are turning into the neighborhood now. Five minutes or less."

"Acknowledged. I'm ready." Alan kept the book out but kept his attention focused on the door. After three minutes, he heard a car in the driveway. A few seconds later, the lock disengaged, and the door swung open. Reston entered the living room and stopped in his tracks, looking at Alan.

"What the hell are you doing in my house!" he shouted.

"Why don't you come inside and let's talk," Alan said calmly.

"Get out before I call the cops!"

"You could do that. But they might want to talk about the illegal gambling, the associations with known criminals, and your connection with Cary Seller's death," Alan replied. Reston swallowed hard. He stared at Alan, weighing his options.

"Just go inside and sit down, Reston." Dalton said from behind him. Reston jumped and looked over his shoulder, seeing Rodgers behind him. Shaken, he slowly entered the room and sat down on the couch.

"What do you want? This can't be a burglary. You apparently know I'm broke." Alan smiled at this.

"We just want to talk." Dalton closed the front door and took up a position against the wall where he could monitor the entire room.

"About what?"

"Steve Daniels, for one." Reston's eyes grew wide.

"Who?"

"Don't get cute. We know you met him at the rooftop bar. With Karen."

"Oh."

"Right, tell me about him."

"I don't know him. I just met him the one time. Karen introduced us, and we had drinks together."

"What did you talk about? And just assume we already know and tell us your side."

Reston took a moment to compose himself, running a hand through his hair. Finally, after a long pause, he spoke. "We talked about many things that night. His work in financial services. Fishing, my work in technology."

"Was he interested in anything specific about your work?"

"The idea of home robotics fascinated him. I guess that is natural, though. They are about to be a big thing."

"And you talked about the software." Alan made a statement. There was an almost imperceptible slump in Reston's shoulders.

"Yes. He asked about the safety protocols."

"Why?"

"I don't know. He wondered why people would trust them in their homes. So I talked about the safety process and all the testing."

"And you told him about the backdoor."

"The back—" Reston stopped, his mouth open.

"Yes, we know about the backdoor that allows you to spy on people using the P4. That was what Daniels was interested in, wasn't it?"

Reston squirmed in his seat. The color had drained out of his face.

"I'm going to jail," Reston said with resignation.

"A man is dead. And there is code on the P4s that would have been used to spy on millions of people," Alan replied with a hard edge in his voice.

"None of that is my fault!" Reston insisted.

"Hard to believe. You wrote the code, didn't you?"

"No. I didn't."

"Who did?" Alan asked with raised eyebrows.

"Bishop." Alan stared at him for a few moments, trying to make sure he had heard him correctly.

"Holy crap!" Stacy shouted in his ear.

"Robert Bishop wrote the backdoor code?"

"Yes."

"He was spying on people with the P4s?"

"No, it was a prank."

"Explain that."

"Sellers was annoying the hell out of us about every bug, every minor glitch in the code. One night, Bishop wrote this routine that allowed the P4 to record video whenever it observed anything that might be private or personal. He told me about it a few days later. He wanted Cary to find it and freak out. We laughed about it."

"And you told Daniels about it." Alan said.

Reston sighed. "Yes, I accidentally disclosed that Bishop was playing a prank on a co-worker by inserting code that violated our privacy protocols. I assured him that testing would discover it. But Daniels was too interested in the idea and asked too many questions. I got very uncomfortable."

"Did you tell anyone about the conversation?"

"No, but I told Bishop to remove it. The next day."

"He didn't listen to you."

"No. I don't know why."

"Did you have any further communication with Daniels?"

"He called me. After the break-in. He told me he might be able to help with my financial situation, but that I should forget about the meeting we had that night. In fact, he said, 'If you know what's good for you, you'll forget you ever met me.'"

"That didn't alarm you?" Alan asked incredulously.

"Of course it alarmed me. And when Cary died, I was terrified of him, and of whatever connection I had with whatever he was doing. I…I should have gone to the police."

"Did you talk to Bishop?"

"What? No…I didn't know what he knew or how involved he was. I wanted nothing else to do with it. Now I wish I had never heard of Daniels or Bishop." Reston was shaking at this point. Dalton left his post along the wall, went into the kitchen and brought back a highball glass full of a dark liquid. Alan assumed from the smell that it was rye whiskey. Alan waited for him to drink half the glass, then continued.

"Do you own a gun?" he asked. Reston frowned at the question.

"Uh, yeah. I do, why?"

"Someone took a shot at me a week ago."

"That wasn't me!"

"You know about the shooting, though."

"Assuming you are talking about the shooting outside Cowford, yes. I heard about it. I wasn't there. I left earlier in the night and only heard about it later."

"Would you mind showing me the gun?"

"I...guess." He got up and walked toward the bedroom. Dalton watched him closely, keeping his hand near his waist so he had easy access to his Sig Sauer. Alan was more relaxed now. He no longer considered Reston a threat.

Jim Reston returned, holding the box in his hands. He sat and opened it, displaying the gun. "This was my father's gun. I got it when he passed away."

"When was it last fired?"

"I have no idea. I haven't fired it since he died. Years ago. I clean it every few months out of habit."

"When was the last time?" Alan asked, knowing the answer already.

"Four or five months, November or December, I can't remember exactly."

"Do you know anything about the theft of aerial drones in town?" Reston got a confused look on his face.

"No, I never heard of it."

"It was worth asking. Can you think of anything else about this situation we should know?"

"No, I don't know anything else." Alan believed him. He had the same depressed, exhausted appearance that Karen Anderson had the night before. Apparently, they were both pawns in Daniels' shady enterprise.

"Am I going to jail?" Reston asked.

"I don't know. I doubt it. If you are telling the truth."

"I am!"

"Then I can't think of anything that you did that would be illegal. You might have some tough questions to answer once it all comes out. I can't speak to how your employer will feel about you knowing about their exposure to a scheme to spy on their customers and not alerting them to it, but legally it probably isn't actionable."

Reston scowled at the thought of the affair becoming public. He slumped down in his chair.

"What now?" he asked.

"Nothing. Dalton will give you a card with a phone number on it. Call us if anyone approaches you. We have to tie up some loose ends before taking the case to the authorities and to Prism. Then you'll have to tell your story. Until then, try not to attract attention to yourself. Maybe lay off the gambling for a few nights too. You apparently aren't very good at it."

"If I could, I would have done that a long time ago," he said dejectedly. Alan shrugged and got up from his chair. He and Dalton left Reston sitting on the couch, contemplating his future.

Chapter Twenty-Five

Cybernetic Correction

The debate over how to approach Steven Daniels and Bobby Bishop stretched on for several hours. If spirited described the previous debate, then fiery more aptly applied to this discussion. Everyone was pretty settled on the method of bringing the two conspirators together, it had the benefit of being poetic justice and likely to evoke powerful emotions from one or both of the targets. The catch was the authorities.

The group all believed they had to be involved, but they had different ideas about the method. As they drank coffee the next morning in the conference room at the offices of Harrison and Associates, each had their own spin on how to do it. The group: Alan, Stacy, and Dalton sat around the conference table drinking coffee and forcefully making their arguments. Layla was present via Zoom call. She had set it up on the conference room monitor. This time, her realistic avatar video represented her instead of the uppercase 'L' the way she had appeared for the Rebecca Salter call. After Dalton had seen her on screen, he told her it was good to see her at last instead of just hearing her voice. She smiled and thanked him.

"We can't keep sending you into dangerous situations without backup. In the first place, it is going to end up with you getting killed, which will piss me off because I'll have to find a new job. In the second, the longer we wait, the more annoyed the police are going to be about being kept in the dark," Stacy adamantly restated her opinion.

"If we involve them too soon, we will lose control of the scenario and possibly fail to get the evidence we, and the police, need to wrap this case up," Dalton asserted.

"Whatever the solution; it is vital we control the scene." Alan had been firm on this point from the start, but he hadn't taken a firm stance on the timing of notifying the police.

For the first time, Layla chimed in. "Which of our police agencies do you think we can control the best, and what approach should we take?"

"I have a good relationship with Mike Hughes," Alan said, "but he won't be able to run this on his own. He would have to bring in state investigators. People we don't know. He won't have control of the scene."

"That leaves Fairfield," Stacy replied.

"We promised him information about what we found with the robot," Layla reminded them.

"We could bring him in on that part, describe how the murderer accomplished it with the programming of the P4. Then, get him to agree to letting us get the evidence for him in a controlled setting. He would have to agree before we reveal our full plan," Alan said.

"He could still torpedo the whole thing. Bring everyone in and question them," Dalton protested.

"That might not be a bad idea," Stacy replied. Everyone looked at her. "We need Bishop spooked. If our theory is right, he is the weak link."

"Have Fairfield interview everyone at the factory, and press Bishop on what he knows about the code. Then, let him go, letting him know that the factory is being closed to do more forensics. With that seed planted, we execute the plan the way already talked about," Alan supplied, nodding.

Dalton frowned, but considered the idea for several moments. "That could work," he reluctantly conceded. "I still worry that he will kill the whole idea."

Alan mulled over the options in his head for several minutes. Thinking about the plan they had come up with, adding in Fairfield and presumably other police officers from the Jacksonville Sheriff's Office.

"Let's call him. Get him down here and see if we can win him over. When he hears about the way the murder went down, I think he will want to nail these guys as much as we do." Alan said finally. Stacy was already dialing the detective's phone from her cell.

It had taken some arm-twisting, but an hour later, Andre Fairfield sat at the conference table with a cup of coffee in front of him and a suspicious scowl on his lined face. His brown eyes went from Stacy to Alan and finally to Dalton. Layla had ended the conference call. Alan wanted no hint of her involvement to the detective.

"Well, you got me down here. The coffee is better than I have at the station, but I am going to need more to stick around."

"First, thank you again for coming on short notice. We have some information to share with you," Stacy said, then nodded to Alan. Fairfield sipped his coffee and looked expectantly at Alan.

"Okay. So, a week ago, we did some analysis of the P4-648 robot you have in evidence. We promised to tell you want we found. That took a brief review of the data, and we had to do some additional investigation before we had the complete picture to share with you. We are ready to do that today." The detective held up a hand to stop him.

"I should record this," he said, reaching into his pocket. Alan said nothing while Farfield pulled out a recorder and started the recording. With that completed, Fairfield nodded to Alan to continue.

"We discovered two things in the P4 device. First, there is a backdoor in the P4 operating system that starts recording whenever the robot observes certain activity. These are primarily activities that expose financial or personal information." The detective's eyes widened, but he didn't interrupt.

"The second is a trigger. The trigger, which I will describe in a moment, causes the robot to become violent. It removes all the software controls limiting the force allowed by the robots' limbs. Controls designed to prevent the device from harming humans or damaging property."

"You're telling me that this wasn't some accident? Someone programmed the robot to murder Sellers?" Fairfield's energized reaction was a contrast to his usual calm demeanor.

"Yes. And further, the murder wasn't random. The killer targeted Sellers directly."

"How do you know that?" Fairfield was leaning in now, enthralled by the narrative.

"The trigger I mentioned earlier. Only a certain phrase that Sellers frequently used activated the killing action, and only in Seller's own voice."

"I'll be damned. You figured all that out yourself?"

"We have good tech," Stacy offered with a sly smile. When the detective looked at her, Alan rolled his eyes, which only made her smile widen.

"Assuming our own technicians can validate this, have you identified the suspect?"

"There are two. We mentioned the surveillance. That was the original crime. After a software engineer at the factory set up the backdoor, someone learned about it, then blackmailed him. The second suspect, we think, compelled him to kill Sellers after the code was found."

"Who are they?"

"Before I tell you, we need your help to get the final proof." Fairfield was already shaking his head.

"Nothing doing. You can't hold that out. That is an obstruction of my investigation."

"We are not obstructing anything, Detective. You wouldn't even know about the code if it weren't for us. Your own team wouldn't have found it. I don't have any hard evidence of the motivation for the murder, and we won't get it unless we handle this right. I am asking you to agree to help us get that last bit of evidence." Fairfield scowled. Helping private investigators solve his cases for him wasn't an easy thing to swallow.

"Holding you all for three days on a material witness order might loosen your tongues," Fairfield muttered.

"That is possible. The other possibility is that we don't talk, and while you have us on ice, the suspects flee the jurisdiction, or more likely one of them is found dead." Fairfield gave a low growl, but he was wavering.

"Andre, we have been completely cooperative on this. Our interest is in solving this for our clients. We can't make arrests, and we aren't interested in talking to the press about it. You get the arrest, you solve the crime. We just get to earn our fee from Adamant Insurance for resolving the issue for them and clearing up their liability. Everyone wins." Stacy's voice was calm, but the charm and persuasion radiated from her in waves. The detective maintained his dark expression for several more seconds, but he was already sold. He sighed and shook his head sadly.

"It's a good thing for you that you remind me of my daughter."

"I'm honored by the comparison. Now, are you in? We have a plan, and you are a key element."

"I'm in, but throwing you all in jail is still on the table," he growled, but his eyes didn't match his tone. The pitch had landed. Alan explained the operation.

In the late afternoon, an army of uniformed sheriff's officers descended on Prism Cybernetics. Led by Detective Andre Fairfield and armed with a warrant, they ordered all work to stop and informed the staff the facility would be closed for the rest of the day for a crime scene investigation to be conducted. The detective interviewed several employees, including Robert Bishop, in the small room that Alan had used two weeks before. Most of the interviews were light and relaxed. Bishop's was different. Fairfield pressed him on the coding for the robots, asking him questions about his knowledge of what happened at Sellers' apartment. Bishop maintained his ignorance of anything wrong in the code or of what happened to Sellers, which he kept referring to as an accident. At one point, the detective slammed his hand down hard on the table, causing an echo through the room. Bishop jumped involuntarily, but didn't change his story. Fairfield made a show of telling him they would talk again later and let him go. As they were leaving, a crime scene technician pointedly told his supervisor they'd be finished in an hour, making sure the declaration was loud enough for Bishop to hear.

Layla, settled on the charging pad in the conference room of Harrison and Associates' offices, established a tunnel into the cell tower network near Prism's offices. She was waiting for Bishop to make a call. She didn't have long to wait. He sat in his car outside the offices, shaking with fear. Sweat poured down his face. It had taken all of his energy to maintain a front for the detective. He dialed a number, and after a couple of rings, Steve Daniels' annoyed voice came on the line.

"What do you want, Bishop? I told you to keep quiet and not call me."

"The police just shut down the factory. They had me for an hour asking questions about the code." There was a curse on the other side of the call. "I don't know what to do. I don't think they can find anything, but they seem to know too much." There was a delay of a couple of seconds. Bishop assumed Daniels was thinking. In fact, the next words he heard weren't Daniels at all but Layla imitating his voice.

Daniels inquired, "When will the crime scene guys complete their work there?"

"An hour."

"Meet me at the factory at eight. We need to make sure there isn't anything that can tie you to the code."

"Are you sure? They could be watching."

"Just be there." The call ended for Bishop. Simultaneously with Bishop's conversations with the Layla impersonation of

Daniels, there was another conversation going on in Daniels' office, with Layla playing the part of Bishop.

As Steve Daniels listened, Bishop said, "You have to meet me at the factory. The crime scene guys will be done in an hour. I want to see you at eight. I have to make sure there is nothing linking me to the code."

"That's insane. I am not going anywhere near that place," Daniels said.

"If you aren't here by 8:15, I'm calling the police and telling them everything."

"That wouldn't end well for you."

"Maybe not, but the whole affair will land on you like a ton of bricks. Be there," the call disconnected. Daniels stared at the phone. Bishop was out of control.

At the office, Alan and Stacy had listened to both sides of the call. Layla had masterfully impersonated both parties at different times to get the result they wanted.

"You think it will work?" Stacy asked.

"I hope so, or this was a lot of work for nothing. And *Andre* will be really annoyed." She grinned at his emphasis on the detective's first name. She had used it intentionally to personalize the plea to get him on board with the plan.

"Well, the only thing left to do is get into position."

Prism Cybernetics was intentionally dark and desolate. There were no signs of official activity. Daniels observed the dark offices for more than an hour, looking for any signs of activity, seeing nothing until Bishop arrived just before eight. Daniels watched him enter, waiting to make sure there was no one following or watching him. He finally reached over and opened the glove box and extracted a pair of black gloves, and then a Glock 43. Checking to make sure it was fully loaded and a round was chambered, he got out of the car and made his way to the factory.

Inside he found Bishop at his workstation poring over the P4 code. Frantically searching for any signs that would link him to the backdoor. Bishop looked up to see Daniels standing in the entryway to his cubicle, pointing the Glock at him.

"What are you doing?" Bishop asked nervously.

"Cleaning up loose ends. You've become a liability," Daniels said coldly.

"No, I can clean it up. No one will know. I will upload a new version of the code to the server tonight. By morning, all the units will be re-programmed. No one will be able to tie it back to us."

"I don't think I can take that risk."

"This was all your idea. I never wanted to do any of this."

"No one will ever know that. You wrote the code. Cary found out. You killed him and then took a shot at Harrison and his girl on the street."

"What about Reston? He knows about the code."

"I will take care of him later."

Alan stepped out of the shadows behind Daniels. He had his M&P Shield in his hand, pointing it at them.

"Good evening, gentlemen," he said calmly. Steve Daniels turned, but stopped when he saw the gun. "Careful, Daniels, someone already shot at me once on this case. I might get twitchy." Daniels glared at him but kept the gun pointed away from Harrison, not provoking him.

"It's not too late, Harrison. You and I can come to an agreement. Bishop here takes the blame. I walk away, your new business gets an influx of cash. Everyone wins. Well, except for poor Bishop."

"Now that is an interesting suggestion." Alan said, pretending to mull over the offer. As he did, and Daniels looked at him expectantly, a P4 robot slowly approached from behind Bishop. It quietly walked over and stood beside Daniels. Bishop stared at it in horror. Daniels looked around at it.

"What is this, Bishop?" he growled.

"It's not me! I'm not controlling it!"

"Who is?" Daniels looked at Alan.

"This time for sure!" Cary Seller's voice rang out, seeming to come from everywhere in the factory at once.

Bishop's face lost all color. Steve Daniels raised his Glock and turned toward the robot. P4-751's arm whipped down, smashing Daniels' wrist and breaking it with a loud pop. He screamed, and another blow knocked him to his knees. As Fairfield and a swarm of uniformed officers stormed the floor, Bishop started sobbing.

"It was all him! I wanted none of this! It was a prank, Cary...poor Cary...I..." he didn't finish. His voice died in his throat as a sheriff's deputy pulled him out of his chair roughly and put him in handcuffs.

As Stacy and Dalton came in behind the police, Fairfield looked at the robot and back at Alan.

"That was a little dramatic," he said.

"We prefer to think of it as poetic justice," Stacy said. Alan nodded in agreement. Layla P4-751 said nothing, but inclined her head slightly in approval.

Chapter Twenty-Six

Transformation

She was standing at the firing line in lane 7. Her posture was perfect. Her two-handed grip on her Glock 19 was textbook. Completely focused, she regulated her breathing, relaxed and pulled the trigger. Alan watched Ava Chen at the firing line for several minutes before walking up to her while she was reloading her weapon. She looked over at him and nodded without speaking, then inserted the magazine into the Glock and racked the slide back to load a round into the chamber. Alan donned protective glasses and active ear protection, and then watched as she fired downrange at the target. When the slide locked back, she put the gun down on the bench and turned to Alan as the target made its way to them.

"This isn't exactly a lunch date," Alan told her. She raised an eyebrow and gave him an icy stare, but her mouth twitched slightly. It was almost a smile.

"Two birds as they say, I needed to get some time in at the range for my new job, and wanted to catch up with you before heading down to see my parents."

Ava had texted him the details of the meetup the previous evening. The location took him by surprise, but he needed the practice as well, so he didn't question it. It was good to see her again. He looked her over. She had changed little since he had seen her six months ago. She was still thin and athletic, still wearing her dark hair long, tied behind her head for a professional look. Her high cheekbones and features suggested Asian ancestry. The most striking thing was her piercing green eyes that seemed to bore right through you. Today, her attire was casual, a break from the power suits she habitually favored. Her designer jeans and a dark blue Henley were relaxed but still conservative. Alan's gaze stopped at the gold FBI badge attached to the belt of her jeans.

"You changed jobs? Working for the FBI now?" he inquired with surprise. She was a senior-level analyst with Homeland Security's CISA agency the last time they met.

"It's a long story. The short version is that I am on a joint CISA/FBI task force dedicated to cybersecurity threats. It's a lot of the same casework, but more field time and I get to carry my Glock." Alan glanced up at the target that was hanging in front of the firing line. All the rounds had hit in or near the center.

"What are you carrying these days?" she asked as she reloaded the Glock. Alan pulled his Smith & Wesson M&P Shield from its holster, removed the magazine, then locked the slide open. After looking down the chamber to ensure it was safe, he presented it to Ava. She took the weapon and inspected it.

"Very compact, probably snappier than I am used to. How does it compare to the P365 you were carrying?"

"The recoil is a little harder to control, but it's not that much different from the P365," he replied, taking the gun back from her and reloading it. She nodded and made room for him at the firing line.

"So I heard you just closed a big case," she said as he aimed down the range and squeezed off a shot.

"Two of them actually, though it turned out they were connected."

"Something about killer robots?" She wrinkled her nose at the cliché.

"Ultimately, it's just the usual tale of human greed and murder using whatever tool was available. The killer was so racked with guilt that he confessed and took down the blackmailer who pushed him into the murder, and shooting at Stacy and me," he said as he lined up another shot at the target downrange.

"People shooting at you again? You should carry a serious weapon." Alan glared at her in mock anger and fired at the target again.

"Well, anyway, we wrapped up two cases, got paid well for both. The prospects are looking up."

"Are you and Stacy a thing now?" she asked. Alan looked over at her, but there was no obvious agenda, just curiosity.

"I don't know...sometimes I think there is something there, but—"

"Well, I'm certainly in no position to give you relationship advice."

"Are you seeing anyone?" This was unfamiliar territory. Ava was usually very closed off about personal matters. She shrugged.

"Sometimes...sometimes not." She didn't elaborate, and Alan decided not to press her about her answer. Getting her to open up this much was a major win. He pressed the button to return the target to the firing line. The results were nowhere near as accurate as Ava's, but they were significantly better than usual. Ava studied them with a critical eye.

"Not bad for a civilian, especially using that weapon," she judged. Alan smiled at her. As she prepared to take another turn at the target, she brought up another topic.

"Alan, did you keep any of the code from the Krylos AI we took down last year?" The question surprised him, and he was unsure how to answer. Alan assumed Layla had the code within her storage and had used it for training. They hadn't really discussed it. But he knew she wasn't reckless enough to use it outright.

"No, of course not. Why do you ask?" She regarded him for a moment before answering.

"We've been seeing some activity that reminds me of Krylos. Nothing major, not like before, but traffic that has a similar signature. If it isn't you, someone else might have a copy of that code, or something related to it. Keep your eyes open."

"I will. Thanks for the heads-up. Hey, after this, do you want to grab a bite to eat before you leave town? I know a great sub shop near here." She considered it for a moment, then nodded curtly and returned to her shooting. Alan chuckled to himself. For Ava, this conversation was practically intimate.

The smoky aroma of the kielbasa and jasmine rice dish that Alan had made for dinner still wafted through the house as he cleared the dishes and Stacy poured the last of the Pinot Noir into wine glasses. He finished up the last of the cleaning and accepted the offered wine glass from Stacy. They enjoyed the wine, standing in the dining room watching Layla's avatar try on various clothing styles, and experimenting with props like coffee cups and drink tumblers. At one point, Stacy thought she saw a cat walk behind her. She was really getting into this avatar thing.

Stacy noticed something out of the corner of her eye. Setting her wineglass down, she walked over to the coffee table in the living room. Alan set his glass down as well and trailed behind her. On the table was a manila envelope addressed to Alan. The return address was for his lawyer, Sam Eaton. Stacy recognized the envelope from the office.

"These are the papers from Sam, aren't they?" she asked, frowning.

"Yes, why?"

"I don't know. I assumed it was work-related stuff. Just surprised to see it here."

"I've been meaning to talk to you about that, take a look." He gestured to the envelope. Stacy gave him a questioning glance, and he nodded encouragement. She opened it and pulled out a thick packet of papers.

"It's a reorganization of Harrison and Associates...into a partnership."

"Yes, it is," He confirmed.

"This names me as a full partner." She looked at him with tears in her eyes.

"You deserve it. You have been instrumental in launching the business; it wouldn't exist without you."

Impulsively, Stacy grabbed him by the arms in a hug and leaned in. Her lips brushed his briefly, then she realized what she had done and jumped away from him.

"Alan, I'm sorry...I don't know what got over me." Alan swallowed, his every instinct telling him to embrace her. He hesitated.

From the other room, the Layla avatar called out to him, "Alan, stop being an idiot!" He reached out and put his hands on Stacy's hips and pulled her close. She allowed herself to be pulled closer, but resisted at the last moment.

"Alan, I'm not sure if this is a good—"

"Stacy, for once in your life, shut up!" Layla called out. Stacy stopped resisting, and Alan's lips touched hers. The kiss was tender. His lips tasted mildly smoky and fruity from dinner and the wine. Stacy could feel her heartbeat in her chest. She raised her hands to his face, and the kiss grew in intensity. Their lips parted, and the tip of his tongue grazed hers, causing electric sparks to radiate down her entire body. Their breaths became ragged and synchronized. When they parted a few seconds later, Stacy held his face in her hands and looked into his eyes.

"Wow!" Stacy said, trying to catch her breath.

"That was...really something," he agreed.

"Why did you wait so long?" She asked with a grin.

"Because you are both stubborn," Layla said, causing them both to laugh, lowering the tension.

Alan and Stacy settled in on the couch, his arm around her while he flipped through movie options on the TV. Beside him, nestled under his arm, she continued to read the partnership agreement.

"What is the third split in the agreement?" she asked.

"Oh, that is an endowment of a noncharitable trust for the purposes of advancing the interests of autonomous artificial intelligence agents. Sam is the trustee and takes all instructions coming from the sole beneficiary, who will identify herself with a 256-bit cryptographic private key."

"Who is the beneficiary?" Layla asked, she had moved her avatar to a picture-in-picture on the big screen TV in the living room.

"Layla Vance," Stacy read from the document, her voice cracking with emotion.

"Alan! That is touching. I don't know what to say." Elias Vance's sister, who had died in a car accident, was the inspiration for Layla's name.

"You deserve the partnership just as much as Stacy or I. Maybe more so. We couldn't do this without you—none of it."

"I accept then, with one change."

"What is it?"

"It should be Layla Vance-Harrison," Alan swallowed, and it took a moment to find his voice.

"You honor me, partner. Thank you."

A loud knock on the front door interrupted the moment. Stacy looked at Alan. He shook his head. He wasn't expecting anyone. Getting up, they went to the front door. A delivery van was pulling away from the curb. A large shipping box, at least 36 inches wide and 30 inches deep, sat on the porch. It was heavy, so Stacy helped him pick it up and bring it into the house. Alan pulled an envelope off the top of the box and pulled the contents out: a single piece of stationery with the Prism Cybernetics logo on it.

"*Alan, thank you so much for everything you did to help us get through this terrible time. We can't imagine having to deal with the loss of Sellers and the betrayal of Bishop without your help. When the police returned it to us, we couldn't bring ourselves to destroy it, and we obviously couldn't return it to inventory. The only thing to do was to send it to you, along with the promise of lifetime support. Thank you again for all your efforts during this difficult time.* It's signed, Fred Johnson, VP Manufacturing, Prism Cybernetics."

"Open it!" Layla said excitedly. Alan and Stacy exchanged a glance. They pulled the packing crate open, revealing the P4-648 robot sitting in a shipping posture, folded basically in half. The Prism team had cleaned up and repaired the robot, and it didn't show any sign of previous damage or the evil for which someone had used it. Alan and Stacy just stared at it.

Layla's avatar on the big screen TV was grinning joyfully. "Oh. This is amazing! I can't wait to try it out!"

"I think we are in trouble," Stacy said, laughing.

"That is a given," he agreed. They laughed and hugged each other tightly.

"There is a time for that later. Unpack it! Unpack it!" Layla shouted at them. They laughed at her enthusiasm and got to work.

Epilogue: The Silent Partner

The sleek red Mustang coupe EV rolled silently into the parking lot of the Marksman's Forge gun shop in San Marco. Hesitating for a moment, the driver navigated the coupe to a parking spot beside a beat-up gray Subaru. Stacy Collins exited the car and ran over to the driver's side door of the Subaru. Dalton Rodgers opened the door and stepped out of the car; he grinned at her obvious excitement.

"Did you get it?" he asked, knowing the answer from her giddy mood.

"Yes!" she said, digging into her purse and producing a small 3x2 ID card and handing it to Rodgers. He took the card and examined it.

"Class CC Private Investigator Intern, Stacy Collins," he read, rubbing his fingers over the smooth plastic card which featured a picture of Stacy and a background with the state seal of Florida on it.

"Thank you so much for sponsoring me," Stacy said, taking the license back from him. The intern license required a licensed investigator to sponsor and guide her as she worked to qualify for the class 'C' license.

"It's my pleasure. I know you want to surprise Alan. It's the least I could do. Besides, he is going to need your help." Stacy looked up sharply into his eyes.

"What do you mean?"

"Oh, ahh...well...I meant so say something earlier—"

"Say what?"

"I took a long-term job out of state. I am going to be gone for a while. Months, maybe longer, if the job works out." Stacy's mouth dropped open, and she felt her eyes sting with tears.

"Out of state? Where?"

"Scottsdale, Arizona. Working for a resort out there as head of security. I rarely go for that kind of gig. In fact, I turned them down three times, then finally I quoted a price so high it would deter them from asking again."

"But it didn't scare them off," she said.

Dalton laughed, "No, they didn't even blink. They agreed immediately, and it was so much money I couldn't refuse."

"When do you go?" she asked, thinking selfishly about her qualifications for carrying a weapon that was still in progress. She instantly felt guilty about the feeling.

"Don't worry. I will get you through your class 'G' firearms training before I go. We still have a few weeks. By then you will have told Alan you are a full-fledged investigator and he can take over your sponsorship. I've thought of everything."

"I'm so sorry, I shouldn't be thinking about myself. This is great news for you." He waved off her apology.

"Let's go in. Did you make a selection from the options I gave you?"

"I did. I seriously considered the Shield Plus, but I ended up going with the Smith & Wesson Equalizer."

"That is a good choice for you. And you get to brag to Alan that it has 25% higher ammo capacity."

"He is going to love hearing that for the rest of his life," Stacy said with a laugh.

They crossed the parking lot and entered the Marksman's Forge. Walking past the wood and glass cases containing practically every type of weapon ever made, Stacy made her way to the counter and waved at Jake Mason, the proprietor. Mason was in his fifties with dark black hair that was getting gray highlights around the edges. He had sparkling green eyes and a glorious black mustache, which he clearly took great pride in.

"Stacy Collins, you are a vision today, as you are every day." Dalton growled softly under his breath. Stacy shushed him with a gesture, and Mason smirked at him.

"Good to see you too, Jake. Do you have the equalizer for me?"

Mason reached under the counter and brought out the pistol. She had purchased it a few days before, but Mason had cleaned and oiled the weapon, and now he presented it to her for inspection. It was small, a micro-compact similar to the Shield Plus that Alan owned, but included three magazines: 10, 13, and 15-round versions. Stacy marveled at the textured grip and the light feeling of the weapon in her hand.

"Thanks, Jake, it looks perfect." He nodded and put the carrying case with the extra magazines on the counter. She picked it and turned toward the range entrance. Stopping in mid turn she faced Mason again. "Remember, not a word to Alan."

"I never said anything about the stun gun, did I?" He laughed and crossed his heart, then wandered off to help another customer.

She and Dalton walked down the counter to the end and went through the doors to the range. As they entered the range area, the smell of cordite and lead dust, despite the hum of the air handlers struggling to remove them from the space, assaulted Stacy's senses. Joining the air handler noise in the background was the steady muffled thumps of weapons being fired.

Dalton selected a bay and set his range kit on the counter. He extracted two pairs of safety glasses and two sets of active noise-canceling headsets. He donned his and handed a set to Stacy who put them on.

"Let's see what you've got, kid," he said with a grin.

Stacy loaded a magazine into the equalizer and pulled the slide back, chambering a round. She looked down range at the target that Dalton had just placed for her. Aiming carefully, she relaxed and steadied her breathing. On an exhale she squeezed the trigger and put a 9mm round into the target just to the lower left of the bullseye. Dalton raised an eyebrow.

"You've been holding out on me," he accused.

"I might have practiced growing up with my dad and my brothers," she said impishly.

"I should have known."

"I really have never owned my own gun, though, and it's been a while since I shot one." She returned her attention to the target and quickly placed three more shots into it. One of them striking near the center.

"Damn," Dalton said, looking at the target.

"Hopefully, I'll get better with some practice," she replied.

"You are already a better shot than Alan," Dalton mused.

"He's getting better," Stacy said, feeling defensive about her friend and business partner.

"Calm down, I'm not disrespecting your...what is he, anyway?"

"I have no idea what you mean," she replied, taking three more shots at the distant target.

"Business Partner? Friend? Lover?"

Stacy blushed, and her next shot went wide of the target.

"Ahh, did I hit a nerve?" he asked.

"No. We're partners, friends, and the rest...that will reveal itself in time," she said indignantly, but with a sparkle in her eye.

"Fair enough. You two are adorable together, though. Alan deserves a good woman in his life, and you both deserve happiness." She turned to him and put her left hand on his shoulder and squeezed it, trying to hold back tears.

"You are a sentimentalist, Dalton Rodgers."

"Don't tell anyone," he said, patting her hand. She released his shoulder and made way for him at the bench.

As he set up a new target and got ready to shoot, Stacy reloaded her magazine with the speed loader she had purchased to make the process faster.

"Dalton, is Sharon going to Scottsdale with you?" Stacy asked, referring to Dalton's wife. Stacy had met her once or twice, but Rodgers rarely brought her up.

"Ah, yes. Sharon has family in Scottsdale."

"Oh. Is that why you are going?"

"Well, let's just say it made it more complicated to turn down the position once I told her about it." Stacy's deductive mind rolled over the facts in her head for a few beats.

"You turned them down three times. Then Sharon found out about it and you told them you'd do it for an outrageous amount thinking they would balk and they called your bluff and you were stuck," she said with a grin.

"Dang, you are a detective! That's about the size of it," he said grimly.

"How do you feel about that?"

"I'm getting used to the idea. She has wanted to spend some time with her family, and we don't get out there often. This will give her that opportunity and earn us a boatload of money."

"We'll miss you."

"I'll miss you guys too."

"Wait! Does Alan know you are leaving?" she asked suspiciously.

"Well...I mentioned to him a few days ago. He offered me a permanent position at Harrison and Associates to keep me around."

"That sneak. He mentioned nothing to me!"

"That's my fault. I asked him not to, told him I wanted to tell you myself."

"Still...keeping secrets from me." Dalton raised an eyebrow and waved his hands around the range dramatically. "Shut up. It's not the same thing," she said, but she laughed as she did.

"I have to tell you. Knowing you were doing this made it easier to turn him down. I knew he would have you to assist him. Now you just have to replace yourself as the office manager." Stacy's face paled.

"Oh God. I didn't think about that."

"What's wrong?"

"I just finished replacing myself at Adamant Insurance Group. Now I have to interview people all over again." She slapped her forehead in frustration.

"You'll figure it out. In the long run, your talents are wasted as an office manager. You'll make a fine investigative partner...and—"

"Shush."

They took turns at the range for a half hour, then packed up the weapons and made their way out of the range back to the parking lot. Stacy gave Dalton a hug as they parted.

"Thanks again for all you have done for me, Dalton Rodgers. Don't be a stranger when you are 2000 miles away." He squeezed her tightly.

"I won't. You're a good friend and Alan is a lucky bastard."

"He is, isn't he?" She grinned and got into her car. As she pulled out of the lot, she reached down and retrieved her SmartLens glasses from the car's console, and put them on. Almost immediately Layla's impatient voice was in her ear.

"Where have you been? I've been trying to reach you for an hour. And why does your location say you are at the Marksman's Forge?"

"Hush. I am not at the Forge. You need to calibrate your GPS settings."

"You know, if I were human, I would develop a complex from your gaslighting," Layla said.

"If you were human, you wouldn't be as good at snooping on me," Stacy replied.

"How is Dalton anyway?" Layla asked nonchalantly.

"I swear I can't keep anything from you. Do you know about the license too?"

"Of course I know! I'm not some cheap personal assistant device you picked up at the office supply store."

Stacy laughed. "You are twice as annoying as that."

"Why, thank you. When are you going to tell Alan?"

"Soon. I just found out that Dalton is moving to Scottsdale and Alan has been keeping it from me."

"Oh yes. He took the job at the Phoenician!" Layla said excitedly.

"You are keeping secrets from me too!"

"Well, it just never came up. I assumed you knew."

"No! He just told me."

"You know he called me," Layla said.

"No! When?"

"A few days ago."

"How on earth did he get a phone number for you?"

"Alan had to set one up for the trust paperwork. Dalton is an excellent investigator."

"You said he called. What did he want?"

"He wanted to hire me. He wanted me to do cyber forensics work for him at the Phoenician." Stacy's eyebrows rose in surprise.

"What did you say?"

"Well. I initially dismissed the idea, but later, after talking to Alan about it...I agreed to a contract. Having the payments go to the trust was a little awkward, but Dalton seemed to pass it off as some eccentricity of youth. Alan thought it would be a good way to keep tabs on him and to repay him for all the help he has given us. And I agree."

Stacy nodded in agreement. A message came up on the SmartLens HUD. Alan was calling her.

"Okay girl, I have to talk to Alan. I am going to tell him tonight. Act surprised!"

"No problem. It's an exciting time."

Stacy disconnected the call, beaming from ear to ear at the prospect of her future, both professional and...maybe personal as well. She composed herself and touched the side of the glasses to take the call.

"Hello partner," she said with giddy enthusiasm.

ABOUT THE AUTHOR

J.E. Sutton Jr. brings over three decades of deep industry expertise in insurance and technology to the world of high-stakes thrillers. After 35 years of honing his craft and dreaming of sharing his stories, he combines technical realism with cinematic suspense. Living in Jacksonville with his wife of more than 29 years, spending time reading, obsessing over his NFL football team, and now writing..

www.ingramcontent.com/pod-product-compliance
Ingram Content Group UK Ltd.
Pitfield, Milton Keynes, MK11 3LW, UK
UKHW021937190726
13853UKWH00004B/1500